GEOFF RODKEY

THE CHRONICLES of EGG
NEW LANDS

PUFFIN

PUFFIN BOOKS

Published by the Penguin Group
Penguin Books Ltd, 80 Strand, London WC2R ORL, England
Penguin Group (USA) Inc., 375 Hudson Street, New York, New York 10014, USA
Penguin Group (Canada), 90 Eglinton Avenue East, Suite 700, Toronto, Ontario, Canada M4P 2Y3
(a division of Pearson Penguin Canada Inc.)
Penguin Ireland, 25 St Stephen's Green, Dublin 2, Ireland (a division of Penguin Books Ltd)
Penguin Group (Australia), 707 Collins Street, Melbourne, Victoria 3008, Australia
(a division of Pearson Australia Group Pty Ltd)
Penguin Books India Pvt Ltd, 11 Community Centre, Panchsheel Park, New Delhi – 110 017, India
Penguin Group (NZ), 67 Apollo Drive, Rosedale, Auckland 0632, New Zealand
(a division of Pearson New Zealand Ltd)
Penguin Books (South Africa) (Pty) Ltd, Block D, Rosebank Office Park, 181 Jan Smuts Avenue,
Parktown North, Gauteng 2193, South Africa

Penguin Books Ltd, Registered Offices: 80 Strand, London WC2R ORL, England

puffinbooks.com

First published in the USA by G. P. Putnam's Sons,
an imprint of Pengiun Young Readers Group, 2013
Published simultaneously in Great Britain by Puffin Books 2013
001

Text copyright © Geoff Rodkey, 2013
Map copyright © David Atkinson
All rights reserved

The moral right of the author and illustrator has been asserted

Set in Minion Pro
Printed in Great Britain by Clays Ltd, St Ives plc

British Library Cataloguing in Publication Data
A CIP catalogue record for this book is available from the British Library

ISBN: 978-0-141-34252-8

www.greenpenguin.co.uk

Penguin Books is committed to a sustainable
future for our business, our readers and our planet.
This book is made from Forest Stewardship
Council™ certified paper.

ALWAYS LEARNING   **PEARSON**

For Tal

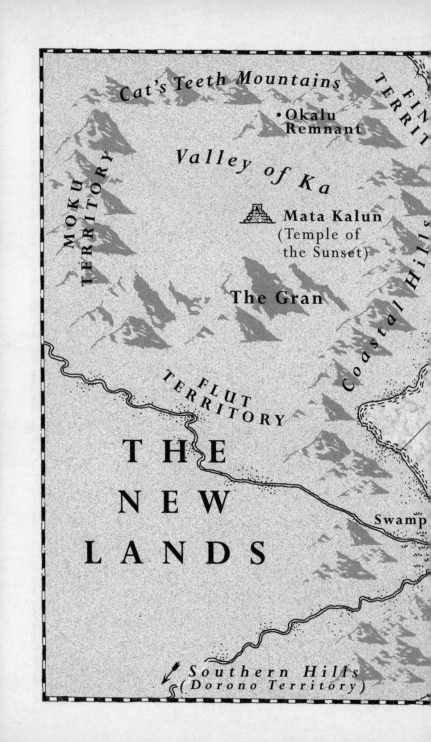

CHAPTER 1

BUGGING

I hung my head over the side of the *Thrush* and watched the prow carve the seawater into a hissing spray. Viewed up close, the Blue Sea wasn't all that blue, and I wondered – for the umpteenth time in the past few days – who had named it that, and why they hadn't bothered to get it right.

They should have called it the Greenish Blue Sea. Or the Almost Blue Sea. Or the It Only Looks Blue From A Distance Sea.

It was stupid, I know. But it kept my mind off the other stuff.

Like the man who wanted to kill me.

And his daughter, Millicent, who I was in love with.

And the map in my head, which was the cause of all the trouble, and which I wasn't even sure I was remembering right. Especially the tricky part in the middle.

Three squiggles down left, four dashes up . . .

Or was it four squiggles and three dashes?

It turns out it's a bad idea to try and memorize something

written in a language you don't even speak. I'd been practising the map twenty times a day, tracing it with my finger on the deck of the *Thrush,* so you'd think by now I would've had it hammered into my head pretty good.

But it was getting harder, not easier.

Still hanging over the gunwale, I shut my eyes and tried to imagine the original, its crooked lines of Okalu hieroglyphs painted on the gloomy wall of the Fire King's tomb.

Dash dot feather, cup, two dash dot firebird . . .

"Done yet?"

It was Guts. He was standing behind me on the deck.

"Almost," I said. "Just let me throw up again."

He snorted. "Wot's yer problem? Food ain't *that* bad."

"It's not the food," I said, although the food was awful. The crew were all bone-skinny, and after three days of eating their smelly turtle meat and wormy biscuits, it was no mystery why.

"Seasick?"

"Not that, either."

"Then wot?"

I'm scared out of my mind and I think we should just forget about finding this stupid treasure and run away.

But I couldn't actually tell Guts that.

I couldn't admit that I was terrified we were doomed – that if we set foot in the New Lands, we'd be killed long before we could find an Okalu Native to translate the map, and that the only sane thing to do was to bug out and flee down to the Barkers, or maybe even further, someplace where nobody was gunning to kill me for an ancient treasure I barely understood and wasn't even sure existed.

I couldn't admit any of that.

Or could I?

I retched over the side one last time to make sure I was done. Then I straightened up and turned to face my partner.

Guts was bobbing on the balls of his feet, eyes twitching under his tangled thicket of white-blond hair. He raised his arms in a fighting stance. The steel hook on the stump of his left hand glistened in the morning sun.

"C'mon," he said. "Let's tussle!"

I sighed. "Again?"

"Need to practise!"

He'd bought the hook from a field pirate just before we left Deadweather Island. He was getting pretty handy at fighting with it, which I guess was helpful. Except that I was his only sparring partner, so the fact that he was getting better meant my shirt was ripped in three places, and there were a dozen puncture marks and several deep scratches on my forearms. He kept promising he wouldn't make contact, but he couldn't seem to help himself.

"Not now," I said. "We need to talk."

"'Bout wot?"

"I think we . . . it's . . . I forgot the map."

"Nah, ye didn't."

"I did!"

"Said that yesterday. Then ye remembered it."

"I thought I did. Then I forgot again. And this time it's worse."

"Said *that* yesterday, too. C'mon, ye *porsamora*! Fight me!"

One of the crew had taught him how to swear in Cartager. He was as excited about that as he was about his new hook.

"C'mon! Lucy needs a workout!"

He'd named the hook "Lucy". I kept telling him it was ridiculous, but he didn't care.

"I'm serious! We need to talk!" I insisted.

Guts lowered his arms and frowned. His eyes twitched one more time and then went still. When we first met – when Ripper Jones and his pirate crew had made us fight almost to the death, and had done who knows what else to Guts before that – he twitched constantly. Eyes, shoulders, head . . . sometimes the whole upper half of his body would shudder.

Now it was mostly just his eyes, and sometimes he'd go a good two minutes without a twitch.

Sometimes, he almost seemed normal.

Not me. Not lately. I was a wreck. And the closer we got to Pella Nonna, the worse I got.

I'm scared out of my mind and I think we should just run away.

Guts was still staring at me.

"So talk," he said.

I took another deep breath.

I HADN'T STARTED the trip scared out of my mind. In fact, when we first boarded the *Thrush* three days earlier, I'd been feeling pretty cocky. Mostly because right before we left Deadweather, Guts and I had managed to stand down Roger Pembroke and a hundred Rovian soldiers.

How we got to that point is kind of a long story. Pembroke had killed my whole family – sent them off to their deaths somewhere out in the Blue Sea, in a runaway hot-air balloon that he'd rigged so it looked like an accident – and when I didn't die with them, he'd gone to an awful lot of trouble to finish me off.

4

I don't think it was anything personal. He just wanted the Fire King's treasure. And he figured the map to it was somewhere on my family's ugly fruit plantation, which was why he wound up sailing to Deadweather with a hundred soldiers and marching them up to our front porch.

But somehow, Guts and I escaped, with the only surviving version of the map lodged between my ears.

The "somehow" was mostly Millicent's doing. She was Pembroke's daughter, and the person I loved more than anything else in the world. I think that must have been true for Pembroke, too, because he let her talk him into slinking off empty-handed, packing his whole company of soldiers onto a boat back to Sunrise.

The truth was, if it weren't for Millicent, Guts and I would have been dead as rocks.

But I wasn't thinking that when the *Thrush* showed up to take the ugly fruit harvest to Pella Nonna in the New Lands, and we hitched a ride on it. And I wasn't thinking it was just blind luck that a ship had appeared at exactly the moment we needed to get off Deadweather, headed for exactly the place we wanted to go.

I wasn't thinking we'd only got this far because of blind luck and Millicent. Not yet. Instead, I was patting myself on the back for how clever Guts and I were to have pulled it off.

And considering what we'd just got away with, I figured the rest of it – finding an Okalu Native, translating the map, tracking down the treasure – would be no trick at all.

So I spent most of that first day at sea sunning myself on the deck like a lazy turtle, daydreaming about what I'd do once the treasure had made us fabulously wealthy.

I'd marry Millicent, that was obvious. I didn't bother to stew over minor obstacles like our being thirteen and her father wanting to kill me, let alone whether she'd say yes in the first place.

To my mind, the real challenge was figuring out where to build our mansion.

Deadweather was out of the question. Too many pirates, not enough food, the weather was lousy, and until I'd left for a while and come back again, I'd never realized just how much the smouldering volcano made the whole island stink like rotten eggs.

Sunrise wasn't an option, either. It was beautiful and all, but the people were terrible snobs. And since Roger Pembroke had plastered WANTED FOR MURDER posters with my face on them all over the island, it was likely to be awkward for me at dinner parties and such.

There were the Fish Islands, up north. But the name made me think they probably didn't smell too good, and I didn't know anything else about them. I knew even less about the Barkers, down south . . . Pella Nonna was full of Cartagers . . . and the rest of the New Lands were nothing but Native tribes and wilderness.

So that just left the Continent. We'd have to sail forty days across the Great Maw to get there, but once we did, we could live in Rovia itself – the setting for almost every novel I'd ever read, a rich and fabled land with glamorous cities and a countryside of gently rolling hills (I wasn't sure what "gently rolling" meant, but it sounded awfully nice) supposedly chock-full of ancient castles. If any of those were for sale, we wouldn't even have to build a mansion first. We could just move right in.

I figured I'd get a place like Timberfield, the mountaintop fortress where Billicks the Brave wound up at the end of *Throne of the Ancients*. I'd pass the days with a lot of hunting and falconry, and at night, Millicent and I would curl up in our massive library and read books to our hearts' content, surrounded by our six children.

The kids would read books, too, even the little ones.

I was just getting around to naming our firstborn when the quartermaster banged on the dinner plate. Starving, Guts and I quickly gathered under the mainmast with the eight haggard-looking crewmen for our first night's meal.

And that's when things started to go sideways.

FIRST, CAPTAIN RACKER demanded fifteen silver from us for the right to eat while we were on board. We forked it over, but when we saw what we'd paid for – the biscuits were so maggoty that if you set one down, it'd slither off under its own power – Guts just about buried his hook in Racker's head.

I managed to keep Guts from drawing blood, but then the jokes about my name started.

"Egg, eh? Was mummy a chicken?"

"Nah! She was an omelette! Haw, haw!"

Just the mention of my mother, who I'd never known except as a story Dad told over her grave, made me angry.

"It's short for Egbert," I said, trying to sound polite.

"That's even worse! Haw, haw!"

"Why stick ye with a name like that? Didn't they love ye none?"

It was a fair enough question as far as my dad was concerned. But that just made me madder. I had to bite my lip to keep quiet.

Then the conversation turned really unsettling.

"Why you headed for Pella?" asked Racker. "Got an itch to die young?"

"What do you mean?"

"Short-Ears'll kill ye 'fore ye get off the dock," snorted a snaggletoothed crew member.

Pella Nonna was a Cartager port, the same way Sunrise Island was Rovian. And Cartagers all had freakishly small ears, which was why everybody called them that.

"Wot they want to kill us fer?" Guts asked.

"For the shape of your ears," said Racker. "Haven't you heard of the Banishment Law? Ever since the Barker War, Rovians are banned from the New Lands on pain of death."

"Nuts to that!" spat Guts. "Islander, I am. Never even been across the Maw."

"It's not where you're from, boy – it's how you look. And talk. You got Rovian ears, Rovian skin and a Rovian tongue."

"But that makes all of you Rovian, too," I said. "And you're going to Pella."

Reggie the quartermaster shook his head. "Nah. Droppin' anchor offshore. Cartagers run boats out, load the ugly fruit. Then off we go. Try to put in, Short-Ears'd hang us dead."

A heavy lump of dread settled in my gut. "So if we go to Pella . . . they'll hang us dead, too?"

The crewmen all nodded eagerly.

"Might even torture ye first," said the snaggletooth, with a wide-eyed grin that told us he found the idea pretty exciting.

"Could you . . . maybe drop us on the coast? Farther north?" I was thinking we might be able to avoid Pella completely. After all, we didn't need a Cartager to translate the map. We needed an Okalu.

"What? And get eaten by Natives?"

"They'd actually *eat* us? The Okalu?"

8

"Okalu, Fingu, Flut – any of them tribes. Bunch of cannibals."

"Now, hang on, cap," the quartermaster chimed in. "They don't eat the whole of ye. Just yer heart."

"Reggie's right," agreed the snaggletooth. "Cut it out yer chest, munch it down while it's still beatin'. That's how they do it."

"Tell the other one!" Guts snorted.

"True enough, boy. They're not called savages for nothing." Racker shook his head. "If you're dead set on going to the New Lands, you're best off in Pella. Might stand a chance there if you keep your ears covered. And you speak the language."

He leaned forward and looked down his thin nose at us. "You *do* speak Cartager, don't you?"

We didn't.

GUTS REFUSED TO WORRY that we were sailing to our deaths.

"Gonna be fine," I heard him say as we lay awake that first night in the hammocks we'd strung up in a corner of the cargo hold. It was pitch-black down there – I couldn't see my hand in front of my face, let alone Guts in the next hammock.

"How can you say that? What's going to stop the Short-Ears from stringing us up?"

"Lucy, fer one."

"Will you stop calling it that? It's a *hook*."

"Yeh – hook named Lucy."

"But it's stupid! Might as well name your pants."

"Pants ain't gonna get me out o' no scrapes."

"And a hook's not going to kill a city full of Cartagers."

"Don't need to – that's wot her brothers an' sisters are fer."

"What brothers and sisters?"

"Ones in the sack."

We had four pistols and a pair of knives in the rucksack we'd brought with us, but I didn't see how it changed the odds much.

"You're out of your mind," I said. "And how are we even going to feed ourselves? Only got fifteen silver left."

"Got the necklace. Want money, just sell off a stone."

Guts had taken a necklace from the Fire King's skeleton back on Deadweather. It was a long string of gems, crowned by a three-inch firebird pendant made of rubies, diamonds and the like. After a hundred years in the tomb, the gems were crusted with dirt, and rotted feathers hung from it like clumps of dried seaweed. But it was obvious, filthy as it was, that it was valuable.

"Don't be stupid! We need that for the Okalu. It belonged to their king – it's got to be precious to them. If we hack off parts of it to buy food, think how mad they'll be."

Guts didn't say anything.

"And that's if they don't cut our hearts out at the sight of us. Or is Lucy going to get you out of that fix, too?"

He still didn't say anything.

"Are you even listening to me?"

I waited for an answer to come through the darkness.

Then I heard him snore. Unbelievable.

I didn't sleep that whole night. But not because of the snoring.

What the crew had said about the Cartagers in Pella sounded true enough. In all my favourite books, from *Basingstroke* to *Red Runs the Blood*, Short-Ears were villains – every one of them vicious, black-hearted and cowardly. Killing us for being Rovian seemed like just the kind of thing they'd do.

I hadn't read any books about Natives, or even laid eyes on

one, unless you counted the distant glimpses I'd got of the silver mine workers slogging away up on Mount Majestic, above Sunrise Island. But there was no reason to doubt what the crew said about them, either.

I started to wonder if we shouldn't scrap the whole plan and go back to Deadweather. But I knew if I did, Roger Pembroke would find me.

Then again . . . what was going to stop him from hunting me down in Pella Nonna? Or anywhere else?

As I thought about it, lying there in the dark, my heart started to pound like a drum. Because I realized no matter where I went, he'd be coming for me. Pembroke wanted that map badly enough to kill for it, and as long as he was rich and powerful, and I had the only copy on earth, I was in danger.

Pretty soon, my heart was pounding so hard I could hear it in my ears. I tried to settle it down by telling myself I'd managed to outwit him so far.

But then I thought about everything that had happened over the past few weeks – *really* thought about it – and I realized I hadn't outwitted anybody.

I hadn't been clever. I'd just been lucky. And sooner or later, I was going to run out of luck.

Or maybe I already had. Something was going horribly wrong with my body – my heart was racing, I couldn't move, I couldn't think, I couldn't breathe . . . My chest felt like somebody was stacking cannonballs on top of it.

I needed air. I thrashed against the hammock until it dumped me out on my head. Guts mumbled groggy words at me, but I didn't answer. I flailed around, knocking against boxes and crates and ceiling beams and who knows what else until I finally found the stairs and managed to stagger up to the main deck.

At that hour, the Blue Sea was black.

I thought about that as I puked under the moonlight.

I SPENT MOST OF that first night at sea retching over the side. I was still at it when Guts finally got up the next morning and joined me on deck.

It wasn't any easier to talk sense into him than it had been the night before.

"If they'll hang us just for being Rovian –"

"How they gonna know?"

"It's *obvious*! What are we going to do, cut off our ears?"

"Can't see our ears – too much hair. Problem solved."

"It's not just our ears. We don't speak a word of Cartager!"

That stumped him for a while, and he wandered off. Half an hour later, he came back with the snaggletooth, whose name was Mick, and who Guts had just hired – for ten silver, no less – to teach us Cartager.

Mick said he'd picked up the language in a Fish Islands prison, where he'd shared a cell with a pair of Cartager dock thieves. Pretty quickly, the limits of that became obvious.

"*Blun.*"

"*Blun,*" Guts and I repeated.

"Means dung," said Mick. "But ye can use it for anythin' ye don' like – food, weather, prison guards –"

"Right. What else?"

"*Balamunor.*"

"*Balamunor?*"

12

"Means dog-brains. *Shroof.*"

"*Shroof.*"

"Means a coward. Man wit' no honour. Big on honour, Cartagers are – want t' get under someone's skin, *shroof*'s worse'n *balamunor*. Wot else . . . ? *Wanaluff.*"

"*Wanaluff?*"

"Means cow-ears. Prob'ly hear it a lot – on account o' to a Cartager, two o' you got cow ears. Man calls ye *wanaluff*, try callin' him a *porsamora.*"

"*Porsamora?*"

"Yeh! Means he likes pigs. And not just fer eatin', if ye know wot I mean. Now, if ye *really* wanna insult a man –"

"Do you know any words that aren't insults?" I interrupted.

"Wot ye mean?"

"I mean, we're trying not to get killed. So what we really need are useful words."

"*Porsamora*'s dead useful! Good in all sorts o' situations. Man don't have to actually like pigs fer ye to call him that, ye know."

Mick was looking at me like I was thick in the head. So was Guts.

"But insults aren't going to help us get on with Cartagers," I said.

"Wot is?" Guts asked me.

"Things like, 'Can you help us?' Or 'We're friendly'."

Mick curled his lip in disgust. "Gonna say *that* to a Short-Ears?"

"*I'm* not," declared Guts.

"Can you at least teach us to say, 'Do you speak Rovian?'" I pleaded.

Mick scrunched his eyebrows together. I seemed to have stumped him.

"Why don't we just forget the whole thing?" I suggested. "Give us back the silver, and –"

"A-a-a-a-a! Give it a chance, boyo!" Mick waved his hands at me like I'd just threatened to slug him. "Wot ye want to say? 'D'ye speak Rovian?'"

"That'd be a start," I said.

"Fine. 'Kay. Here it is. It's . . ." He paused, his eyes narrowing into slits. When he finally spoke, it was unusually slowly – like he was making it up as he went along. *"Dee . . . lo . . . spee . . . lo . . . Rova . . . neelo."*

"Deelo speelo Rovaneelo?"

"That's right," he said, bobbing his head confidently. "Wot else ye want to know?"

"More curses!" said Guts. "How ye tell someone he's ugly?"

"Lots o' ways! Lessee . . . *Palomuno,* means horse-face . . ."

I quit the lesson a few minutes later, after Mick's claim that "Where can we find an Okalu?" translated as *"Weerwo feerwo Okaleerwo?"* convinced me nothing he taught us was reliable, except maybe the curses. Guts stuck with it, and eventually picked up a few dozen of what Mick promised him were the foulest insults in the Cartager language.

He was as thrilled with his new vocabulary as he was with his new hook. For the next three days, he practised them both non-stop, usually at the same time.

I spent the days doing a few things over and over myself: practising the map, puking over the gunwale, worrying over who among the Cartagers, Natives and Pembroke was going to kill me

14

first . . . and eventually cooking up a plan for how I could quit the whole business.

The plan itself was simple. Once she'd dropped the ugly fruit cargo in Pella, the *Thrush* was headed south, way down to the Barker Islands. I'd never been, but I knew they were Rovian-held, so at least there wouldn't be any Cartagers or Natives around to slaughter us for no good reason. We'd be that much further away from Pembroke. And from there, it'd be no trick to hop a ship across the Great Maw to the Continent, where even someone as rich and powerful as Pembroke would have a hard time tracking us down.

It was cowardly, I know. I'd be running away from the man who killed my family, when the truly noble thing would be to seek him out and avenge their deaths somehow.

But after a few days of stomach-clenching fear, I didn't want to be noble. I just wanted to not be dead. And I told myself that even if I bugged out now, I could always come back and avenge them some other time. Like in ten years, when I might be rich and powerful myself. Or at least slightly less terrified.

Bugging out would be easy. There was nothing to it. All we had to do was stay on the boat, and not get off when we reached Pella.

The hard part was figuring out how to sell the idea to Guts.

"SO TALK," HE SAID on the morning of the fourth day.

"We can't go to Pella," I said. "*Really* can't. We'll just get ourselves killed – if not by Cartagers or Natives, then . . . by the others."

"Quit bein' a *shroof*! Gonna be fine."

"It won't! And I don't care what you call me. We're not going."

He must have realized I was serious this time, because his eyes started to twitch.

"Wot about the treasure?!"

"Probably just a myth anyway."

"*Blun* to that!"

"Whatever . . . I don't care about the treasure."

"'Cause ye got a whole plantation? That it?"

"I gave the place away! To the field pirates. Remember? Anyway, it wasn't worth much to begin with."

"So ye need the treasure! Set ye up!"

"I don't care about that."

"*I do!*"

He was twitching badly now, worse than he had since we'd boarded the *Thrush*. And he must have really been getting hot, because he started swearing in Rovian again.

"Ye — —! Wot about yer family?"

"What about them?"

"He killed 'em! Gonna let him get away with it?"

"*You didn't even know my family!*" It came out so loud I could see crewmen turning to stare from all the way down at the stern.

But once I got going, I couldn't stop – everything I'd been trying to stuff down inside came up at once.

"I am *sick to death* of running, and fighting, and people trying to kill me – I don't want treasures, or maps, or revenge – I just want them to leave me alone!"

My arms were shaking, and I had to cross them over my chest and stuff my hands under my armpits to get them to stop.

Guts twitched a few more times. Then he lowered his voice.

"Wot about yer girlie? Gonna let her down, too?"

16

He knew me pretty well by now. Other than avenging my family, Millicent was the one thing that made me think I shouldn't cut and run.

"She'd understand. Anyway, I'll get her back somehow. Just . . . not soon."

Guts cursed a few more times. Then he shook his head, like he was done with the whole thing.

"Fine. Gimme the map, then."

"What do you mean?"

"Gimme the map! You ain't gonna use it."

"You'd go alone?"

"Course!"

It hadn't crossed my mind that Guts might leave me behind. At the thought of it – just when all the other fear was finally starting to lift – a panicky feeling shot through my belly.

"Gimme the map!"

"You can't memorize it. There's no time."

"So get paper! From the cap'n. Write it down!"

"And . . . what? You'd go to Pella? I'd go to the Barkers? We'd split up?"

I could barely see his eyes as they glared at me from under his long tangles of hair.

"If yer gonna bug . . . then yeh. Go it alone."

The panicky feeling in my gut was spreading. As I stared back at him, I started to realize there might be something worse than just being scared.

And that was being all alone in the world.

The look in his eyes said Guts didn't like the idea any better than I did. He lowered his head, staring down at the deck.

"*Need* that treasure. Bad! Set me up. Ain't got nothin' else. No way to make it, neither."

His voice was scratchy and thick. "You an' me had a deal. Partners. Things got hot, I didn't bug on you. Don't you go buggin' on me."

He looked up and met my eyes again, and I knew he was right.

If Guts was dead set on going to the New Lands, I was going with him. Like it or not.

I was opening my mouth to tell him as much when a voice called out from up in the rigging.

"PIRATES! DEAD AHEAD!"

CHAPTER 2

BOARDED

"PIRATES!"

I turned towards the horizon to look for the ship. The deck shuddered with the pounding of feet, and soon the captain was at my elbow, squinting through his spyglass into the late morning haze.

"SURE IT'S A RAIDER?!" Racker yelled, tilting his head up to yell at the crow's nest atop the foremast.

"SHE'S FLYIN' RED AN' BLACK!" the lookout yelled back.

"HARD ASTERN!" cried Racker as he ran for the wheel.

I looked around for Guts, but he'd vanished.

I was trying to puzzle out where he'd gone when the deck suddenly pitched to starboard at such a steep angle I lost my footing. As the ship wheeled around, I spent the next few seconds in a frantic scrabble to grab hold of something so I wouldn't fall overboard.

The *Thrush* righted herself and began to barrel north, bucking and lurching as she crashed over the waves. The crew were scurrying every which way to trim the sails, and I tried to stay clear of them as I scanned the deck for Guts.

There was no sign of him. He'd disappeared before the deck started to pitch, so I figured he hadn't gone overboard unless it was on purpose. And no matter how much Guts hated pirates – he'd been sold into Ripper Jones's crew, and even though he never talked about it, I got the sense that the Ripper was the reason Guts didn't have a left hand – he wasn't the type to drown himself in a panic at the first sign of trouble.

I made my way to the stern, where the captain stood with Reggie the quartermaster, watching our pursuer. I could see her now, coming up hard, her silhouette growing by the second.

Racker looked even more gaunt than usual as he stared through his spyglass.

"Wait a minute . . ." He lowered the glass. "That's a Cartager galleon. One of their warships. Take a look."

"Cartagers . . . ?" Reggie took the glass and peered through it.

"Cargaferf?!" Guts popped up beside me, out of breath and armed to the teeth. Literally – his jaws were clamped down on the blade of one of our knives, his good hand held a pistol and two more were shoved in the waistband of his trousers.

As the three of us stared at Guts's arsenal – a little nervously, because the pistols were cocked and loaded, and he wasn't being too careful with them – he handed me the one he was holding so he could take the knife out of his mouth and wipe the drool from his chin.

"Ain't pirates after all? It's Short-Ears?"

Instead of answering Guts, Reggie went back to looking through the spyglass.

"If she's Cartager Navy . . . why's she flyin' red and black?"

A thought occurred to me. "Can you make out the figurehead on her bow?" I asked. "Is it a skeleton?"

Racker took the spyglass back from Reggie. "Let's see . . . too far to . . . no, wait . . . think it *is* a skeleton."

A wave of relief surged through me. "Thank goodness . . . it's Burn Healy!"

At the mention of the most feared pirate on the Blue Sea, Racker and Reggie both turned to me with terror in their eyes.

"You sure?"

I couldn't help smiling. "No question. That's the *Grift* – he captured it from the Cartagers in the Barker War. We were just on it last week."

As Racker stared at me in shock, Reggie put a hand to his mouth, like he might throw up. Another crewman had been close enough to overhear, and the word spread across the ship in panicked cries:

"DEADWEATHER BOY SEZ IT'S HEALY!"

"*BURN* HEALY?!"

"SAVIOUR SAVE US! IT'S HEALY!"

Boz, the grim-looking first mate who was manning the wheel, looked over his shoulder at Racker.

"Gonna run the white flag, cap'n?"

The crew had pretty strong opinions about that.

"DO IT!"

"QUICK! 'FORE HE SENDS US T' THE BOTTOM!"

"PAINT THE DECK WIT' OUR GUTS, WE DON'T SURRENDER!"

"CALM YOURSELVES!" yelled Racker. "THERE'S NO NEED –"

We never heard the rifle shot that took Racker's hat off his head. Healy's ship was too far away for the sound to travel. But suddenly, the hat was skittering across the deck, and when a crewman picked it up, there were two round, clean holes where the ball had passed through the crown.

That was enough for the captain. "Run the white! Strike the sails!" he croaked from a frightened crouch below the deck rail.

IN THE THIRTY MINUTES it took for the *Grift* to come alongside and tie up to us, half the crew turned religious, wailing on their knees to the Saviour as they begged mercy for a lifetime of sins. The other half had pretty much the opposite reaction, breaking out a hidden store of rum and drinking themselves blind.

Racker made Guts put his weapons away so he wouldn't complicate the surrender. Guts grumbled about it, but we knew Healy marauded under a code that guaranteed the safety of children. Since he'd included us in that category the last time around, Guts and I figured we didn't have much to fear.

I actually felt a little guilty about the situation. While the crew were losing their minds in mortal terror of Healy's arrival, I was looking forward to it. Although I still had no idea why, Healy had gone out of his way to be helpful to us in the past – he'd not only rescued us when we were lost at sea and given us passage to Deadweather, but the pistols we carried were left over from the

crates of weapons he'd sent us to help defend the ugly fruit plantation from Pembroke's soldiers.

Not only that, the food on the *Grift* had been much better than
on the *Thrush*. If things went our way, we might have a shot at a
decent meal.

As the *Grift* tied up to us, Racker ordered the crew to form a
line on deck with our hands over our heads in surrender, Guts and
me included. It wasn't a pretty sight. The religious types couldn't
stop trembling, the drunks were swaying on their feet, Guts was
twitchy . . . Pretty much the only man among us who could hold
still was one of the drunks, and that was because he'd passed out
cold on the deck.

The pirates slid a long plank from their deck to ours, and while
a line of them kept watch with rifles from the deck of the *Grift*,
Burn Healy – a shade over six feet, with wide shoulders, curly
brown hair topped by a black hat and a face that might have been
handsome if the look in his grey-flecked blue eyes wasn't so terrifying – strode across the plank and onto the *Thrush*.

It was a pretty treacherous walk. The *Grift*'s higher deck made
for a steep downward slope, both ships were bobbing in the water,
and over the gap between them, there was nothing to hold on to
or to break a fall. But Healy pulled it off the same way he did everything, with a light touch and a confidence so total you couldn't
help staring at him in awe, or fear, or both.

He was followed by his first mate Spiggs, a barrel-chested man
with a hawklike face. Behind Spiggs came two rough-looking pirates, each with a saber in one hand and a pistol in the other. All
four men carried the Healy mark: a small red flame tattooed on
the side of their throats.

Healy walked up to Captain Racker without so much as a glance at the rest of us and got straight to business.

"Cargo and destination?"

"Mostly timber. Bit of ugly fruit. Headed to Pella. Then the Barkers." Racker's voice was barely more than a whisper, and he didn't seem to know whether to look Healy in the eye or keep his head bowed in submission.

"You trade with Cartagers?" The question itself wasn't threatening, but Healy's tone was so menacing that I felt my stomach drop.

As he watched Healy's left hand slowly travel to the cutlass hanging from his belt, Racker seemed to forget how to talk. His lips fluttered, but no words came out.

"Do you understand the question?"

"Y-y-yeh."

"Meaning, yes, you trade with Short-Ears?"

As he nodded, Racker began to tremble. I could understand why. When he wanted it to, Healy's tone of voice could make even the most harmless-seeming words sound like they were threatening a violent and sudden death.

As I watched the two of them, fearing for Racker's life, I wondered how I ever could have looked forward to an encounter with such a terrifying man.

"Does it please you, being a traitor to the Rovian crown? Or are you so craven that it never crossed your mind?"

"J-j-just t-t-trying . . . t-to . . . earn . . . m-my bread."

"So we're leaning towards craven, then?"

The captain nodded miserably and squeezed his eyes shut, like he expected to be sliced in half by Healy's cutlass and didn't want to see it coming.

Healy just stared at him, expressionless.

In the silence that followed, one of the crewmen uttered a low moan.

Finally, the pirate's eyebrows jumped ever so slightly, dismissing the subject.

"Ugly fruit . . . Bound from Deadweather, I suppose?"

Racker opened his eyes a crack. "Y-yessir."

Healy turned his head, his sharp eyes moving down the line of trembling crewmen. When they reached me, I saw a flicker of recognition – but as his eyes burned into mine, I realized I was risking death by staring back and quickly looked at my feet.

Healy returned his attention to Racker. "You're familiar with a pirate named Ripper Jones?"

Guts growled in his throat at the mention of the pirate who once owned him.

"Only b-by reputation," answered Racker.

"Captains a frigate called the *Red Throat* – three-masted, square-rigged, thirty guns. Have you seen such a ship in the past week?"

"N-no, sir."

"Would you know it by sight if you had?"

"I-I-I th-think, sir. Ha-haven't seen *any* ships this week, other th-th-th . . ." Racker had to pause for a bit to get his nerves under control. "Th-than what was in port at-at Deadweather."

"Which was what?"

"*S-s-sea Goblin . . . Frenzy . . . Blood Lust . . .*"

25

"Nothing under sail?"

"N-no, sir."

"You're quite sure?"

"Y-y-yes."

Healy nodded. Then he raised his voice, addressing the entire crew.

"It's in the interest of every man who sails the Blue Sea . . . that Ripper Jones be scoured from these waters forever."

He turned his head to take us all in with his fearsome eyes. "So if any of you encounter him, or his ship – you will kill him . . . sink it . . . or find me immediately so that I can do it. Do you understand?"

"Yes?" came a frightened squeak from Racker.

Healy looked disappointed – not just at the captain but at the whole crew, who immediately fell to croaking their agreement as loudly as they could muster.

"Yeh!"

"Got it!"

"You betcha!"

They didn't sound too convincing. Then again, it was a pretty tall order. And I wondered whether Healy was hunting down the only pirate on the Blue Sea with a reputation as terrible as his own for personal reasons – everybody knew Healy and the Ripper hated each other's guts – or because of the Ripper's attack on the *Earthly Pleasure,* a passenger ship full of Rovian nobles that Roger Pembroke owned.

Healy and Pembroke had some kind of relationship that I couldn't for the life of me understand. Millicent had once told me that Healy worked for her father, and while I couldn't imagine

Burn Healy taking orders from anybody, at times they did seem like allies. But then at other times, they seemed like the mortal enemies you'd expect a businessman and a pirate to be.

It was mystifying. But so were a lot of things on the Blue Sea.

Finally, Healy let his eyebrows jump again.

"Right, then. Place five bushels of ugly fruit on the deck of my ship, and we'll leave you to your wretched commerce with the scum of the earth."

The crew fell over themselves racing to the cargo hold to fetch the fruit. Guts and I were about to follow them below when Healy stepped in our path.

"Hello, Egbert," he said evenly.

When Healy spoke to me, Reggie was a few feet away, and I heard him make an odd gurgling noise that I think was an expression of shock.

"Hello, sir," I said.

"Come. Have a chat with me."

As Healy strode over to the deck rail, Guts and I traded looks: *was Guts supposed to come, too?* In the end, he settled for hanging back just out of earshot.

When I reached Healy, he was studying the western horizon, his back to the rest of the ship. I stopped an arm's length away from him. The first time we met, I'd watched him throw a pirate overboard without warning. Even though the pirate had deserved it, I didn't want to take any chances.

"Tell me something," he said, his eyes still on the horizon. "Is that captain giving me the truth?"

"I think so," I said. "Haven't seen any ships since we've been at sea."

"What was happening in Port Scratch when you left?"

"The field pirates were on a bender. Roger Pembroke had tried to bribe them, so they had some money, and a lot of guns – thanks for those, by the way."

Healy gave a little shrug. "I had extra. About the Scratch, though – any sign of the Ripper, or his men, any discussion of him? It's important."

I shook my head. "I wish I could help."

He was quiet for a while, still searching the empty sea. I was starting to wonder if the conversation was over when he turned his head, looking at me for the first time.

"How *did* things go with Pembroke, by the way? He seems not to have killed you. Is still trying?"

"Far as I know."

"And I take it you didn't kill him?"

"No," I said. "Sorry – I did *want* to," I quickly added, because Healy had suggested it the last time I'd seen him, and I felt like I'd let him down.

"No need to apologize. It was just a suggestion."

"Your guns were an awfully big help, though. Probably wouldn't be here if it weren't for them."

"Glad to hear it. Did you hang on to any? Or did the field pirates cadge them all?"

"We've still got a few."

"Well, keep the powder dry. Never know when it might come in handy. There's pirates in these waters, you know."

Then he winked at me. It was hard to know how to take that. Here was a man everyone agreed was the most pitiless killer on the Blue Sea, who moments ago had seemed on the verge of

28

slitting Racker's throat just for selling ugly fruit to Cartagers . . .
and now he was joking with me like a friendly innkeeper.

I didn't know whether to feel pleased or terrified.

Healy turned his head to look at Guts, who was skulking by
the foremast, trying not to look like he was eavesdropping on us.

"What happened to the girl you were with?"

"Went back to Sunrise with him."

Healy cocked his head, his eyes narrowing thoughtfully. "Was
she . . . ?"

"Pembroke's daughter."

His eyes widened. Then he shook his head and chuckled. "Hats
off to you, boy. Got a talent for trouble . . . You headed down to
the Barkers now?"

"No . . . Pella Nonna."

The humour left his eyes. "What the blazes for?"

I didn't want to mention the treasure, but I had no idea what
else to say. So I wound up gaping at him like an idiot while my
palms went clammy.

"Going to tell me it's complicated again?" Healy's face darkened, which was a frightening sight. "Are you looking to get in
with the Short-Ears?"

I shook my head hard, even as I wondered what he had against
Cartagers. "No! Not at all. It's . . . I just . . . need to . . . see some
Natives."

He searched my face for a moment. Then the dark look turned
to one of recognition.

"Ahhh . . ." he said slowly. "Let me guess: lost treasure of the
Fire King? Is *that* what it's all about? This business between you
and Pembroke?"

The look on my face must have convinced Healy he'd guessed right. I looked away. As I studied my shoes, I could feel his eyes on me.

"Piece of advice, son. Whatever you think you're after, I seriously doubt it's worth the trouble. And Pella Nonna's no place to be. Especially in the next few weeks."

I looked up, confused by what he'd said, and the look on his face confused me even more. His eyebrows were knitted together, less in anger than what I could've sworn was concern.

Then he looked away, took a deep breath and let it out with a heavy sigh.

Since when did a pirate – and not just any pirate, but Burn Healy – sigh? Over anything? It was even more disorienting than the wink he'd given me.

Healy glanced at Guts, then back to me. When he spoke, it was in a low, oddly wavering voice.

"I imagine you're at loose ends . . . between your family and this Pembroke business . . . If you and your friend want to come with me . . . temporarily, mind you . . . I'm sure I could figure out what to do with you."

It was dumbfounding – not just the offer itself, but the fact that Burn Healy suddenly seemed less than completely self-assured. In fact, he seemed almost as confused by his offer as I was.

I looked up at his ship, at the line of stone-faced killers on the deck with their guns still trained on the *Thrush,* and at the red flag of piracy snapping in the wind over its mast. Then I looked back at Guts.

"Can I . . . talk it over with my partner?"

"Partner? Oh! Yes. By all means. Have at it." Some of Healy's usual verve returned, and he motioned me towards Guts with a wave of his hand.

"Wot is it?" Guts muttered when I'd dragged him off to a corner of the foredeck.

"He wants us to come with him."

"Wot, on his ship?"

"I guess so, yeah."

"Wot the *pudda* for?"

"I don't know. I think he wants to help us."

"Help us how?"

"Well . . . he guessed what we were after. And he said it's not worth the trouble. And Pella's no place to be at the moment. And if we come with him, he'll . . . 'figure out what to do with us'."

"*Blun* to that!"

"Keep your voice down! Look, I don't know what he's getting at, but –"

"I do! Wants the treasure!"

"You think?" That hadn't occurred to me.

"Course he does! S'plains everything! That's why he helped ye against Pembroke! 'Cause he knew ye had the map! So he gives ye the guns ye need to slip the richy, then follows ye out here, makes like he's savin' ye again! And yer so grateful, ye spill yer guts to him! So he gets the map, slits our throats, makes off with the treasure!"

Guts let out a low whistle. "Real *porna mafalo,* he is."

I chewed on that for a while. It did explain a lot. But I just didn't buy it.

31

"I don't know . . . I feel like we can trust him."

Guts snorted. "That's 'cause ye never lived on no pirate ship."

"He's not like the Ripper! You heard what he said to the crew –
he's hunting him down! Burn Healy's not that kind of pirate."

"Don't be a fool! Friendly or not, sooner or later . . ." His face
twitching, Guts unstrapped Lucy and raised his left arm to show
me the rounded stump where his hand should have been.

"Only one kind of pirate in this world," he said.

That settled it for both of us.

There was just one problem.

"How am I going to tell him no? He's Burn – Healy. What if he
kills me?"

"He ain't gonna . . ." Guts's voice trailed off as he considered
the situation.

Then he grabbed my arm in a tight squeeze. "'Fore ye go over
there – draw me the map, will ye?"

"Oh, shut up!" I tore my arm away and started towards Healy.

It was the longest twenty feet I'd ever walked. He must have
heard me coming, because he turned to look at me when I was
still a few steps away.

"What's the verdict?"

"We . . . kind of . . ." Talking to him was suddenly as hard for
me as it had been for Racker. "M-maybe . . . rather . . ."

"Not come?" His eyebrows jumped. But not like he was angry.
Like it was a big relief.

"Well, more's the pity. Best of luck to you."

He gave me a smile and a friendly pat on the shoulder. Then
he took off so fast he was halfway up the plank before I had time
to exhale.

WHEN THE *GRIFT* disappeared for good over the horizon, a cheer of joy went up from the crew. But something had been bugging me almost from the moment Healy had left the *Thrush*, and once the cheers died down, I finally shared it with Guts.

"The thing is . . . he's Burn – Healy, right?"

Guts nodded. "Burn *pudda* Healy."

"So if he wants something, he takes it. And if he wanted the map – why not just kidnap me? Drag me on board? It doesn't make sense."

Guts thought about it. "Nope. Guess it don't."

"I think he really *was* trying to help us. And he warned me about Pella. Said it's 'no place to be. Especially in the next few weeks.' Like something bad was going to happen there."

We were both quiet for a minute.

"I think we should have gone with him," I said.

Guts gave a twitchy shrug.

"Too late now."

He was right about that, anyway.

CHAPTER 3

PELLA

Not long after we parted ways with Healy, the cry of "LAND HO!" went up from the crow's nest. Soon enough, the mountains came into view: a distant range of jagged blue peaks. Racker turned the *Thrush* parallel to the coastline, and we followed it through the night and into the next morning.

It dawned foggy and grey. We couldn't see mountains any more, or anything at all through the haze. By late morning, I was starting to wonder if we'd strayed off course when a massive fortress appeared out of the gloom, flying the purple and orange of the Cartager royal flag.

Its giant walls were brown and smooth, like they were made of clay, and the whole thing seemed to float on the water, unattached to anything. It wasn't until we cleared the far side that I realized it was built on a long finger of rocky land that jutted out at the end of a large bay.

We continued into the bay, and ships began to appear at

anchor. There were a few familiar schooners, but mostly they were strange and exotic-looking: giant galleys with dozens of oars and curved hulls as round as sausages, or lopsided single-masters with towering sterns and squared-off bows so low they didn't look seaworthy.

As we got further in and the whole port came into view, I counted over a hundred ships, moored in the bay or docked at one of a dozen long piers. Tied up at the northernmost piers, by the finger of land that led to the fortress, were three gargantuan Cartager men-of-war, their triple decks bristling with cannon.

Then the city itself peeked out of the fog, starting with a ragged line of buildings, some as high as six storeys tall and all made of the same smooth brown material as the fortress. They were packed so close together that at first I thought they were all one building, like some sort of giant rectangular anthill.

We dropped anchor in the middle of the bay, and Reggie used signal flags to hail a few distant figures on the docks. Guts fetched the rucksack full of our weapons from the hold, and we fidgeted on deck as we waited for a boat to row out so we could hitch a ride to shore.

I thought about asking Guts for one of the guns from the pack, but I was so keyed up my hands were shaking, and I didn't want to accidentally shoot anybody.

The Cartager soldiers came out first, in four long boats. There were two of them in each boat, big men with tiny ears and jowly necks, all so overfed and sleepy-looking I never would have guessed they were soldiers if they hadn't been carrying rifles and wearing long purple uniforms that most of them left unbuttoned over their swollen bellies.

"Don't look like killers t'me," Guts scoffed. "Look like purple slugs."

I had to agree. They seemed too lazy to hang anybody dead. None of them did a lick of work – as far as I could tell, they were only in the boats to keep an eye on their Native labourers, who couldn't have been more different from the soldiers.

The Natives were lanky and trim, with copper skin and wide, flat noses. They went barefoot and shirtless, dressed only in pale cotton breeches that hung loosely off their hips. Two of them manned each boat, handling both the rowing and the loading of the big crates of ugly fruit that just barely fit in the boats.

"Okalu?" I called to a couple of the Natives, but they didn't even look up at me.

I wasn't about to get on a boat with armed soldiers, no matter how fat and sleepy they looked, so once Reggie promised us civilians would be coming out, too, we stayed put and waited for a better option.

Half an hour after the last of the soldiers pushed off, a much smaller boat arrived, manned by a pair of Natives. One of them looked like all the other Natives, skinny and shirtless, but I would've mistaken the second for a Cartager if it hadn't been for his ears, nose and skin – he wore a frilly silk Continental shirt over a big belly, and he didn't even bother to get up when the fruit crate proved too wide for the boat and nearly capsized them.

That sent a few dozen ugly fruit into the water. Fortunately, they floated – and although the silk-shirted Native produced a short club that he shook at the skinny one, he didn't end up using it, because Skinny dived right in to recover the fruit.

Eventually, Skinny got it all loaded in – not just the fruit that had gone overboard, but the entire contents of the crate, which he dumped directly into the boat, filling it almost to the gunwale before he sent the empty crate back up to the *Thrush*.

I didn't like the looks of Silk Shirt's club, so we decided to wait for the next boat. We were watching them cast off when Racker turned to us.

"Change your mind about Pella?" he asked.

"Just waiting for the right boat," I said.

"Right or not, that's the last one," he said. I looked back at the deck and realized there wasn't any ugly fruit left on it.

"Wait!" I yelled down at the Natives in the rowboat, who were pushing off from the *Thrush*'s hull. They looked up at me, confused. Then Skinny raised the oars to row away.

I was just starting to panic when Guts jumped over the deck rail and down into the boat, the rucksack strapped to his back.

He landed ugly, nearly swamping the boat and turning it into a chaotic tangle of fruit, limbs and angry Natives. I stood there gaping at the sight until I realized the boat was already too far from the *Thrush* for me to make it at a jump, and getting further away with every passing second.

I took a deep breath and went into the water.

When I broke the surface, I could hear Guts and the Natives yelling at each other. With a few frantic strokes, I managed to make it to the boat and grab hold of the gunwale above my head. It was too high for me to lift myself up into the boat, and from the angle I was at, I couldn't see much except the bare back of the skinny Native.

The yelling was getting worse. Guts had used up his whole supply of Cartager curses, and the Natives clearly understood them and didn't appreciate it.

"HELP!" I called.

That got Skinny's attention, but not the way I wanted. When he turned and saw me, his eyes flashed with anger, and he raised one of the oars to clock me.

"DON'T, YE —!" That was Guts.

"— —!" That was Silk Shirt, giving a panicky yell in a language I didn't understand.

Skinny's oar froze in midair. He looked over his shoulder, and I heard him gasp.

"Help him up, ye —!" That was Guts again. He had to repeat himself a few times, because Skinny didn't understand Rovian. But eventually, Skinny put down the oar and turned round to help me.

His eyes were wide with worry, and once he'd managed to haul me into the boat – which was so overflowing with ugly fruit there was barely any room for me – I saw why.

Guts had one of our guns in his good hand. He was sweeping it back and forth at the two Natives, like he was trying to decide which of them to shoot.

"Grab a gun," he told me. "Can't cover 'em both where I'm sittin'."

"Are you mad!? You can't shoot them!"

"Don't have to – just gotta look like we might. C'mon! In the pack!"

He was in the middle seat, the ugly fruit piled so deep around him I couldn't see his lower legs. Our pack was on his lap.

"This is bad," I said. "This is *really* bad."

"Could be worse. Could be them holdin' the guns. C'mon!"

He jostled the pack with his leg. I didn't much like his plan, but I didn't have a better one. So I took a gun from the pack and pointed it in the general direction of Silk Shirt, who was sitting up at the bow.

Then I shoved some ugly fruit aside with my free hand and wedged myself into the middle seat next to Guts, facing forward. Guts was facing the other way, his gun on Skinny back in the stern.

"Get rowin'!" he barked, gesturing towards the oars.

Skinny got the point. The boat rocked as he turned us towards the piers.

Silk Shirt was staring at me like he was terrified I'd pull the trigger. I wanted to tell him not to worry, but I figured that'd defeat the whole purpose of pointing a gun at him.

Even so, I didn't want to be unpleasant about it.

"Hello," I said, trying to sound friendly.

He just kept staring – still scared, and confused now on top of it.

"Okalu?" I asked him.

"Neh," he said. *"Flut."*

I vaguely recalled Racker mentioning the Flut in his list of cannibal tribes. But sitting there in a frilly silk shirt, he didn't look much like a cannibal.

"Okalu grawa," he added.

I was about to ask him what that meant when he pointed to my head.

"Wanaluff, neh?"

Wanaluff was Cartager for "cow-ears". I put a hand up where he was pointing and realized that with my hair wet and slick from the water, my ears were exposed. Before I could respond, Guts exploded.

"STUFF IT, YOU!" He whipped round and pointed his gun at Silk Shirt, who reared back in terror and started frantically apologizing.

"Se booya! Wanaluff booya!"

Skinny chimed in from behind me. *"Booya wanaluff! Booya, booya!"*

The way they said it, *booya* might have meant "good", or "okay", or even "calm down" – but whatever it was, they clearly didn't want any trouble.

"Will you take it easy?" I hissed at Guts.

"Ain't nobody calls *me* cow-ears without a fight."

NONE OF US talked much after that. Guts and I kept our guns on the Natives the whole way in, which felt more and more ridiculous. I couldn't imagine shooting an unarmed man, and except for the moment when Skinny was about to clock me with the oar, they hadn't done anything to deserve it.

And when I thought about it from their angle, I realized if it was my boat, and two kids had jumped in it without an invitation, I'd get riled up, too. Especially if they pointed guns at me.

I started to feel terrible about the whole situation.

"I think we should pay them," I said.

"Fer wot?"

"Giving us a ride."

"Doin' it free!"

40

"Because we're holding them up! It's not right. We should at least give them something."

"Only got five silver left."

"How about one?"

"Comin' out o' yer half."

"That's all right."

Guts dug in his pocket and handed me a silver piece. I passed it on to Silk Shirt.

He looked a little wary at first, but he took it.

"*Gadda.*"

I didn't know how to say "you're welcome" in Cartager, so I just smiled.

He smiled back, but it was more of a "please don't shoot me" smile than a real one, and I still felt lousy.

Given the gun situation, I didn't want to take my eyes off Silk Shirt for too long to stare at the city as we rowed in, but I managed to sneak a few glances. The fog was burning off to reveal a reddish-brown forest of buildings that seemed to go on forever.

The place was massive. I'd only ever been to Blisstown and Port Scratch in my life, and you could have fit ten of those towns into Pella Nonna with room to spare. What I could see of the waterfront was thrumming with people, ships, cargo and livestock, all going every which way.

We tied up on a crowded pier in between two fishing boats. The Natives were thrilled to see us go – there were a lot of friendly-nervous *booya!*s and *gadda!*s from them as we climbed the ladder onto the pier. I repeated the words back to them, trying to smile when I did, and wondering if I shouldn't try to get Guts to give them a second silver piece.

Still holding the guns, we hurried down the pier towards the city.

"Let's try not to shoot anybody unless we have to," I told Guts.

He shrugged. "See how it goes."

We turned onto the boardwalk and found ourselves in a churning whirlpool of people, alien-looking and strange in flowing robes and Native breeches and curious hats over weirdly shaped noses, tiny ears, exotic skin . . . all bartering over sacks and crates of things in unusual shapes and colours, along with livestock like none I'd ever seen, needle-nosed pigs and furry long-necked horse-type creatures and powerful little dogs with wide, stubby snouts who barked at us as we passed.

No one so much as looked at us. They were too busy buying and selling and jabbering at each other, mostly in what I guessed was Cartager. There wasn't a single hard letter in the whole language – I tried to listen for the individual words, but they all ran together like liquid dribbling out of people's mouths.

We started up the main road, dodging not just people, but wagons and horses and more strange livestock. On either side of the road, cloth awnings on long wooden poles shaded the storefronts, where men and women in colourful, loose-fitting Native shirts sat slouched on log benches. One or two met my eye as we passed, but most paid us no mind at all.

I was wondering if any of them were Okalu when Guts gave me a sharp elbow in the side.

"Soldiers!" he hissed.

I looked up ahead. Coming towards us was a pack of five purple-uniformed Cartagers, most of them heavyset but still a lot tougher-looking than the ones in the boats.

42

They all had rifles slung over their shoulders. And they were too close, and the street was too crowded, for us to duck the encounter.

The lead soldier's eyes fell on me, and they widened in surprise as he stared at my ears.

I gripped the pistol so tight my hand hurt.

He was three steps away when he broke into a grin.

"Booya damai, wanaluff!"

I didn't know what *"booya damai"* meant, but there was no mistaking his tone. He was being friendly.

The rest of the soldiers repeated the greeting as they passed.

"Booya damai!"

"Booya damai!"

"Boo . . . ya . . . damai," I mumbled back, hoping it was the right thing to say.

The last of the soldiers gave me a friendly clap on the arm as they passed.

Guts and I turned to watch them go. Cartager soldiers, the kind we'd been told would kill us on sight . . .

They couldn't have been nicer.

"Figure those men on the *Thrush* were wrong about this place?" I asked.

"Dead wrong, looks like. Here – stow this." He held out his pistol.

I took the rucksack off my back and put away the pistols. Now that I was a little calmer, I realized I was starving.

"I could use some food –"

"Shhh . . ." Guts had his head cocked to one side, a curious look on his face. "Hear that?"

There was music coming from somewhere. It was too far away to make out anything but the rhythm – a steady, off-kilter chug that sounded as exotic as everything else looked.

Guts grinned. "That's a Cartager beat."

"What's that mean?"

"Means it's good. C'mon! Let's find it."

We followed the sound up the road into the heart of the city. I hadn't heard much music in my life. Growing up, we didn't have instruments in the house, and when I passed the occasional pirate sawing on a fiddle in Port Scratch, it always sounded like a cat getting tortured. When I lived with the Pembrokes, I'd listened in on Millicent's piano lessons, and while they weren't as hard on my ears as the pirate fiddles, the music she played made me want to take a nap.

This was a whole other thing. It had a kind of rolling energy that got my head nodding with the beat as I walked. I looked over at Guts and saw him doing the same, a smile playing across his face.

That was odd. Guts wasn't the type to smile.

As we continued on, the rear corner of an enormous, Continental-style palace came into view. It had soaring windows and fancy trim, and unlike most of Pella Nonna's brown-clay buildings, it was made of gleaming white marble. We followed the street round the side of the palace, and a set of wide steps came into view, spreading across the whole front of the building and leading up to a grand portico fit for a king.

Stretching out in front of the palace steps was a giant court-yard, hemmed in by a tall, fortified city wall and filled with an open-air market that made the bustle down at the docks seem quiet and sleepy. Half the city seemed to be there, either trading, talking, eating or just lounging around.

At the foot of the steps, we found the source of the music we'd been hearing – a band of ten musicians, both Cartager and Native, half of them pounding various drums, a couple strumming guitars and the rest on pipes. A loose cluster of people surrounded them, either dancing to the music or listening with smiles on their faces.

Guts headed for the band so fast I almost lost him in the crowd. When I caught up, he'd snaked his way to the front and was staring at the feet of one of the guitarists.

I followed Guts's gaze to a wide-brimmed hat, upside down on the ground and half full of coins. As I watched, a Cartager girl about my age stepped forward and tossed a coin into the hat. One of the guitarists looked up from his instrument long enough to wink at her, and she blushed as she sank back into a group of other girls, all of them giggling with excitement.

Guts made a noise that sounded like a laugh. Then he elbowed me. "Ain't gonna have no money trouble."

"How do you figure?" I didn't feel right about stealing from them, and anyway if we tried to swipe the hat, fifty people would see us do it.

Instead of answering, he turned back towards the market. "Starvin'. Let's eat."

THE NUMBER OF THINGS for sale in the market was staggering, and there were almost as many kinds of sellers as there were goods – not just Cartagers and Natives, but dark-skinned men with almond eyes who wore long robes and must have come from across the Southern Maw, and Continentals who I could've sworn were Rovian but answered in a strange tongue when we tried to speak to them.

After shopping around for the tastiest-looking food, we used hand gestures to negotiate with a lanky Native for a few cuts from a spit-roasted pig, seasoned with such a delicious hot spice that I swore to eat it for every meal if I could.

But the food cost us two silver – minus some tiny, smooth shells that must have been a kind of money, because the Native handed them to us like he was giving change – and when he wanted a third silver for a jug of water, I realized we were going to be broke by sundown.

"Buy it," said Guts. "Money ain't gonna be no problem."

"Why do you keep saying that?"

He'd wolfed down his food ahead of me and was fiddling with Lucy, tightening and retightening the strap under the hook's leather cowl. Finally, he stopped.

"Get yer water an' I'll show ye."

I bought the water, and when I did, I asked the Native my standard question:

"Okalu?"

He shook his head. *"Neh – Dorono. Okalu grawa."*

That again. Still wondering what it meant, I followed Guts.

The music had stopped while we were eating, and the musicians were taking a break. One of the guitarists, a black-haired Cartager who looked about eighteen, was stretched out on the steps, drinking from a gourd as the cluster of giggling teenage girls fawned over him.

Guts went straight up to the guitarist and barked, "'Ey! Speak Rovian?"

The guitarist eyed him with a grin, then answered with a few slippery words of Cartager.

Guts raised his voice as he looked around.

"Who speaks Rovian here?"

Another young Cartager, a tall kid with a nose as big as his ears were small, looked up from counting the coins they'd collected in the hat.

"I speak. What you want, man?"

He had a thick Cartager accent, so what he said actually sounded more like "I sbee. Wa' yew wa', ma'?"

"Make a bet," said Guts. He pointed at the guitarist with his hook. "Ten gold says I play guitar better than him."

The big-nosed kid burst into laughter, and I felt my stomach clench. Even if we had money, which we didn't, ten gold was a fortune.

"You go' one hand, man!"

"'S'all I need."

"Wha's you name?"

"Guts."

"Gu's? Like –" the kid pointed to his stomach – "on you insides?"

"Guts like I got 'em, ye *bada pudda palomuno porsamora*."

The big-nosed kid just laughed at the mouthful of insults. The guitarist, who'd been turning his head from side to side as he tried to follow the conversation, perked up at the curses and asked his friend a question in Cartager.

Big Nose explained, and the guitarist started to laugh, too.

I expected Guts to blow up at that. But he just smiled bigger.

"Ten gold. Wot ye say?"

I nudged Guts, then whispered in his ear.

"Is this a put-on?"

He shook his head. "Just wait."

Big Nose was shaking his head, like he felt sorry for Guts.

"You wan' lose you money, man? Illy play bes' guitar in Pella."

"Not no more."

The other musicians chimed in, speaking Cartager. I looked around and realized we'd started to draw a crowd. People were trotting over, whispering and chuckling to each other as they pointed at Guts's hook.

Big Nose gave Guts a helpless shrug.

"Okay, man. Ten gold. Hope you can pay. Cos we got big friends."

I whispered to Guts again. "How are we –?"

"Shut up. Gonna be fine."

He was still smiling. In fact, the grin hadn't left his face since he'd first heard the music on the street almost an hour before. In the whole time I'd known him, I'd never seen him smile for more than a second or two.

It was kind of unsettling, to be honest.

The guitarist sat up straight, put the guitar across his lap, and played a short run of notes, his fingers skittering over the strings. Then he paused for a moment, fiddled with a couple of the tuning pegs, and launched into a song.

Like the rest of the music I'd heard that day, it had a hypnotic, chugging rhythm, over which he played a dancing line of notes that I would've found beautiful if I weren't so worried about what Guts had got us into. As the Cartager played, I looked around at all the happy strangers and wondered how many of them would help beat the ten gold out of our hides when it was over.

Some of the men were pretty huge.

The guitarist finished his song, and the crowd clapped and hooted their approval. He stood up, handed his instrument to Guts with a wink and a smile, and motioned for him to take his place on the steps.

Guts sat down. A hush fell over the crowd. I took a quick look around to figure out the best direction to run when it was over.

Straight back, towards the far corner of the courtyard.

I waited for Guts to look up at me so I could signal the getaway route.

But he kept his head down, focused on the neck of the guitar, where he was testing the straight edge of the hook against the strings. It was just long enough to cover them all, and as he ran it down the length of the neck, it made a squeaky noise that didn't sound much like music to me.

There were titters in the crowd. Big Nose shook his head and sighed, half-amused and half-pitying.

Guts stretched out the fingers of his right hand. Then, with the hook pressed against the strings on the neck, he picked out a few tentative notes.

One of them struck false. Guts stopped smiling.

There were a few more titters, but also some pained looks.

I hoped I could run on a full stomach without throwing up.

Guts pulled Lucy away from the guitar's neck. Reached under the cowl to loosen the strap. Readjusted the hook. Tightened the strap one more time.

Then he took a deep breath and began again.

It started with a single note – a long, keening wail that shimmered in the tropical air before it slowly fell away into silence.

Then another. And another. And another, rising to a patter that slowly built into a flood, the notes sliding in and out of each other as the hook flashed back and forth across the neck while the fingers of Guts's good hand tripped the strings in a fast-rising blur of movement.

I don't know what he played, what kind of music it was or where it came from, but it was gorgeous and ecstatic and terrifying, sometimes all at once, ranging in size and shape from towering shards of barely controlled fury all the way down to delicate, plaintive whispers so quiet I could hear the rustle and creak of people in the crowd rising up on tiptoe as they strained to hear.

There was a moment of silence when he finished, followed by a roar of pleasure like I'd never heard before. People were stamping and cheering, crowding around Guts to congratulate him. Even the guitarist he'd beaten couldn't stop himself from flinging his arms round Guts in a friendly hug.

In the middle of the celebration, Guts caught my eye. His grin widened as he gave me a knowing look that said, *Gonna be fine.*

CHAPTER 4

THE LETTER

*D*ear Millicent,
A lot has happened since the last time I saw you.

It was only a sentence, but it took me two hours at a desk and ten pieces of parchment just to get that far. Part of the problem was that I'd never written a letter before, or even seen one, so all I had to go on were the ones I'd read about in books.

The greeting alone gave me fits. *Dear* seemed much too fussy, like something an old lady would write.

I tried *Cheerio, luv,* which was how Eustace started his letters to Gwendolyn in *The Crisps of Upper Mattox,* but I didn't know what it meant. And since I'd always thought Eustace was full of himself, I decided it was a bad risk to copy him.

I started again with *My darling Millicent,* but that looked too gushy.

And *To she for whom no sacrifice is too great and death is not*

51

to be feared should it hasten our blessed reunion felt like overkill. Besides which, the character who wrote that (Miles Cavendish, in *A Storm Upon the Heath*) wound up jumping off a cliff, and I didn't want to give Millicent the wrong idea.

So I was stuck with *Dear.*

Then there was the opening sentence, which had chewed up even more parchment. First I tried:

I love you.

But I was afraid that might scare her off.

I think about that moment when you kissed me a hundred times a day.

Too honest. Also likely to scare her off.

There are a lot of pretty girls in Pella Nonna, but seeing them just makes me miss you more.

That felt wrong for a bunch of reasons. Once I crumpled it up, I decided to avoid the whole subject of my feelings for her, at least up front. So I started again with:

How's the weather on Sunrise?

But that just seemed chatty. And the truth was, I didn't care what the weather was like on Sunrise. I just wanted to let her know what was happening with us. So after a few more failed attempts, I decided to just do that, and to quit tossing out parchment left and right, because it didn't come cheap and I was running low on it.

A lot has happened since the last time I saw you. Guts and I have been in Pella Nonna for two weeks, and although we'll be leaving soon to get the map translated,

I hoped that was true. The question of when we were going to leave had been a real sticking point between me and Guts.

it's been amazing to visit here. You know how in books, Cartagers are always villains? Well, the ones back in Cartage might be, but in Pella, they're not like that at all. They're friendly, and easygoing, and they like to listen to music and eat and drink and have a good time.

No one works very hard, which they can get away with because there's gold everywhere – the Cartagers bring it in from mines somewhere in the southern hills, and there's so much of it lying around that traders come here from all over the world to sell their goods, and even the servants seem to be pretty well off.

Guts and I were definitely well off. I was writing the letter with a peacock quill and a silver inkpot, which I'd found in a drawer of the fancy hardwood desk in the huge living room of the apartment that Salo – he was the tall, friendly, big-nosed band member who spoke Rovian – had helped us rent using the money Guts made from playing music.

There are people here from all over the world, including places I never even knew existed. Mandars, Gualos, Ildians, Umbergians . . . pretty much every kind of people except Rovians. I'm not sure why there aren't more Rovians, because everyone's been very nice to us in spite of our ears.

I'd asked Salo about it. He agreed it was odd that there weren't any Rovians around, but he'd never heard of the Banishment Law. And when I told him about Racker's warning that we'd be killed if we set foot in Pella, he laughed.

"That captain smart, man. He lie to crew, keep them on ship. Crew stop in Pella, crew never leave. Pella *booya!*"

Booya meant good, tasty, delicious. Pella was definitely *booya*.

There are tons of Natives, too, from a dozen different tribes, and I was surprised to find out they're all as different from each other as Rovians are from Cartagers. Some of the ones in Pella are labourers, but a lot are traders and businessmen, and some are even richer than the Cartagers.

The problem for us is that none of them are Okalu. When I got here and started asking around, people kept telling me "Okalu grawa".

It turns out "grawa" is Cartager for "dead".

You know some of the history already,

Millicent had once told me the story of the Fire King's tribe, but I'd forgotten most of it. It took a lot of walking around and awkward conversations with people who didn't speak my language before I managed to track down a Fingu shopkeeper who not only knew Rovian, but could fill me in on what had become of the Okalu.

but the Okalu are blood enemies of another tribe, the Moku. They both come from the mountains north of Pella, and back when the Fire King was alive a hundred years ago, the Okalu ruled the Moku (and most of the other tribes, too). After the first Cartager invasion, the Okalu Empire fell apart, and ever since then the Okalu have been fighting with the Moku for control of their territory in the north.

A few years back, some Continentals (the man I talked to wasn't sure if it was Cartagers, Rovians or someone else) started helping the Moku by giving them guns and cannon. After that, the Moku won the war – they took over the Okalu's territory and killed almost all of them.

People say there might be a few Okalu left, up in the northern mountains, but nobody seems sure of it. I'm going to go there to look for them with Guts just as soon I can get him to leave town.

Oh, one other thing: it turns out Guts is the greatest guitar player anyone in Pella Nonna has ever seen. And that's saying a lot, because there are tons of guitar players here. Anyway, he's famous here now, which is

I almost wrote *really annoying*. But I didn't want to sound bitter.

And to be fair, Guts being famous had its advantages. We were staying in this amazing apartment, and he gave me all the money I needed to buy things. And I had to admit the days were pretty good, because the band played in the square, and I could lounge on the palace steps and listen to them, and eat tasty food, and take in the sights.

But at night, he went out to play at private parties for rich people, and I wasn't invited. After a while, it got boring sitting home alone. I couldn't even read, because all the books in the apartment were written in some weird squiggly language that I think was Mandar.

So I'd go to bed early, because I was alone and there was nothing else to do, and I'd fall asleep thinking about Millicent.

And then in the middle of the night, Guts would come home, along with half the band and the giggling teenage Cartager girls who followed them everywhere, and they'd have a party in the living room that was impossible to sleep through, and sometimes went on until dawn.

Even worse, now that Guts was famous, and making good money from playing his music, he didn't seem all that worried about finding the treasure any more.

But I didn't want to get into any of that with Millicent. So I just wrote:

interesting. He uses a steel hook to make the notes. I've asked him how he learned to do that, and whether he started playing back when he still had two hands, but he won't talk about it. Although he did say that before he got his new hook, he sometimes played with a knife strapped to his forearm.

I guess sometimes it's better not to know things. And I'm glad I was never a cabin boy for Ripper Jones.

Speaking of things I don't know . . . if there's any way you can get word to me about what your father is up to

56

I stopped writing in midsentence, because I'd just realized there was no point in going on.

I couldn't send a letter to Millicent. It was madness. And not just because I wasn't sure how to send one in the first place – I knew from books that people got letters "in the post", but I wasn't too clear on what that meant, or how you went about finding a post, or what you did with the post after you'd put the letter in it.

I couldn't send it because the chances were better than good that her father would intercept it. And then he'd know exactly where I was, and what I was doing.

Not that it would have been too hard for him to figure out I was headed for Pella in the first place.

My heart started to thump, like it always did when I thought about Roger Pembroke and how long it'd be until he came looking for me and the map.

Along with the fear came another emotion – a dark, nagging guilt that had been eating at me the whole time we'd been in Pella, and that lately had started to haunt me even more than the fear.

It had to do with my family.

They weren't the greatest. Dad had always been a mystery, gruff and distant and impossible to read. He didn't treat me ugly like my brother and sister did, but he wasn't exactly kind, either.

Venus and Adonis were pretty horrible all around – vicious and stupid, each in their own special way. When she wasn't insulting me, Venus used to spend her time fantasizing out loud about how some day a Rovian prince was going to pluck her from the muggy stink of Deadweather and make her his princess. If anybody suggested the odds of that were awfully long, she'd screech like a howler monkey and try to claw their eyes out.

I'm not sure Adonis was smart enough to even have fantasies. But if he did, they probably involved stomping on people who were smaller than he was. It was the one thing that never failed to put a smile on his face.

Both of them blamed me for our not having a mother, because she'd died birthing me. Pointing out that I was only a baby when it happened just made them more convinced I was evil.

So it wasn't like I missed having them around.

But as nasty as they were, they didn't deserve what they got from Roger Pembroke, which was death by drowning once the hot-air balloon he'd tricked them into boarding finally dropped from the sky somewhere in the Blue Sea.

And he'd got away with it. He murdered three people, the only family I had, and nobody – not on the islands or the mainland or anywhere else – was going to come after him for it. Nobody was going to make him pay.

Unless I did.

I wasn't sure how to avenge my family. But I knew I had to try. I'd always known it, even on the *Thrush*, when I was so scared I wanted to bug out and run away. At times like that, the fear was strong enough to push that dark, nagging guilt to the back of my head for a while.

But it always came back. And the longer I stayed in Pella Nonna, the worse it got. After a while, lying in the sun and listening to music with my belly full of food didn't make me happy so much as anxious. And not just because I was sure Pembroke was still looking for me, but because I had a job to do and I wasn't doing it.

I put aside the half-finished letter to Millicent and started to practise the map again – not on the parchment, because I was afraid to leave a physical copy for someone to steal, but traced with my finger on the dark wood of the desk.

I was halfway through the map when the front door burst open and Guts entered, along with Salo, Illy, two other band members and half a dozen of the gigglers.

"WHOOOOOOOO!"

They were in high spirits, which was annoying.

Salo slapped Guts on the back. "Tell Egg man big news!"

"Playin' the palace tomorrow!" Guts said with a grin and a twitch. Lately, he only twitched when he was excited.

"We get you in, too, Egg man! You gon' meet *Li Homaya*! Eat his food! *Se booya!*"

"Who's *Li Homaya*?" I asked.

"Big man in palace! Leader of Pella. Been two months gone with army. Tribes in south give trouble, so *Li Homaya* go make them know who is in charge." Salo pounded the air with his fist.

"I thought Cartagers got along with all the tribes," I said.

"Ones that don't give trouble, yeah. Other ones . . . pow." Salo swung his fist again.

It was news to me that the Cartagers and Native tribes weren't totally at peace, and I might have asked Salo more about it if I hadn't had other things on my mind.

"Guts – can you not have the party here tonight?" The band and the gigglers were starting to settle into the overstuffed couches in the living room, and I knew once they made themselves at home, there'd be no getting them out.

"Wot's yer problem?"

I lied. "I'm sick. I think it's catching."

Salo looked concerned. "Hey, Egg man – don't make band sick. Big show tomorrow."

"Well, maybe you should – HUUARCH!" I broke off the sentence with a loud, hopefully not too fake-sounding cough.

That did the trick. They were out of the door in seconds. Guts was going to go with them, but I managed to get him to hang back.

"Wot's yer *pudda* problem?" he asked once we were alone.

"We can't keep putting it off. We've got to go find the Okalu."

"Gonna. In a bit."

"You said that last week."

He shrugged. "Good week, tho'."

"I'm glad you're having fun." That probably sounded a little too sarcastic.

"So's you! Good here! Good fer you, too."

"It's nice and all," I admitted. "But I've got to get on with finding that treasure."

"Been missin' a hundred years. Ain't like it's –"

"He's going to come looking for me!"

Guts winced. I didn't have to tell him who I was talking about.

"I don't want to go it alone," I said. "But if I have to –"

He shook his head firmly. "Ain't gonna have to. Partners." His eyes twitched a couple of times. "Can I just play the palace 'fore we go?"

"When is it? Tomorrow night?"

He nodded. "Go the next day. First thing. Awright?"

"All right," I said. "And . . . thanks."

"Don't gotta thank me. Partners."

LI HOMAYA – THE TITLE meant "The Highest One" in Cartager, and it made me wonder how the King of Cartage felt about
one of his colonial governors calling himself that – returned to
the city late the next morning. An hour before he arrived, a pair
of soldiers on horseback galloped into town through the city's
big double gates and started barking orders at the merchants in
the marketplace. As the merchants hurried to pack up their tents
and wagons, clearing out the courtyard, I asked Salo what was
happening.

"*Li Homaya* coming," he said. "Everybody have to stop work.
Say hello."

Soon a wide lane had been cleared down the middle of the
courtyard, from the gates to the palace steps, and columns of
soldiers from the fortress stood at attention on either side of the
lane. Most of them looked sweaty and rumpled, like they'd all
been woken from naps and forced to run there at double speed.
But at least their purple uniforms were actually buttoned over
their bellies for a change.

We stood with the band, packed in alongside the rest of the
crowd behind one of the columns of soldiers. Guts was scowling.
He hadn't wanted to quit playing.

"*Pudda* stupid."

Salo lowered his voice. "Quiet, Guts man. Soldier hear you,
end up in dungeon."

"Seriously?" I asked.

"Yeah, man. *Li Homaya* big boss. Make all the rules." He
pointed behind us, where a soldier was dressing down a

frightened-looking merchant who he'd caught still trying to do business.

Salo elbowed Guts in the ribs. "Smile for *Li Homaya*, man! You go dungeon, whole band lose money."

Guts wouldn't smile, but he managed not to scowl as much.

Then a bugle and drum announced *Li Homaya*'s arrival. He galloped in, a large man with a moon-shaped face and a billowing cape, riding a white stallion. A squad of cavalry officers followed him.

As the crowd cheered – more out of duty than joy, it seemed like – he dismounted at the foot of the palace steps, handed the reins of his stallion to a waiting soldier and climbed the steps to the portico.

His officers followed him up the steps while the rest of the cavalry entered the courtyard – a couple of hundred surprisingly lean and tough-looking soldiers whose horses kicked up so much dust that an epidemic of coughing broke out in the crowd.

Once the dust had settled and the senior officers had taken their places behind him on the portico, *Li Homaya* faced the crowd and raised his hand in the air.

Everyone went silent. Their leader's big head swivelled from side to side, taking in the scene. Even from a distance, it was pretty clear he was full of himself.

Then, in a booming voice, he began a long and boring speech, complete with a lot of fist-shaking and dramatic pauses. I couldn't understand a word of it. The pauses were meant to give the crowd a chance to cheer him, and they did – but as I looked around, I saw a lot of stifled yawns and glassy looks.

Finally, he finished with a double pump of both fists, turned on his heel, and marched into the palace. The moment the door closed behind him, the cheering died away, the cavalry rode out, and the soldiers began to file back to the fortress.

Within minutes, the market was returning to normal. As the band got ready to play again, I noticed a line had formed at the palace's main door. It snaked across the portico, a curious mix of people, both young and old, Native and Continental, with a few Mandars thrown in for good measure. Some waited in pairs, but not friendly ones – as they stood there, they bickered with each other, a few of them pretty viciously.

I asked Salo what they were doing.

"Want to speak to *Li Homaya*," he said. "They have problem, need him to solve. He make rules. Decide everything."

Soon the soldiers at the palace door started letting people in, and the line began to move. Every few minutes, someone would exit the palace, looking either joyful or angry – for the people in pairs, it was usually one of each – and another one would enter.

As the band played, I watched the people go in and out, amusing myself by trying to imagine what business they'd brought before *Li Homaya*.

Then a group of three Cartager men joined the line. They were a rough bunch, their clothes torn and dirty and their belts sagging with pistols and knives.

My heart skipped a beat as I realized all three of them were staring in my direction. They looked familiar, but I had no idea why.

I was racking my brain to think of where I'd seen them before when one of them pointed – not at me, but just past me – and when I looked over my shoulder and saw Guts playing in the band, I remembered.

They were pirates from Ripper Jones's crew.

I tried to get Guts's attention, but he was lost in his music. The band had drawn a pretty big crowd, and I didn't want to make a scene by interrupting. They were still playing an hour later when the three pirates emerged from the palace.

They sauntered down the steps, pushed their way to the front of the crowd, and stood sneering at Guts.

The second he noticed them, he stopped playing. Gradually, the rest of the band did, too.

"Ay, Gussie," the tallest of the pirates called out. "Where you get tha' hook, boy? You got new frien'?"

"We you frien'," said another. "You come back wi' us! Play for Ripper."

Guts's face was twitching up a storm. "Die first, ye *bada* scum."

The pirates' smiles disappeared, and they moved to draw their weapons.

Guts leaped up, raising his hook with a snarl – but in an instant, a dozen band members and townspeople had jumped in to stand between him and the pirates.

Some of the townspeople had weapons of their own, and angry threats rained down on the pirates from all around.

For a moment, the Ripper's men stood frozen, stunned to discover that Guts wasn't the friendless outcast he'd been on their ship.

The facts of the situation began to sink in. They all took their hands off their weapons and began to back away, towards the street that led to the docks.

"You got lots new frien', eh, Gussie? No worry. We see you a'gin."

Guts looked too angry to speak. I decided to answer for him.

"Not likely," I called out to them. "Burn Healy's looking for your lot."

Their leader turned towards me with a knowing glint in his eye.

"We loo' for him, too. He gon' have bi' surprise wen he fin' us."

"We got new frien', too," added another, jerking his head in the direction of the palace.

I watched the pirates make their way out of the market, wondering what they meant by that.

Guts spat on the ground where the pirates had stood. "*Pudda* them *porsamoras*. I'm playin' the palace tonight."

CHAPTER 5

THE PALACE

*L*i *Homaya* lived well. We were in a room the size of a small town, drenched in gold – gold statues, gold wall hangings, gold plates, gold silverware . . . all gleaming under the light of a dozen gold chandeliers.

There was a raised stage in the middle of the room, surrounded by big round tables set for ten. A couple of hundred guests, all elegantly dressed and much older than us, milled around while servants in crisp uniforms snaked through the group, offering trays of fizzy red drinks in long-stemmed glasses.

I was the only non-band member who'd been allowed to tag along. As I watched the adults stare at us, I thought to myself that it was a good thing Salo had made us all take baths and buy new clothes. We still stuck out, but at least we smelled okay.

After we'd spent a few minutes standing around like awestruck cows, a palace official in a high-collared suit appeared and began to herd everyone into a line starting at the door.

Once we were all lined up, the official bellowed an announcement, and *Li Homaya* entered the room.

Up close, he looked like a well-dressed toad – tall and fat, with a bloated neck that spilled upwards out of the stiff collar of his uniform, nearly drowning his chin. He had tiny Cartager ears and wide-set eyes with a twinkle in them that managed to be both jolly and menacing at the same time.

On his left elbow was a haughty-looking military aide. On his right was a slender teenage girl in a purple velvet dress. She was Native, from a tribe I figured must be Dorono, because Salo had once said they were the prettiest. She had big dark eyes over a broad nose and a prominent, full-lipped mouth. Her black hair fell in thick waves down to the small of her back, and as I looked down the line of band members in front of me, I could see them all staring saucer-eyed at her.

Li Homaya slowly made his way down the line, letting the military aide introduce him to each guest, who all bowed deeply as they shook his hand.

The girl followed them, rarely speaking, and at first I wondered if she was *Li Homaya*'s daughter, even though she didn't look a thing like him, or possibly his wife, although that seemed a little gross considering how young she looked.

It didn't occur to me that she might be a translator until it was time for Guts's introduction, and she spoke up instead of the first aide.

"His Excellence, *Li Homaya* Somio Malalo, Instrument of His Majesty King Illon and Viceroyal Authority of the Lands of New Cartage, welcomes you to his palace, to enjoy his food and drink and to offer the gift of your talent in return."

She spoke in a clear, confident voice, and her Rovian was so perfect that if it hadn't been for her accent, I would've guessed she'd been born there.

Guts grunted a nervous hello and bowed like he'd seen the others do.

A string of words burbled up from *Li Homaya*'s throat. Then he chortled, reached out to grab Guts's hook, and raised it up so he could examine it while the girl translated his comment.

"*Li Homaya* wonders how you make music with this hook, as to him it looks good only to catch fish."

Li Homaya guffawed again, clapping Guts on the shoulder with a meaty fist. As Guts scowled, the girl quickly added, "I think it is smart if you laugh now."

As Guts stared at her, dumbfounded, *Li Homaya*'s eyes started to crinkle. And not in a good way.

I quickly jumped in with a loud laugh, raising my hand to my belly so I could give Guts a discreet elbow in the side.

He snapped out of it, managing to produce a half-decent fake laugh that seemed to salvage the situation. *Li Homaya* turned away and bellowed something as he gestured towards the stage.

The band immediately started for their instruments. The girl explained to Guts:

"*Li Homaya* wishes to hear a song before dinner."

Guts nodded and went to join the band. *Li Homaya* swaggered off after them, leaving the guests who were still waiting for their introduction – which was most of them – looking annoyed.

I was wondering what I was supposed to do when I felt a hand on my arm. It was the Native girl.

"You are also from Rovia, yes? *Li Homaya* has invited a fellow

Rovian to dine with you. You will find Mr Angus Bon at the last table to the left."

The table she pointed me towards was still empty when I reached it, but I found name cards at each place, written in fancy script and sporting names like "Sera Orellalo Mamoya Horrenio". I circled the table until I found one that read "Ser Angus Bon", and next to it, one that said "Ser Ug".

I figured I was "Ug" and took my seat, excited to finally have another Rovian to talk to after two weeks in Pella.

Soon enough, the rest of the table filled with well-dressed, snotty-looking men and women speaking Cartager. The middle-aged man who sat in the place marked for Angus Bon had Rovian ears, grey-streaked red hair, and a thick, droopy moustache.

"Excuse me, sir, but – are you Rovian?" I asked hopefully.

"Mmm," he said in a bored voice. "Suppose you're the new one?"

I nodded.

"Barely out of the cradle, are you?" He looked at my name card. "What kind of name is Ug?"

"It's really Egg," I said. "Short for Egbert. Masterson."

"Masterson? No one prominent by that name. What province are you from?"

"Deadweather Island."

He got a look on his face like I'd just thrown up on his shoes.

"Smashing," he said.

Then he turned away from me and started speaking Cartager with the man on his left, a mound of flesh with jewelled rings on every finger.

My cheeks flushed hot. I felt angry and stupid at the same

time. But I didn't know what to do about it, so I just stared at my plate until the band began to play.

They weren't quite as sharp as usual – I think partly because they were nervous, and partly because the audience reacted to them like a bunch of dead fish – and I spent most of their opening song trying to think of something smart to say to Angus Bon so he wouldn't think I was an idiot just because I was from Deadweather.

I came up with something I thought was surefire, but he was so determined to ignore me that it wasn't until after the main course had been served that I managed to find an opening.

"Mr Bon, could you tell me: is it possible to buy Rovian books in Pella? I'm quite starved for a good read."

"There *are* no good reads in Rovian," he said with a sniff.

"What do you mean?"

"It's all second-rate knockoffs. The only Continental literature worth reading is Cartager."

I was shocked – and insulted, because Rovian books were all I'd ever read, and the best of them I loved like they were people. By the time I recovered, Angus had gone back to chattering with his neighbour, but I interrupted him, blurting out, "What about *Basingstroke*?"

He turned back just long enough to give me a look of scorn. "Wouldn't wipe my dog's feet with that book. It's rubbish."

Then he went right back to ignoring me.

My cheeks burned again. I wanted to get up and leave, but there was nowhere to go. So I sat and stewed, and tried to think up some clever insults.

A few minutes later, dessert arrived, on covered dishes with silver lids. One of the servants had been announcing each course in Cartager, and his description of the dessert stirred up a lot of excitement.

In spite of my anger, I got excited myself. For all its fantastic food, the one thing lacking in Pella Nonna was good dessert, and I dared to hope the palace might serve us jelly bread.

Then the lids came off, revealing sections of an oversized citrus fruit sprinkled with mint on a bed of whipped cream. I couldn't believe my eyes, and I had to taste the fruit to be sure I wasn't mistaken.

It was ugly fruit. And judging from the faces of everyone at my table as they worked their jaws over it, they thought they were eating something rare and exotic.

Angus Bon was as pleased as the rest of them. I couldn't help smiling.

"You know, that's ugly fruit."

"Mmm?"

"It's ugly fruit. Comes from Deadweather. Mostly pirates eat it. But only because they can't afford oranges."

He stopped chewing for a moment, watching me out of the corner of his eye.

"Don't be ridiculous," he sneered through his full mouth.

It didn't matter that he wouldn't believe me. I knew the truth. And any man who thought ugly fruit was a delicacy had no business telling me what books were worth reading.

AFTER THAT, I was as happy to ignore Angus Bon as he'd been to ignore me. But while the band played its set after dessert, it occurred to me that as nasty as he was, he might be able to answer a question that still stumped me.

71

So when the final course of coffee and nuts was being served, and his Cartager companion had tottered away from the table for a moment, I asked Angus:

"Why aren't there more Rovians in Pella?"

"Ignorance," he said. "Most of them don't realize the Banishment Law was never meant to apply to honest men. And more's the –"

"There really *was* a Banishment Law?" So much of what Captain Racker had told us turned out to be wrong that I'd figured it was just something he'd made up to scare his crew.

"Course. There still is – but it was only meant to stop the slavers. Instead, it just drove out all the accountants. Now, *there's* a field where Rovians excel –"

"Wait – what slavers?"

"The ones on Sunrise. I mean, if there's one thing this town needs, it's some decent accountants. The Short-Ears –"

"There's slavers on Sunrise Island!?"

"Course! How else would they keep that silver mine going? Don't interrupt." He must have had a lot of wine by this point, because his speech was getting slurry. And he wouldn't stop going on about accounting.

"The Short-Ears, for all their cultural superiority, cannot add or subtract to save their lives. Their bookkeeping's *disastrous* –"

"Who are the slavers? Is it Roger Pembroke who's behind it?"

"Haven't the slightest idea. Wouldn't set foot on Sunrise if you paid me. All that new money. It's crass . . . But the thing with the Cartagers – it's like they've got some kind of religious objection to proper financial recording –"

"And the slaves come from over here? In the New Lands?"

"Stop changing the subject!"

"Just tell me where the slaves come from!" I'd stopped caring about being polite. I just wanted to know what he knew.

He sighed, then propped his elbow on the table and put his chin on his hand.

"Far as I know . . . or care . . . the slavers have a racket going with one of the northern tribes. Moku. Nasty business, that bunch. Real savages. Not like the Flut – now, *there's* a tribe with business sense. Actually some decent accounting talent if they're properly –"

"So the Moku sell slaves to men from Sunrise Island?"

"You really are quite tedious. It's a miracle they let you in here. Are you somebody's nephew?"

"But why would they sell their own people to Roger – I mean, to Rovians?"

"No, no. Don't be stupid. Moku don't sell Moku. They sell their blood enemies. Okalu."

The bejewelled Cartager had come waddling back. Angus gave him a boozy look of relief and turned away from me.

"So there's still Okalu left? Up north? And the Moku sell them as slaves to Roger Pembroke?"

Ignoring me, Angus started up a new conversation with the Cartager.

I raised my voice. "Are there still Okalu? Up north?"

He turned back to me, exasperated. "I don't know! Ask Kira!"

He gestured across the room at *Li Homaya*'s pretty Native translator. She stood with her back to us, talking to Guts while a few of the band members slunk around nearby, hoping for an audience with her.

"Why would she know?"

"Because she's one of them!"

MOST OF THE CROWD was getting up to leave. I practically ploughed over a few of the older guests as I raced to Guts and the Native girl. Guts's eyes were twitching madly as he spoke to her.

"Anytime, yeh, great. Whenever –"

"Hello," I blurted out.

Guts glared daggers at me, and I heard one of the band members curse me for not waiting my turn. But the Native girl turned to me with a polite smile.

"Hello. You are Mr Guts's friend?"

"Partner, more like," grumbled Guts.

"I'm Egg. Hi."

"I am Kira." She extended her hand.

"Are you Okalu?" I asked before I'd even finished shaking her hand.

A flicker of surprise crossed her face. "Yes."

Guts's eyes bugged out as they swerved away from me and back to her.

"You know of my tribe?"

I suddenly realized I had no idea what I should say. "Sort of . . . I mean, not –"

"Got a map!" yelped Guts.

She turned to him. "I'm sorry?"

I put a hand on Guts's arm to warn him that I should do the talking. But he yanked it away.

"Got a map. Can't read it, tho'. From the Fire King's tomb –"

"Guts, can you –?"

"There's a treasure! Look here –"

Before I could stop him, he pulled the Fire King's necklace from his pocket. He carried it everywhere because we couldn't think of any safer place. We'd cleaned it a while back, removing all the dirt and scraggly feathers, so the stones glittered in the candlelight as he held it up.

Kira stared at it, her big dark eyes going wide with disbelief. I tried to grab the necklace away – flashing it around seemed like a terrible idea – but when I reached for it, Guts jabbed at me with his hook like he meant business.

"Will you let me –?" I started to mutter, but she interrupted.

"Where did you get this?"

"Told ye. Fire King's tomb."

"Guts –!"

"That's impossible," she said. "The Fire King disappeared a hundred years ago. No one knows where –"

"Found it! Back on Deadweather. Me an' him."

"Guts, be quiet!" I hissed.

"Do you have the Fist?" Her eyes were wide and grave.

"Nah – got a –"

"What Fist?" I interrupted, trying to sound like I didn't know what she was talking about. According to Millicent, the Fist of Ka was the most important part of the Fire King's treasure – some kind of magical totem with supernatural powers.

She turned to me. "The Fist of Ka. The Power Giver."

The way she said the words made me realize the Fist was every bit as important as Millicent had said.

"Let's just say –" I began.

"Fist's part o' the treasure, yeh? Got a map! Shows us where it is!"

"Shut up!" I would have smacked him, but he glared back at me with a look that was so wild I figured I might get a hook in my throat if I did.

"Show me this map," she demanded.

"That's not –"

"Ain't on paper. In his head. Got it memorized."

"Shut up!" For the life of me, I couldn't understand why Guts – ordinarily the most suspicious, untrusting person I'd ever met – was telling her everything we knew, without even being asked.

She turned back to me again. "Is this true?"

"Maybe." I felt like a fool.

"Where does the map lead?"

"Dunno. Can't read it," said Guts. "We ain't Okalu."

I wanted to strangle him.

"Wait here. Just one moment. Please don't move."

She slipped away through the crowd, band members flocking after her like seabirds chasing a ship. Guts's eyes stayed locked onto her until she disappeared.

I grabbed him by the shoulders and shook him. "Are you a complete idiot?!"

"Stay away from her! Ain't fair! Met her first!" His eyes twitched with fury, and I immediately figured out what the problem was.

"You fancy her, don't you?"

"No! Course not! Yech!" His cheeks were turning bright red. "Just – ye – don't – back off!"

"I don't care in the slightest about that. Honestly! But you're

76

giving everything away! How do we know we can trust her? She works for *Li Homaya*! She could have us locked up!"

The anger slowly left his eyes. He looked worried.

"Ain't gonna happen," he muttered, none too certain.

"How do you know?"

"Won't tell her no more."

"There's nothing left to tell!"

"Didn't . . . not . . ." He stared at the floor, grimacing. "She's all right," he said.

"Maybe. We don't know. Will you let me do the talking?"

He nodded, his face twitching. She returned just then, holding a piece of parchment, an inkpot and a quill.

"This way. Please."

She led us to the furthest table, now empty and cleared of plates. She shooed away the clutch of band members following her with a few words in Cartager that sounded polite but made them all hang their heads in disappointment as they shuffled off.

"Sit. Please."

All three of us sat down. She looked around to make sure no one else was within earshot. Then she put the parchment and ink on the table between us and held out the quill.

"Will you draw me this map?"

"No," I said.

"Why not?"

"Because it's valuable. And we don't know you."

"I don't know you, either. How can I be sure you have what you say?"

I took the quill from her, dipped it in the ink and drew the first four hieroglyphs across the top of the parchment.

Dash dot feather. Cup. Two dash dot firebird. Spear.

I put down the quill and slid the parchment over to her. She stared at it for a moment.

"This says nothing of the Fist."

A hollow feeling started to grow in my stomach. *What if the map wasn't what we thought it was? What if it wasn't a map at all?*

Back at the tomb, one of the only hieroglyphs Millicent had been able to identify was a lightning bolt over a man's fist – what she'd said was the symbol for the Fist of Ka. In the entire sequence of the map, it reappeared half a dozen times.

I picked up the quill, took back the parchment, and drew the lightning fist hieroglyph below the others. Then I put down the quill again.

Kira pursed her lips. "You say you do not read Okalu. But you know this is the Fist?"

"It's the only one I know. That, and –" I pointed with my finger to the firebird I'd already drawn – "the Fire King."

She was quiet for a moment, staring at the parchment. Then she raised her eyes to mine.

"Draw me the whole map, and I will pay you handsomely."

Guts and I looked at each other.

"Not fer sale," he said.

"Not for a thousand gold?"

The number was jaw-dropping. I was still reeling from it when Guts spoke again.

"Not fer ten. Ain't fer sale."

She raised her eyebrows in surprise. "Why is it so important to you? When you are not Okalu?"

I looked at Guts. I'd been as surprised as she was that he turned down that much money without a second thought. He jerked his head, letting me know it was my job to answer her.

I thought hard before I opened my mouth. "No matter what it's worth in gold . . . a man killed my family for this map. I have to make sure he doesn't get it."

"I can promise this."

I shook my head. "Not good enough."

She stared at me for a while. Her eyes were impossible to read.

"The Fist of Ka belongs to the Okalu. It has for all eternity. Since we lost its protection, we have fallen from Ka's favour. Now we are only a few, and our enemies are many. If my people do not recover the Fist, we will surely die."

She leaned forward in her chair, her eyes burning into mine. "Do you think your claim is stronger than mine?"

I felt the hollowness in my stomach, worse this time. But Guts leaned forward, staring past me to her. "Make ye a deal. Read this map for us, an' we'll find it together."

I nodded. "You get the Fist . . . and we get the rest of the treasure."

"What more do you think there is?"

"The Princess of the Dawn's dowry." According to the legend we'd heard from Millicent, this was the other part of the treasure the Fire King had vanished with – a massive stash of gold and jewels originally meant as an offering to the sun god Ka.

Kira's look darkened. "If this is about money, I will give you gold –"

"No," Guts interrupted. "*We* got the map. *You* tell us wot's in it. *All* of us find it together."

I nodded. "That's the deal. How about it?"

Kira was silent for a long time. First she looked at Guts. Then me. Then she stared at the table.

"I cannot do this," she said quietly.

"Why not?"

"Because I cannot translate it," she said. "I know a few symbols –" She pointed to what I'd drawn. "The Fist . . . Hutmatozal, the last of the Fire Kings . . . But the others . . ." She shrugged. "Only the scribes and elders can read them. I do not have this learning."

"Where can we find someone who does?"

"In the north. Beyond the mountains of the Cat's Teeth."

"Will you take us there?" I asked.

She nodded. "How soon can you leave?"

KIRA DIDN'T WANT to waste any time. Half an hour later, Guts and I were back in our apartment, our rucksack packed with guns, knives, money, spare clothes and what little food we had, waiting for her to knock on our door.

"Don't bring more than you can carry," she'd said. "And make sure you've got weapons and money."

"What for?"

"The usual reasons. I'll meet you in an hour."

She'd rushed off into the night before I could ask what the usual reasons were, and I was still wondering about them as I watched Guts settle back in his favourite chair, his guitar across his lap. But instead of playing, he just stared at it with a sad look.

We'd both been quiet since we left Kira. All sorts of thoughts were running through my head, and not just about the weapons and money. There was also the fact that we didn't really understand what the Fist of Ka was. The way Kira's voice sounded when she spoke of it made me worry we'd got ourselves into something that was too big for us, and that we had no business messing with.

Then there was the fact that we knew next to nothing about her – where she'd come from, why she was working for *Li Homaya*.

And leaving at a moment's notice, in the middle of the night, seemed reckless, and maybe even stupid.

Guts looked conflicted, too. But I figured it wasn't about any of that. He ran his fingers over the headstock of his guitar, like he was scratching a favourite pet.

"Been good here," he said.

"We can always come back afterwards," I said.

He nodded, perking up a little.

"Maybe you should bring the guitar," I said.

"Maybe. Need a strap, tho'. Illy's got one." He stood up. "Think I got time to –?"

There was a knock at the door.

"Guess you don't," I said.

"Probably ain't her yet. Bet it's the gigglers."

I smiled at the thought of the Cartager girls who followed Guts around. They annoyed me to no end, but I knew they'd be sad when he left.

"Try to let them down easy," I said.

As Guts went to answer the door, I turned away to get a drink of water from a jug in the kitchen nook. I had the jug in my hand, my back to the door, when I heard Guts begin to say –

"Who the –?"

There was a loud, sickening crack.

I turned just in time to see Guts crumple to the floor. A massive, wide-shouldered Native in a dark Continental shirt stood over him, holding a wooden club.

An even bigger Native was halfway across the room, headed straight for me.

I remember his eyes, which were big and black and angry.

He must have had a club, too. But I don't remember it, or anything else for a long time after that.

CHAPTER 6

CHAINED

I woke up with a throbbing ache in my head. Something was thudding against my face, over and over.

I opened my eyes, but there was only blackness. And when I tried to raise my hand to my head, I found out I wasn't just blind, but paralysed.

I tried to scream – but the sound stuck in my throat. I couldn't move my tongue or close my mouth.

I panicked and started to wriggle like a fish on land. When I did, I felt myself start to slide down – *or was it up? Which way was up?* – and then someone grabbed hold of me, which was actually comforting for a second until they slugged me, hard, in my lower back. As the fresh pain surged through me, I heard a muffled growl, and I got the message that if I didn't want to get slugged again, I'd better cut out the wriggling.

I tried to calm down by breathing deep, but I couldn't take in any air through my mouth. Gradually, I figured out that the problem was that some kind of cloth was stuffed in it, which also explained why I couldn't talk or move my tongue . . . and then I realized I couldn't see because something was covering my head . . . and I couldn't move my arms or legs because I was tied up.

And I was upside down. Or at least my head was.

Eventually, I figured out that the thing hitting my face was the side of a horse. And it wasn't hitting me so much as I was hitting it – I'd been jackknifed across its back like a sack of potatoes, wedged between the horse's neck and the legs of what I guessed was one of the big Natives who'd attacked us.

Realizing I wasn't blind or paralysed was a relief, but other than that it was a pretty bad situation. My arms and legs were numb, and all the blood vessels in my head felt like they were going to burst, especially around my left temple, which throbbed with pain where I must have taken the hit that knocked me out.

Since I couldn't see, there was no way to anticipate the horse's movements, so whenever it shifted course my head banged against its flank, which made it hurt even more.

Judging by the heat of the sun on my back and the heaviness of the air, I figured we'd travelled through the night. This gave me some hope that whoever had kidnapped us – I could hear the clop of another horse, so I was counting on Guts being with us – would stop soon so they could rest, or eat, or at least pee, and when they did, they'd turn me right side up.

But they didn't stop. For a while, we seemed to be climbing uphill, then down again. We crossed two rivers, one loud and roaring, and the other so deep that my head got dunked a couple of times.

Then, as the heat slacked off and I figured the sun must be setting, we entered a swamp – at least, that's what I gathered from the buzz of insects and the *spluck* of the horses' hooves.

By the time we reached the swamp, I'd had the whole day to think about what had happened. Not that I needed much time to figure it out. The Natives who'd attacked us had big dark eyes, just like Kira's, and the fact that they'd shown up right after we told her where we lived made it pretty obvious they were Okalu, too, and she'd sent them to kidnap us.

The kidnapping seemed pointless. They were probably taking us to their territory, somewhere in the northern mountains, but we'd been planning to go there anyway. The senselessness of it – *why tie us up and carry us someplace we were happy to walk to?* – didn't leave me too hopeful that they were reasonable people.

I realized I'd been thinking of the Okalu as somehow friendly, or at least harmless – like the fact that they were so hard to find, and had fallen from power and were losing their death struggle with the Moku, meant we had nothing to fear from them.

But there was no good reason to believe that. As I thought about it, dangling upside down with a throbbing head, it seemed just as likely that the Moku were trying to wipe them out because the Okalu were the worst of the worst, the most savage of the savages.

Then I remembered what the crew of the *Thrush* had said about Natives cutting out our hearts and eating them, and I started to get panicky.

I tried to puzzle out some way to bargain with them for our lives, but we didn't have much to offer. Once I'd coughed up the map – and I figured they'd torture me until I did – we were useless to them. Even if they didn't go so far as eating our hearts, they'd almost definitely slaughter us without a second thought.

Maybe they like music, and they'll let Guts live if he plays guitar for them.

But what are the odds they brought the guitar? Not good.

Maybe we can make one.

Make a guitar? Ridiculous.

Maybe they'd go back to Pella and pick it up?

Even more ridiculous.

How do I know Guts is even with us? Maybe they already killed him. Maybe she told them to take just me, because I'm the one with the map.

We're doomed. We never should have trusted that girl.

What was it Millicent said to me? On the lawn of her mansion, the day we met?

The memory came bright and clear, right down to the green stripe on the croquet mallet perched on Millicent's shoulder, and the sun in her hair and the freckles on her nose as she scrunched it up, a teasing grin on her face:

"Come now, Egg. All the books you've read, and you don't know beautiful women are evil?"

I should have told Guts that, before he'd gone and shot off his mouth to a pretty girl and got us killed for it.

But it was too late.

And now I was never going to see Millicent again.

I tried to picture her in my head, the way she looked that first day we met: the deep brown eyes, the sharp cheekbones, the honey-gold hair that fell down to the middle of her back.

And the way she smelled . . . I don't know if it was perfume, or something the servants in Cloud Manor used to wash her clothes, but she always smelled like flowers. And not the sickly sweet ones they sold in the shops in Blisstown, but the wildflowers, up on Mount Majestic, clean and crisp and –

The horse stopped moving. I heard the shriek of a bird, practically on top of us. Then an identical shriek, somewhere in the distance.

Then another one, close by, only this time I realized it wasn't a bird but a human imitating one.

For a while after that, there was no movement except the horse swatting bugs with its tail and occasionally shifting position, stirring the water.

Then there was splashing up ahead, followed by muttered voices. I could've sworn one of them sounded Rovian. But that was impossible.

I felt arms pick me up and hand me down from the horse. Then someone was carrying me, splashing through the water, and they set me down – on my rear, with my head up, which was a huge relief after all those hours upside down – on something hard and dry.

I was still trussed up, and my legs felt dead and useless. I was starting to worry I might tip over when a voice barked, "Sit up! Hold still!"

I felt swoony and off-balance, but I did my best to sit up straight. A moment later, something heavy came down next to me, and I felt everything lurch downwards, then pop back up again, and I realized I was in a boat, bobbing in the water.

I heard the voice again. "Sit up!"

It didn't make any sense. Why were the Okalu putting me in a boat?

And why did they sound so much like Rovians?

The boat bobbed again as someone got into it. I heard the creak of wood against metal, followed by the sound of oars pushing through the water.

"'Bout time," a voice grumbled. "Sick o' this bog. Skeeters eatin' me alive."

"Dunno we're leavin'," said another.

"Ain't this the lot of 'em?"

"Reckon. Lotta work afoot, tho'."

"Not fer us. Fer the soldiers. I ain't stormin' no –"

"Shhh! Ain't s'posed to jaw 'bout it."

After that, it was quiet for a while. The numbness slowly left my legs, but when it did, they started to feel like they were getting stabbed with a thousand needles.

Then there were more voices, from somewhere above us. The boat knocked hard against something, and I almost fell over.

Then I was getting picked up again, and turned and prodded, and suddenly I was jerked up off my feet, squeezed tight across the chest by whatever I was tied up in, yanked higher and higher into the air – and then in an instant all the pressure released and I fell in a heap onto a wooden deck.

"Get that sack off 'im. See wot we got."

What felt like several pairs of hands picked me up and shook me out of whatever I'd been stuffed inside. Then they dropped me back to the deck, my arms and legs still tied.

It took a moment for the starbursts in my eyes to clear, and when they did, I wished they hadn't.

I was staring up at four Rovian men, large and rough-looking. Three of them I'd never seen before.

The fourth was Birch.

Birch, who worked for Roger Pembroke.

Birch, whose twin brother had pushed me halfway off a cliff, only to wind up at the bottom instead of me.

Birch, who'd tried to kill me with a knife the last time I'd seen him.

He cocked his head to one side as he peered down at me. A smile slowly crept across his thick lips.

"Been waitin' fer you," he said.

Then he kicked me in the belly with his boot, so hard it knocked the wind out of me. I gagged on the rag in my mouth, and my nose started to run and my eyes teared up and it was hard to breathe and I thought I might puke but I tried to hold it down because with the rag stuffed in me there was no place for it to go.

I was curled up on my side, fighting to breathe, when I felt something go *thud* on the deck next to me and start thrashing every which way, and somewhere at the back of my head I felt a pang of relief, because I knew it was Guts and he was still alive.

"Even better," I heard Birch say. Then he kicked Guts like he'd kicked me. Only he didn't stop at just one.

When he was finished, I heard him growl an order.

"Put 'em below. On the plank."

MOST SHIPS' HOLDS smell awful. Even the cleanest ones carry a tang of puke, along with some undercurrents of rotting food and bilgewater. But the hold of this ship was beyond foul, and not just from the usual filth. There was something worse in the air.

It smelled like death. And as I lifted my head from the plank where they'd chained me, my neck straining against a steel collar to see through the dim light of a small oil lamp hanging from an overhead beam, I understood why.

We were in a long compartment made up of two wide rows of low planking with an aisle running between them. The planks were big enough for several dozen men to lie side by side across them. Three sets of chains ran the length of each row. The first held manacles for the feet; the second, manacles for the wrists; and the third, steel collars for the neck.

There was no question the hold had been built for human cargo. We were on a slave ship.

At the moment, the only slaves were me and Guts.

Birch's three henchmen had cut me free so they could properly chain me to the end of one plank. With the steel collar on my neck, I was able to raise my head just far enough to watch them chain Guts to the end of the plank opposite me.

They'd taken his hook away, and his stump was giving them trouble – without a left hand, they couldn't chain him by the wrist. In the end, they had to get a longer chain and clamp it on his arm above the elbow. As they did, Birch watched impatiently, arms crossed, leaning against the ladder that led to the upper deck.

Guts didn't give them much of a fight, which made me think he was either waiting for the right chance, or he was hurt pretty bad.

Once they'd chained us up tight, Birch pocketed the keys to the locks and ordered the others upstairs to prep the ship for sailing.

Left alone with us, Birch took a seat on the edge of the plank by my feet and looked back and forth at me and Guts with a satisfied grin.

"Ye stupid — —s," he cursed us, slowly shaking his head. "Coulda been clean away by now. Halfway to the Continent, all the time ye had. And wot ye do? Set up in Pella, make a spectacle o' yerselves."

He leaned across the aisle and smacked Guts on the bottom of his feet. "Ay! Ye like bein' toast o' the town? Was it worth it? My boys didn't even need to ask round! Says they walked in the square, saw ye struttin' the palace steps like a peacock!"

"It wasn't her who helped you?" I asked, meaning Kira. I don't know why I thought he'd answer the question. Or why I thought it mattered.

Birch looked at me quizzically.

"Wot, yer girlie friend? Won't see her no more. Daddy put her on a ship to Rovia. Some fancy boardin' school. Ye'll be long dead 'fore she comes back."

By the time I realized he was talking about Millicent, he'd stood up and walked around to the side of the plank so his face loomed directly over mine, staring down at me with his yellow eyes.

"Speakin' o' Daddy . . ." Up close, I saw his face was pitted with tiny scars. It was hard to tell whether they were from the kind of craggy pimples my brother, Adonis, used to get, or a blast of grapeshot Birch had caught in the face. "Boss got plans fer you. Special-like. Shame of it is, I ain't s'posed to lay a hand on ye."

Birch's mouth split into a grin, showing two crooked lines of grey teeth. "Course, he'll never know long's I don't leave no mark."

He brought his fist down like a hammer in the soft middle of my belly, right where he'd kicked me.

This time, the pain was bad enough that I went fuzzy for a

while. When things finally came back into focus, Birch was on the other side of the hold, sneering down at Guts.

"... 'Member when ye bit me?" Birch pushed back the sleeve on his right forearm to reveal a deep, ugly wound, still unhealed and sewn together with ragged black stitches. It was the bite Guts had given him to stop Birch from killing me back on Deadweather.

"Like a dog, ye was. Gonna show ye wot I do to dogs. 'Cause the boss don't care a whit fer *you* – I can do whatever I like to yer dirty carcass."

He reached into his coat pocket and pulled out Guts's hook. He waved it over Guts's face.

"Maybe I'll use this. How ye like that? Pluck yer eyes, fer starters . . ."

I turned my head away, sick with horror. Guts was going to be ripped apart, just a few feet from me, and there was nothing I could do to stop it.

Soon enough, they'd kill me, too. Roger Pembroke would get what he wanted. And I'd never see Millicent again.

When you added all that to the pain in my gut and the lack of food, water and sleep, it's no wonder I started to hallucinate, seeing things I knew weren't really there.

It started with a flicker of movement in the gloom beyond the ladder that led to the upper deck. Then it slowly grew until it entered the dim circle of light cast by the overhead lamp and hardened into the ghost of a man, short and skinny and dressed in sailor's leggings and a baggy shirt.

It lurched slightly as it moved, hands pressed together to hold a tightly knotted burlap sack, swollen with something bulbous and heavy-looking.

As it passed under the lamp, it rotated its head towards me, and I nearly gasped when I saw it had Millicent's face – only pale and wraithlike, with terrible dark circles under its eyes. What would have been her long golden hair was matted and dull, bunched up in a straggly ponytail.

The ghost stared at me with hollow eyes. Then it slowly shifted the sack to one hand and raised a finger to its lips.

I couldn't have made a peep even if I'd wanted to.

It started moving again, through the pool of lamplight towards Birch. It was still lurching, like the sack it held was a chore to carry.

Birch was bent low over Guts, still taunting him with Lucy.

". . . Nah! Not yer eyes! Then ye can't watch the fun! How 'bout I start lower down? Carve me name in yer belly? Then when ye die . . ."

The ghost came to a stop just behind Birch and slowly hoisted the sack up over its head.

". . . an' ye go to the devil, he'll know it was me wot sent ye! How ye like –"

In one swift, violent motion, the ghost swung the sack down against the back of Birch's head. To my surprise – heavy as it seemed, I figured it was a phantom sack that would pass right through him – it collided against his skull with a crunchy thud.

Birch staggered to one side. The ghost followed, raising the sack to hit him again.

The second blow brought him to his knees. Then there was a third, and a fourth – I imagined I was hearing the ghost utter a fierce little grunt with every swing – and with the fifth strike, the phantom sack seemed to burst, dissolving into a shower of tinkling shards that clattered to the floor around Birch's unconscious body.

I could've sworn I heard the ghost mutter "Oh, blast!" but I knew that wasn't possible, because ghosts couldn't talk any more than they could grunt.

It crouched down over Birch's body, facing away from me. I couldn't see what it was doing, but I figured it was sucking the everlasting soul from his body, because I'd read a story once about ghosts, and I knew they did that kind of thing.

"Where the *blun* did *you* come from?" I heard Guts sputter. I was about to call to him when suddenly the ghost rose up in the air and began to lurch towards me.

As haggard and hollow-eyed and sallow-skinned as it was, it looked so much like the real Millicent that for an instant, I thought it actually was her – and that she was leaning over me, lowering her head towards mine, so she could kiss me.

But when it got close, its breath was so rancid and sour I knew it must be some kind of unearthly demon, because the real Millicent never could've smelled that bad.

It pressed a clammy palm against my head, pushing it to one side, and I recoiled in horror, certain the demon was about to suck my soul out through my ear.

Then I heard jingling, and out of the corner of my eye, I saw the ring of keys it was holding, taken from Birch's pocket.

And when the demon barked, "Saviour's sake, Egg, move your fat head so I can unlock this stupid collar!" I realized I hadn't been seeing things at all.

 CHAPTER 7

WATER AND FIRE

It took Millicent some doing to get the chains off me – she kept fumbling the keys, and when she finally got my neck free and moved on to my wrists, she tried the same key over and over, even though it clearly didn't fit into the lock and there were two more on the ring.

"Maybe try the others," I suggested.

"What do you think I'm doing?" she snapped. She wasn't herself – the surly attitude wasn't all that unusual, but the horrid breath and ragged appearance definitely were. Worse, she was woozy and unfocused – even though I knew it was her in the flesh, her normally sharp eyes still looked ghostlike and vacant.

"Hurry!" hissed Guts. "He's gonna come to!"

I couldn't tell if Birch was stirring, but even if he wasn't, there was no telling how much time we had before someone came down the ladder and found us. So when Millicent finally got my wrists free, I asked her for the keys.

"Why don't I do the rest?"

"Ugh! Fine." She handed them to me, then wandered off towards Birch's body. I unshackled my ankles and sprang up to free Guts. I had to step round Millicent to get to him – she was kneeling on the floor by Birch's legs, stuffing her pockets with the scattered contents of the burst sack.

They turned out to be hundreds of newly minted silver pieces, although just then I was too frantic to appreciate that Millicent had saved us by coldcocking Birch with a sack of her father's money.

As I went to work on the lock for Guts's neck collar, I heard what sounded like voices of alarm somewhere far above us.

We had to find a way off the ship, and fast.

The instant I unshackled Guts, he jumped up from the plank and started to stomp on Birch's head with his bare foot.

"Cut it out!" I hissed. "You'll break your foot!"

As I looked around the deck for portholes, I felt a smack on the back of my leg. It was Millicent, still kneeling on the floor and stuffing her pockets full of coins.

"Help pick these up!" she demanded.

"There's no time!" I told her. "And we don't need it!"

"Course you do! You're poor as pantry mice!"

She reached up and shoved a fistful of coins into my pocket.

Guts was still stomping on Birch's head. I couldn't blame him for it, but it was as big a waste of time as picking up the coins.

"Come on!" I slugged him on the arm, then moved to the lantern, taking it off its hook so I could explore the rest of the deck.

I started forward with the lantern, and I heard Millicent curse behind me as she lost the light she needed to gather the coins.

Guts followed me, strapping on his hook, which he'd plucked from the floor where Birch dropped it.

Beyond the ladder were two more lengths of planking with chains for slaves. Past those, the ship began to narrow, tapering towards the bow. Small, floor-to-ceiling storage compartments ran along both sides. I opened one and found nothing but a pile of stone blocks with steel rings embedded in them. Some of the rings had manacles attached on short chains.

I kept going. Two compartments from the bow, I found a little cabin with a short bed and a hinged table. There was still no porthole, but it gave me hope that I'd find something else – and when I opened the final compartment, there it was.

I'd found the head. It was a cramped space, half of it filled by a boxlike structure just the right height for sitting, with a round hole in the middle about a foot across.

I peered down through the head. Since it was night, I didn't expect to see anything except blackness – but to my surprise, the water was clearly visible about ten feet down, light dancing on its surface.

It was flowing past the hull at a good clip, foam spraying up off the prow. That was bad.

"We're moving out to sea," I told Guts.

"Wot!?" He looked past me down the head, then cursed.

"Can't fit through that," he warned me. "Too narrow."

"I'll bust out the seat. You get Millicent."

We both started back towards the middle of the deck. As Guts continued on, I stopped at the storage compartment where I'd seen the heavy stone blocks. I'd just picked one up when I heard Millicent's voice.

"Let go, you sod!"

I found them near the ladder. Guts had Millicent by the waist and was trying to drag her backwards as she struggled, spitting venom.

"Get your hands off me!"

"Yer outta yer tree!" he said.

"Quiet! Both of you!" I could hear an increasingly loud commotion somewhere on an upper deck, and I was terrified someone from the crew would hear us yelling and come down to investigate.

"She was halfway up the ladder!" Guts exclaimed. "Had to pull her off!"

"I'm just going to the galley," Millicent said, as if it was the most reasonable thing on earth.

"Are you out of your mind?!"

"I'm *starving*! And I'm *sooooo* parched!" she said, with an exaggerated roll of her head that only made her seem more crazy.

"Yer mad!"

It was worse than mad. It was suicidal. And yet Millicent was looking at us like we were the crazy ones.

"I won't take much. They'll never miss it."

Her eyes fluttered just then, like she might faint, and I suddenly realized what was wrong. She must have been hiding on the ship for days, and she'd gone batty from lack of food and water.

As I reached out to steady her, I heard footsteps on the deck above us. We were running out of time.

"So if you don't mind –" she started to say, lunging for the ladder.

"Food and water's this way!" I said, yanking her back towards the head.

She stumbled, unsteady on her feet. "No, it isn't!"

"Yes, it is! *Tons* of it!"

"*Pffft!*"

Guts got the idea and joined in. "Oh, yeh! Seen it! Cakes and all. Big feast!"

Once we'd got her staggering in the right direction, I left her to Guts and rushed ahead with the stone block. When I got back to the head, I brought the block down hard against the wood surrounding the hole.

It made a terrible racket, and I felt the shudder up through my feet. But the wood didn't budge.

I panicked and started to bang on it so wildly that when the wood finally gave way, I fell forward and almost dropped the block into the water. With a few more shots, I managed to open up a hole big enough to fit through.

By this time, Millicent had figured out she'd been swindled.

"That's the loo!"

As I stepped out of the head, I heard a voice calling down from the top of the ladder.

"Mr Birch! Need ye up top!"

"Through the hole! Quick!" I told Millicent.

"You're not serious! People poop out of that!"

"*Mr Birch . . . !*"

"Go!" I said to Guts.

He squeezed past me and vanished through the hole.

I heard feet on the ladder.

"Come on!" I begged Millicent.

She looked offended. "If you think for a moment I'm going to jump in a privy –"

I picked her up by the waist, swung her round and dropped her through the hole. By the time I went after her, there were feet pounding across the deck towards me.

The ship was moving fast enough that I didn't hit Millicent when I came down, but as I kicked back up towards the surface, I conked my head pretty good against the passing hull and had a panicky moment of fear that the rudder would knock me cold as it went by.

I started kicking and paddling in the direction I thought was sideways to the boat. It seemed to be taking an awfully long time to break the surface, and I realized my shoes were dragging me down, so I kicked them off.

Finally, I surfaced and started gulping air, and there was light – far too much of it for the middle of the night – and I turned to look around and discovered why.

The boat was on fire. Even as it continued to move out to sea, its two topsails were burning out of control.

I trod water, which was harder than it should have been, and looked around for the others. There was no trace of them.

"Millicent! Guts!"

Someone broke the surface about ten feet away. I swam towards them, and as I did, I could feel my trousers sucking me downwards. I was about to shed them, too, when I realized the problem was the silver coins Millicent had shoved in my pocket. I quickly dug them out and let them sink.

"Guts?"

"Help!" he gurgled, and I realized he had Millicent in his good hand and was trying to pull her head above water.

I got a hand on her as well, and we struggled together for a moment until we managed to get Millicent's head up. She coughed water, so I knew she was breathing. But she was heavy as a stone.

"Swim!" Guts urged her.

"Trying . . . !" she grunted, and as I readjusted my grip on her, my hand scraped against something hard near her waist, and I realized her clothes were still packed full of the silver coins.

"The coins! In her pockets!"

I felt around until I found a pocket and started pulling coins from it.

"Need those!" she protested.

I ignored her. "Kick your shoes off!"

"*Need* them!"

Instead of arguing, I dived under and pulled her shoes off, getting a hard kick in the cheekbone for my trouble.

After we got her shoes off and the coins out of her pockets, she seemed able to stay afloat on her own, so we started to swim. The boat had been anchored in a wide inlet, and while most of the area was swamp, there was a stubby finger of land nearby that had some elevation and looked dry.

When we first started for it, I thought I saw a light flickering on its shore, like there was a fire burning, but when I looked again, I didn't see it.

Guts and I swam as fast as we could, but we quickly began to leave Millicent far behind, so we flipped over on our backs and slowed down to let her catch up.

The ship was a couple of hundred yards out to sea by now. But the flames had eaten most of the sails, and it was drifting to a stop.

When Millicent caught up with us, she was panting hard.

"Stop awhile," she gasped.

I wasn't keen on the idea, but I might have agreed to it if I hadn't seen movement in the water off the ship's stern.

Guts saw it the same time I did.

"Somebody's swimmin' for us!"

"Come on, Millicent!" I urged her. "They're following us!"

She just looked at me helplessly with those wiped-out eyes.

"Hang on to my shoulders," I ordered her.

She grabbed hold, and I started to swim with her hanging on my back. It was tough going.

"Can you at least kick?"

She tried to kick, but I don't know how much good it did. Mostly, she just seemed to get her legs tangled in mine.

Within a couple of minutes, I was panting hard, and the shore didn't seem to be any closer. So when Guts growled, "Gimme a turn," I was happy to let him.

After Guts took over, I flipped onto my back to check the progress of whoever was swimming after us. They'd closed a third of the distance already – and back at the ship, where the last burning shreds of the sails were peeling away from the mast, I could see a davit swinging out with a rowboat attached.

"They're putting a boat in. And the swimmer's closing on us," I told Guts.

He grunted. He was having as much trouble towing Millicent as I had.

"Millicent, can you swim? They're going to catch us," I said.

"Okay," she said.

She did her best. But it wasn't good enough to stop the swimmer from continuing to close the gap. A minute later, when I chanced a look back, he was just fifty yards from us.

Behind him, the rowboat was in the water and pulling hard in our direction.

"Faster!" I yelled.

Guts and I gave it everything we had, and soon I felt my hand brush the sandy bottom.

I stood up and ran splashing through the water towards shore. Guts was just ahead of me.

Up near the tree line at the top of the beach, I could see flames licking out of the ground like there was a fire burning in a pit, but I didn't see any people around it.

I looked back over my shoulder for Millicent. She was still twenty yards out. The swimmer was coming up fast behind her.

I waded back out towards her. I was waist deep when she reached me, and I pulled her up by the arms so we could run.

But it was a mistake, because it was even slower going than if I'd let her keep swimming. We struggled together, our legs churning against the water, and I didn't dare look back because I knew the swimmer was almost on top of us.

I could see Guts up ahead in the moonlight. He was standing by the little fire on the ground, yelling at us, but I couldn't hear him over the surf.

Then the water was just shin deep, I had Millicent's hand in mine, and I thought we were going to make it when suddenly she fell, dragging me down with her.

We were on our backs, scrabbling backwards through the

shallows. The swimmer was looming up over us, shirtless, barrel chest heaving with his breath. He was taking his time, not even bothering to reach out and grab us because he knew we were trapped.

Then I heard a *whoooosh* in the air behind us, and his chest exploded in flames.

He plummeted backwards into the surf, and when he hit the water, whatever had struck his chest quickly fizzled out.

For a moment, I thought I'd just imagined he'd been on fire.

But then there was another *whoooosh,* and a second fireball sailed over our heads and struck something in the rowboat.

"RUN!" I heard Guts scream. I got up and grabbed Millicent's hand, pulling her to her feet, and we stumbled across the beach towards the trees.

We were halfway to Guts when I realized there was a second person next to him, crouched over the pit of flames, wreathed in smoke and kneading something on the ground.

Then she rose up, and I saw her face.

It was Kira. She held some kind of twinned rope in her hand. A smoking, fist-sized object dangled from the end of it.

"Move!" she yelled, motioning us aside.

As we ducked out of the way, she took a few quick steps towards the water, then cracked the rope like a whip.

I heard the *whooosh* again, and I turned just in time to see the fireball ignite as it whistled through the air.

This time, it sailed wide of the rowboat and fizzled into the sea.

She cursed in a strange language, then crouched down again.

"Fire another!" Guts yelled to her.

Kira popped back up, her hands full. She handed Guts a fat skin of water, then hoisted a large woven bag onto her shoulders.

"I don't have more," she said. "We have to outrun them."

I looked back at the rowboat. The men in it were crouched low, so I couldn't tell how many of them there were, but two sets of oars were still pushing through the water. It was less than fifty yards out.

I turned back in time to see Kira disappear, crashing through the thick scrub of the trees. Guts followed her.

"What's happening?" asked Millicent in a bewildered voice.

"I don't know," I admitted. "But I think we'd better follow her."

CHAPTER 8

IN THE REEDS

I had to follow Kira and Guts mostly by sound – not just because it was dark, but because I was holding one arm in front of my face so my eyes wouldn't get poked out by one of the stiff branches we were crashing through.

I had to practically drag Millicent behind me with my other arm. She was still so loopy she couldn't seem to get it through her head that we were running for our lives, and she complained with every step.

"Ow . . . ! Will you let go?! Egg! Quit snapping the – OW! Stop . . . !"

"*Quiet!*" Kira growled at us from somewhere up ahead.

"Who *is* that?" Millicent whined.

"She's an Okalu," I said.

"She's a snot."

Kira and Guts stopped to let us catch up, and we nearly bowled them over when we did.

"Will you quit –" Millicent started to say.

"*Shhhhh!*" Kira's hiss was so fierce that even brain-fogged as she was, Millicent shut up.

We all listened, frozen in place.

From somewhere behind us came the sound of snapping branches.

Kira took off again, holding her pack in front of her as a battering ram against the thick brush. The seriousness of the situation must've finally sunk in with Millicent, because she stopped complaining, and I didn't have to pull her along any more.

It was slow going for another fifty feet. Then the brush began to thin out – but as it did, the ground under my bare feet turned squishy and slick.

All of a sudden, the brush fell away, and I could see past Kira and Guts to a vast, moonlit swamp full of thick reeds looming up out of the water.

I was wondering how we were going to cross it when Kira plummeted out of sight. There was a loud splash. Then Guts disappeared with a second splash.

I tried to stop myself, but the ground was too slick, and I slid off the edge of the embankment just like they had, plopping down into the swamp with Millicent right behind me.

We were waist deep in water, the tall reeds so thick it was hard to push my feet down through them. Kira headed off at a sharp right angle. We followed her, and the reeds quickly swallowed us, reaching a foot or more over our heads. We were about thirty feet from the embankment when I heard several splashes, and I knew whoever was following us had hit the swamp, too.

Kira led the way, zigzagging through the thick reeds. Pretty quickly, I got disoriented – I kept my ear tuned to the sound of the surf hitting the shore, but it was hard to tell if we were heading towards it, away from it, or something in between.

I had faith, though, that Kira would lead us to safety. I'd never seen anything like those fireballs she'd cooked up back at the beach, and when you added that to the fact that she'd managed to track our kidnappers, when they were on horseback and she was on foot, carrying a heavy pack, over a full day and night . . .

I didn't know if her powers were magical, or just beyond my understanding. But they were awesome enough that at that moment, I would've followed her anywhere.

Which was why, as the water got deeper and deeper, it took me a while to get worried.

The water was up to my rib cage the first time Kira stopped. We were clumped together so tightly that I bumped into Guts before I stopped, too.

We could hear the *splish* of the men somewhere behind us.

I expected Kira to start moving again right away. But she didn't.

The seconds stretched out.

I felt Millicent's hand press down on my shoulder. When I turned to look back, her eyes were questioning and afraid.

The men were getting closer.

I was about to nudge Kira when she finally started to move, at such a sharp angle that we were practically going backwards.

For a couple of minutes after that, the water didn't get any deeper.

Then it did.

It was nearly to the top of my chest when Kira changed direction again.

When she turned us a third time, it was up to my neck.

Then she stopped for good.

In the dim moonlight, I could see the water lapping gently against the back of her head. The pack she'd strapped to her back was completely underwater.

She turned to look at us. The water was at her chin, and for the first time since we'd left the beach, I got a good look at her eyes.

There was fear in them.

Just like that, I knew there was nothing magical about her powers.

And she hadn't stopped as part of some grand plan.

She'd stopped because if she kept going, she was going to drown.

And she didn't know what to do next, any more than we did.

We could hear the men moving through the water behind us.

I looked at Guts. The water was nearly to his chin, too. His eyes twitched as he stared back at me.

Millicent's hands were pressing down on my shoulders.

The sound of the men kept getting louder.

Kira began to wrestle with her pack, agitating the water. I couldn't tell what she was working at, but the soft splashing noise made me grit my teeth with worry.

Then her arm rose up from the water, holding a foot-long machete in a sheath. She held it out for Guts.

He raised his arm and took the knife by the handle. As Kira started digging in the bag again, he turned towards me, jerking his chin urgently. He wanted me to unsheathe the blade.

I slid the sheath off. Guts raised the machete over his head and stepped round me, in the direction of the men.

Then Millicent's hands slipped off my shoulder, followed by a *plunk* that sounded like a gunshot in my ear.

I twisted round, grabbing her under the arms to hold her up as I heard a voice call out:

"That way!"

The sound of the men in the water instantly grew twice as loud. They were headed our way fast.

We stood frozen in place, not daring to move. Guts was in front of me, the machete by his ear. Out of the corner of my eye, I could see Kira had a machete of her own now, poised to strike.

My arms were tangled up with Millicent, and I could feel her body trembling.

The splash of the men got more measured – they'd slowed down a bit – but they were headed straight for us.

They were close now.

Ten feet? Less?

The reeds began to wave gently. The water rippled towards us as the movement of the men stirred it up.

A few more seconds and they'd find us.

Guts raised the machete higher.

The ripples got bigger.

I felt something bump against my neck. It was the sheath from Guts's machete – I must have dropped it when I turned to help Millicent, and now it was floating on top of the water right beside me.

Almost without thinking, I raised my arm out of the water, grabbed the sheath, and threw it off to the right, on a high arc over the reeds.

It came down about twenty feet away, with a rustle as it fell through the reeds, then a loud *plop* when it struck the water.

I heard a whispered voice in the reeds, not more than an arm's length from us.

"Wassat?"

The water stopped rippling towards us.

"There."

"Sure?"

"Listen!"

The silence that followed was agonizing.

Millicent took a hand off my shoulder. I was afraid she was going to fall again, but a moment later, her hand rose up from the water and threw something in the same direction I'd tossed the sheath.

As it tumbled through the air, I caught a glint of it in the moonlight. It was a silver coin. Guts and I must have missed it when we emptied her pockets.

The *plop* when it landed was even louder than the sheath had been.

I heard the voice again, practically in my ear.

"There!"

They splashed off to the right.

We waited and listened.

I felt a sharp pinprick on my cheek. A mosquito was biting me.

I twitched my face, trying to make it fly away. But it didn't budge until it drank its fill.

The sound of the men was fading away.

We stood there, frozen and silent, until a long time had passed since we'd last heard them.

Then we started moving. I took the lead, walking us back to where the water had only been up to my chest. By then, I was trembling from hunger, and we stopped so Kira could pass around a water skin and a few packets of food – corn pancakes, wrapped in banana skins, that were so soggy from the swamp water I could barely tell what they were. But I was glad for them just the same.

After that, we moved inland as best we could, zigzagging when the water got too deep for us to pass.

The swamp seemed to go on forever. We must have waded through it for hours, long past the point where we couldn't hear the surf behind us any more. Every so often, we stopped and listened for the men.

The water slowly grew shallower. By the time the sky turned from black to purple, it was only up to the top of my thighs, and I could almost see over the reeds.

Then the sky was pink, the water was shallow enough that my head cleared the reeds and I could make out high ground a few hundred yards ahead. It was much slower going by then, because in such shallow water, we could barely move at a walk without making noise.

Halfway to the higher ground, we stumbled on a flock of birds, which caused such a racket when they took flight that my heart jumped into my throat. We spent several minutes after that crouched on our knees in the reeds, terrified the noise had alerted the men looking for us.

But we didn't hear the men anywhere, and once we started moving again, we quickly reached the firm but muddy ground.

The brush was as thick and tangled as the stuff we'd crashed through when we first came ashore. Trying to move through it silently would be a challenge, and with the sun up, we'd be easy to spot.

And we were exhausted.

So we found a little hollow under one of the larger shrubs, with no more than a few feet of visibility in any direction. Then we curled up together like a litter of wet mice and drifted off to sleep.

CHAPTER 9

ON THE MOVE

When I woke up, I wasn't sure if it was morning or afternoon. I itched all over, but especially on my face, which was riddled with mosquito bites and little scratches from the run through the brush. My mouth was dry and cracked, and I was shaky from hunger.

Millicent was asleep to my right, lying on her side with her back to me. Her sailor's shirt was splotchy and stained, and as I watched her shoulder rise and fall with her breath, I tried to puzzle out why I wasn't more thrilled to see her.

It was all wrong somehow. I'd spent the past three weeks pining for her, cooking up all sorts of fantasies about what would happen when we finally saw each other again.

Not one of them involved cowering in a bug-infested swamp.

And all my fantasies were about a completely different Millicent from the one who'd actually shown up. In my dreams, she was perfect – beautiful and clever, sharp-tongued and self-assured, light on her feet with that wicked glint in her eye.

She was never haggard or weak, brain-fogged or bewildered, sallow or stringy-haired. And she *definitely* never smelled bad.

But the Millicent lying next to me had been all of those things – and practically none of the good ones.

It was confusing.

It was worse than confusing. I was almost mad at her.

And I was mad at myself for feeling that way, because I knew there was something cruel about it. But I still couldn't help feeling it.

A noise near my feet startled me.

It was Kira. She must have been awake for a while, because she'd had time to unload everything in her soggy pack and set it out to dry. As she crouched near my feet, fussing over a few small tins, I looked over her provisions.

There was a big, soaking wet blanket that must have taken up half the space in the pack; what looked like a couple of Native cotton shirts; a second full skin, probably of water; two more banana-leaf packets of corn pancakes; a few tins and a corked jar that I guessed held food; a pair of flints; a small drawstring sack filled with something that rattled softly when she moved it; and some rolls of cloth.

Then there were the weapons: two machetes, one of them now missing its sheath; a few twinned strings of rope with pouches sewn to one end that must have been slings; and a pistol, along with a canister of shot and a powder horn.

As I watched, Kira uncapped the powder horn and turned it sideways, tapping it gently.

After a moment, a glop of sludgy black goo dribbled out. It was useless – and without it, so was the pistol.

Kira cursed under her breath. Then she looked at me with her big dark eyes.

I was full of questions, but the first one that came out was: "How'd you make the fireballs?"

Even whispering – I didn't want to make too much noise for fear the slavers might be nearby – my voice cracked from the dryness in my throat.

She pointed to the little corked jar.

"That's pitch," she whispered. "You know pitch? It burns easily. You soak pieces of cloth –" she pointed to the rolled-up cloth – "in it. Then you heat stones in a fire. When they get hot, you wrap them in the cloth and use the sling to throw them. If the stone is hot enough, and you throw it fast enough, it catches fire in the air."

"Can I have a go at that?" Guts was sitting up to my left, his voice croaky and dry like mine.

Kira shook her head. "It's very hard to throw so fast. You could not do it."

Guts scowled and twitched at the slight, muttering a Rovian curse. His voice cracked in the middle of the word, which only made him angrier.

Kira shrugged. "It's not an insult. Just the truth. Here." She handed him the full skin. "Drink, so you don't sound like a frog."

Guts's cheeks reddened as he put the skin to his lips, and I remembered how smitten he was with her. I wondered if there was any chance she liked him that way, too. It was hard to tell. She wasn't exactly being sweet with him, but I got the sense that she wasn't the type to act sweet with anybody.

"The hardest part was making the fire to heat the stones," Kira said. "Right away when the Moku handed you over, I knew I had to burn the sails if they ran them. But the ship left so quickly, I almost didn't have time."

"They were Moku?" I asked. "The men who kidnapped us?"

"Yes. Why did they take you? Because of the map?"

I nodded. At the mention of the word *map,* my brain automatically started running through the hieroglyphs: *feather, cup, firebird . . .*

"How'd ye know to follow 'em?" Guts asked Kira as he handed me the water skin.

"I was coming to your apartment when I passed them on their horses. They had you in big, long bags. I thought you were sacks of grain. But at your house, the door was open, things were thrown on the floor . . . I went back, and the men were stopped at the city gate, arguing with the watchmen to open it. I looked closer and thought the grain was maybe not grain. Then I saw them bribe the watchmen with silver coin, and I knew what they were."

Guts and I must have both looked confused.

"A Moku with silver coin works for the slavers," she explained. "They buy my people with that silver."

I handed the skin of water back to her. I'd had enough to wet my throat, but not enough to really stop my thirst.

"Thanks for following us," I said.

She sighed. "It was hard. They did not stop."

Then she opened up one of the tins. Inside was a brick of hard cheese. She cut a few pieces with a machete and offered them to us.

"Here. Eat."

We helped ourselves. She took some herself, then nodded in Millicent's direction as she chewed.

"Who is she?"

"A friend."

"She was on the slavers' ship?"

I nodded. "Her father is their leader."

"Her father is a slaver?"

"He's *the* slaver," I said. "He runs the silver mine that –"

"I BEG YOUR PARDON!" Millicent must have been awake and listening, because she suddenly rolled over and sat up, roaring her objection so loudly that all three of us went *"Sssssshhhhh!"*

"Oh, shush yourselves!" she shot back.

"Quiet!" hissed Kira. "If they find us, they will kill us!"

"They'll kill *you*. They'll give *me* a ride home," snorted Millicent, quieter but no less angry. "And I can arrange that if you don't stop slandering my father with this 'slaver' nonsense."

"Millicent –" I started to say.

"Don't 'Millicent' me, Egg! I'm not saying Daddy's pure as Mandar linen. But accusing him of *slaveholding*? That's ridiculous! He'd never do something *that* vile."

The look on my face must have told her what I thought of that.

"I didn't say he was good!" she protested. "Just not *that* bad!"

"Nuts!" croaked Guts. "You was on that ship. Who ye think they chain up down in that hold?"

"The likes of you! Insubordinate sailors! I don't know! All I know is –"

"Be *quiet!*" Millicent was getting loud again, and Kira was glaring daggers at her.

118

Millicent ignored her. "I have *never*, in all my life, seen a bigger pair of ingrates! I saved your stupid lives, and this is how – *eeegh*!"

Kira sprang forward, and before I knew what was happening, she had Millicent pinned to the ground, with one hand over her mouth and the other holding a machete to Millicent's neck.

"Shut your mouth," Kira told her.

Millicent jiggled her head, her eyes as big as saucers. Having got the point across, Kira got off her.

Millicent glared at me, like it was my fault she'd got jumped on.

"What on earth . . . ?!" she whispered in a quavery voice.

"I don't . . . think that was necessary," I told Kira, even though I was pretty sure it *had* been necessary.

"Thanks for sticking up for me," Millicent muttered.

There was an awkward silence after that. Millicent looked longingly at the last hunk of cheese in my hand. I held it out for her. Instead of taking it, she looked past me to Kira.

"Is there anything to eat or drink . . . ?" she asked.

Kira scowled, but she held out the tin of cheese. Guts offered up the skin of water. Millicent took a long, gulping pull of the water, then started in on the cheese.

"Who are you?" she asked Kira between mouthfuls.

"My name is Kira Zamorazol. I am a translator for the Viceroy of New Cartage. But my people are Okalu. Who are you?"

"I'm Millicent Pembroke."

"Pembroke?" Kira repeated, staring hard at Millicent. "From Sunrise Island?"

"Yes. What of it?" Millicent asked, glaring back at her.

"Your father is Roger Pembroke?"

"He is. How do you know him?"

Kira's nostrils flared as her eyes stayed locked on Millicent's.

"I don't. I only know my father was murdered on his orders."

At first, Millicent looked like she might burst into tears. Then she turned angry – at me.

"*You* put her up to that, didn't you?"

"What?"

"You told her to say that! What's the *matter* with you?"

"I don't know what you're talking about!" I said. "I didn't tell her to say anything!"

"Well, what *did* you tell her?"

"Nothing!"

"About what?" Kira wanted to know.

"About . . ." Millicent shut her eyes and sighed sharply, shaking her head. Kira gave me a questioning look.

"Her father killed my family," I told Kira.

"This is *absurd* . . ." Millicent's voice was quavering again, and her eyes welled up as she glared at me. "Why did I even help you, when all you can do is –"

"*Shhhhhhh!*" Guts held up a hand in warning. He sat up straight, staring past us into the swamp, in the direction I guessed was south.

We all shut up and listened. In the distance, there was a steady and unmistakable splashing.

Something was coming through the swamp towards us.

KIRA WAS UP and moving first, sweeping all the supplies into her pack except the soggy blanket, the worthless powder horn, and the two machetes.

"Gimme the gun," said Guts.

"No powder," she said as she handed me the second machete.

"Why's *he* get the knife?"

"You have the hook."

Keeping the second knife for herself, Kira began to push her way inland through the thick brush.

"That's going to make a racket," I said.

"No choice."

We followed her, making a racket as I'd feared. We didn't use the machetes much – it was faster to just plough through as best we could – and it was hard going.

But by the time we stopped to listen, we couldn't hear the splashing any more, and it didn't sound like anyone was following us through the brush.

We worked our way through it for an hour or so, long enough to cover our faces and arms with more little cuts and scratches, until finally the brush gave way to a forest of thick-trunked trees with low, spreading branches.

It was a relief to be able to move over the more open ground. But it didn't last long. We'd been hurrying through the forest for just a few minutes when I heard the familiar shriek of a bird, somewhere ahead of us. It was the same call I'd heard the Moku use to signal the slave ship.

I stopped. "It's the men."

There was an answering shriek, off to the left.

"They're close," said Kira.

There was no knowing which way to go – not straight ahead, and not to the left. But what if there were more of them off to the right as well?

I looked up. The bottom branch of the nearest tree was easily within reach – and its trunk soared well out of view above the thick cover of its leaves.

"That way," said Guts, pointing to the right.

"Wait – what if we go up?" I suggested.

The others raised their heads and stared up into the tree.

Instead of answering, Kira grabbed hold of the lowest branch and started to climb. The rest of us followed.

We went up about thirty feet, until we couldn't see the ground through the leaves. Then we waited.

Every few minutes, we heard another pair of birdcalls. The first was always more distant, but the answering call kept getting closer.

Then one came from right underneath us.

I stared down through the leaves, trying to get a glimpse of whoever it was. One of the slavers? Their Moku allies?

Birch himself? If so, he'd be in a bad way – Guts had stomped him pretty good while he was laid out on the ship. There wouldn't be any mercy after that. They'd kill Guts instantly. Probably Kira, too.

I'd be next, once they got the map out of me.

I still had the machete, and I tried to think about the best way to fight with it if someone climbed up after us.

Maybe they wouldn't. Maybe they'd just sit and wait us out.

There was a faint tremor of movement through the branch as Millicent, sitting beside me, adjusted her weight. I turned my head to look at her.

She was staring down through the trees. Her eyes were sharp and clear, nothing at all like the hollow stare of the night before.

Then she raised her eyes to meet mine, and in an instant, all the misgivings and disappointment I'd felt about her vanished.

Even dirty, scratched and mosquito-bitten, she was beautiful. But that wasn't what made me ache when I looked in her eyes. Pella Nonna had been full of beautiful girls, and none of them, not even Kira, had anything like the light in their eyes that Millicent had. It was as if there was a furnace burning somewhere deep inside her, and the heat and the light from it shined through her pupils in a way that was brilliant and fierce and warned she was nobody's fool and not to be messed with.

That was the look that kept me up at night thinking about her. The look that – even at a moment when one wrong move or accidental noise could bring disaster down on our heads – was capable of making me forget about everything on earth except her.

As she looked back at me, her eyebrows bunched up, as if to say, *Why are you staring at me?*

There were stray hairs falling across her face. I lifted my hand to reach out and brush them away.

She drew her head back, out of my reach. Then she glared at me, her lips pressed together in a tight frown.

If it weren't for the circumstances, I think she would have smacked me.

I was trying to figure out what I could do to make her less angry when we heard another birdcall in the middle distance. This time, the answering call was at least a couple of trees away from us.

The men were moving on.

We waited until the birdcalls faded away, in the direction I thought was north. Kira handed out another round of soggy pancakes. We ate in silence. By then, the sunlight was starting to weaken – and given the heavy canopy of the trees, pretty soon it'd be too dark for us to see our way out of the tree, much less through the forest.

We held a whispered conference and agreed we should start moving. We climbed to the ground and headed west, towards the sun and at a right angle to where we'd last heard the birdcalls. We went as fast as we could without making too much noise.

The ground gradually sloped upwards, and the forest began to thin. The terrain turned a bit rocky, and Kira paused a few times to pick up fist-sized stones and stuff them into her pack. It wasn't until the third time she did it that I realized she was gathering ammunition for her sling.

It was almost sunset when we topped a short rise with enough of a break in the trees that we could see a line of hills a mile or two ahead, off to the right.

"Should we head for the hills?" asked Millicent. "Or keep going straight?" She pointed in the direction of the sunset.

"We should go north," Kira said. "Into the hills."

"That's where them slavers went," said Guts.

"Will you stop calling them slavers?" said Millicent in an irritated voice.

No one answered her.

"They weren't going to the hills," I said. "They were headed more –" I pointed further to the right, between the hills and the coast – "straight up the coast."

"Right, then. Hills it is."

"Wait," said Kira, looking towards the sunset. She turned to Guts. "Do you still have the necklace?"

124

"Yeh."

"Can I have it, please?"

Guts dug into his pocket and pulled out the firebird necklace. He handed it to her.

Kira slipped her pack off her shoulders, set down her machete and knelt on the ground, facing the sunset. Then she carefully arranged the firebird pendant in front of her.

"We're wasting time –" Millicent started to say.

"'Nuff outta you!" Guts growled at Millicent.

"Oh, stuff it, Guts," Millicent snorted.

Still kneeling, Kira straightened her back, pointed her chin skywards and began to whisper in Okalu.

As the strange words tumbled out of her, she slowly lowered her head and rounded her back until she was flat on the ground, arms stretched out in front of her on either side of the pendant.

I didn't know whether to watch or avert my eyes. I'd never known anyone who prayed like that – come to think of it, I'd never known anyone who prayed at all – and once again, I had the sense that we were involved in something much bigger than us, and that shouldn't be trifled with.

Kira stood up, the necklace in her hand. "May I hold this?" she asked Guts.

He nodded. "Yeh. Course."

As Kira pocketed the necklace, Millicent nudged me.

"He fancies her, doesn't he?" she murmured under her breath.

"Shhh!" I whispered, worried Guts had overheard her. "No! Don't talk about it."

Kira hoisted the pack onto her shoulders, and we headed for the hills.

IT WAS FULLY NIGHT by the time we reached the foot of the nearest hill, and the tree cover was so thick we could barely see far enough in front of us to keep moving. At first, we tried to climb straight up, but the hillside was much steeper than it had looked from a distance, so we had to settle for moving at an angle.

"Do we really want to be going inland?" Millicent whispered to me. We were hanging back, letting Kira and Guts take the lead.

"I don't know," I admitted.

"Well, where are we headed once we lose the men from the ship? Won't we need to find a port? Where's the Fire King's treasure?"

"We don't know yet," I said.

"What do you mean, you don't know yet? What did the map say?"

"Haven't got it translated. That's why we're going to find the Okalu."

"*Find* the Okalu?! I thought she was Okalu!"

"She is. But she can't read the writing."

"So she's illiterate? Oh, *smashing*."

"I wouldn't call her that if I were you."

"Let me get this straight – you hitched your wagon to an illiterate, knife-wielding maniac –"

"I *really* wouldn't call her those things."

"Because why be honest? Is that it?"

That got me mad. "Don't tell me about honesty! When you won't even admit –"

"I swear to you, Egg, say the word *slaver* and I'll beat you on the head with a rock."

I left the sentence unfinished. I'd made my point.

Millicent let out a little huff of disgust. "What on earth have you been doing the past three weeks?"

"Looking for an Okalu!"

And listening to Guts play guitar while I stuffed my face and lounged in the sun. But I couldn't exactly admit that.

"And Crazy Knife Girl's the best you could do? That's *pathetic*!"

"Shut up, Millicent."

"What a clever retort. All that time hanging around illiterates certainly sharpened your wits."

We were both quiet for a minute after that. In the silence, I kept getting more angry. I'd forgotten how annoying Millicent could be.

I wasn't the only one who was getting angrier. When Millicent opened her mouth again, her words dripped venom.

"Should've left you to die."

"What kind of comment is that?!"

"Another honest one. It's one thing to be a fool. But I never took you for a pig. Thanks for proving me wrong."

I was stunned. "What's the matter with you?"

"I'll tell you what," she spat. "I nearly *died* saving you! I didn't have to be on that boat. They were going to send me to Rovia. To the finest boarding school on the Continent! And I gave it up. I ran away and hid in that filthy hold, days on end, no food or water – just to save your stupid life! And you couldn't even be bothered to thank me."

Her voice was husky with emotion. I tried to defend myself.

"I did –"

"You *didn't*! Not once! And worse – you just stood by and let

127

those two rip into me. That shrew was going to slit my throat, and you didn't even try to stop her! You're not just a pig – you're a coward."

There was a sick, hollow feeling spreading in my stomach. I wanted to yell at her, to tell her she was dead wrong.

But I couldn't, because I knew at least part of it was true.

"I'm sorry." The words sounded small and weak.

Millicent let out another huff of disgust. "I should've listened to Cyril," she said.

"Who's Cyril?"

"Nobody . . . Just the boy I'm going to marry."

CHAPTER 10

UPHILL

My brain shut down completely. The sick feeling in my stomach kept spreading, and I had to stop for a second because I was getting dizzy, and I thought I might fall over and tumble down the hill.

Then I realized Millicent had stepped up her pace and was almost as far ahead as Guts and Kira – and all three of them were about to disappear into the darkness.

I rushed to catch up, but I didn't pay enough attention to where I was going, and the broken end of a dead tree branch stabbed me in the forehead. It was excruciating, but the pain seemed to clear some of the fog from my brain. I managed to stagger forward until I was only an arm's length behind Millicent.

"Who's Cyril?" I asked the back of her head. I meant to whisper, but it came out much louder than that.

"Shhhhhhhhh!" all three of them hissed at me.

"Sorry!" I whispered.

I resolved to quit trying to talk to Millicent while our lives were still in danger.

But I couldn't help myself.

"Who's Cyril?" I asked again a minute later, this time managing to pitch my voice low enough that Guts and Kira couldn't hear.

"What do you care?" Millicent whispered over her shoulder.

Because you're supposed to marry ME!

I couldn't actually say that. It wasn't like we'd ever discussed it. "Just . . . curious."

"He's a boy from Sunrise. Well, a man, really – he's nearly seventeen. Six feet tall, wealthy, brilliant . . . has his own boat. We've known each other forever."

"How come I never heard of him?"

"Why would you?"

"I did live in your house."

"He was away at school then. In the Fish Islands. Just came back – they kicked him out for seditious behavior. He's *terribly* rebellious. But not in a stupid way."

"Shut up!" Guts growled from up ahead. "Both of ye! Gonna get us killed!"

I quit trying to talk to her after that, not only because Guts was right, but because I didn't know what else to say.

I felt awful, in all sorts of different ways. I wanted to throttle Millicent for betraying me by taking up with some other boy – and worse, for never having told me about him in all the time we'd spent together.

And I hated this Cyril person even more. I tried to conjure up an image of him just so I could imagine him getting eaten by sharks.

I hated myself, too. I couldn't believe I hadn't thanked Millicent for saving us. But when I ran through the past day in my head, I not only couldn't remember thanking her, I couldn't recall having said anything nice to her at all.

It made me sick and ashamed, and somehow I felt like if I'd just been a better person – more kind and considerate, and not full of cruel thoughts about things like her breath, which was much better now, and which I knew had only turned foul because she'd gone days without food and water to save my life – maybe she'd want to marry me instead of Cyril.

And I hated myself for not being older. And taller. And rich. And having my own boat.

That business about the boat was particularly irritating. Who had their own boat? His parents must have bought it for him.

How big was it? Did it have a crew?

Maybe I could get Kira to teach me how to make fireballs so I could burn it down.

I fantasized about that for a while. It was a lot easier to imagine than a shark attack, and more satisfying, too – or at least it kept me from focusing on the awful gnawing sadness in my gut.

I was numb and exhausted by the time we reached the top of the hill. It was as thick with trees as the hillside had been, but we found a good-sized rock jutting out over the far slope and climbed it to get a look around.

Below us, a wide, flat valley seemed to stretch west forever under the moonlight. Straight ahead, the north side of the valley was bordered by a distant range of craggy peaks. I wasn't good at figuring distances, but it looked like at least a two-day hike across the valley to the mountains, and possibly more. The thought of walking that whole way made me even more tired than I already was.

I wasn't the only one. "We should rest," Kira said.

We climbed down from the rock and settled into a sheltered spot to one side of it. Kira handed out half our remaining food, which wasn't much. I ate my share in a few quick gulps, then curled up to go to sleep between Millicent and Guts.

"I'm sorry about everything," I whispered to the back of Millicent's head. "I really appreciate your coming to save us."

"Shhh," was all she said in reply.

I was drifting off when I heard Guts whisper to Kira.

"How'd Pembroke off yer dad?"

She didn't answer. He started to apologize.

"Sorry! Didn't mean nothin'. Stupid."

"It's all right," she said. "It was four years ago. We were in Edgartown. In the Fish Islands. My father was a diplomat."

Her voice was so low I had to strain to hear it.

"Wot's a diplomat?"

"An elder who goes to other tribes and tries to form alliances with them. When I was little, I almost never saw him. He was always travelling, and I stayed home with my mother. It was better for the Okalu then – there was always war with the Moku, but the fighting rarely touched us. We still lived in our homeland, in the Valley of Ka – on the other side of those mountains in the distance."

She sighed. "Then came the Dark Time. Do you know about it?"

"No."

"It was after the war between Rovia and Cartage."

"You mean the Barker War?" I whispered.

It was silent for a moment before Kira answered. I don't think she'd realized I was awake and listening.

"Yes. Before the war, sometimes slavers would come from the islands and try to capture Natives – from all the tribes, not just Okalu. The tribes would fight them, and so would the Cartagers. *Li Homaya* didn't want Rovians in the New Lands, and his army had good relations with the Natives, so his soldiers would come north from Pella Nonna to drive away the slavers.

"But after the war, Cartage was much weaker, and *Li Homaya* stopped sending his troops to the north. He kept them in the south, to protect Pella Nonna and the gold route.

"Then something worse happened. The slavers made an alliance with the Moku. They gave the Moku guns and cannon to fight us – and in return, the Moku gave the slavers any Okalu they captured.

"For hundreds of years, the Moku had tried and failed to defeat us. But the guns and cannon changed everything. In just a few weeks, the Moku drove us from our lands in the Valley of Ka – they captured our temple, burned our homes, took the men for slaves . . . and slaughtered the women and children."

She paused. I heard her take a deep breath before she continued.

"When the Dark Time began, my father was away, on a mission to another tribe. My mother was killed in the fighting, and I fled with the others across the Cat's Teeth. Eventually, my father joined us. By then, the elders knew we had no hope from any alliance. No one would help us against the Moku and the slavers.

"But my father had been told the King of Rovia hated slavery and outlawed it among his people. My father believed this king was just and fair, and if he knew his own subjects were making slaves of us, he would stop them. So my father went to Edgartown, in the Fish Islands, to seek an audience with the Rovian Governor General and ask him to stop the slavers.

"Because my mother was dead, my father took me with him. He thought it would be a simple thing to speak with the Governor. But it wasn't. We were in Edgartown over a year before my father got an appointment. To pass the time, he hired a tutor, and I learned both Rovian and Cartager.

"When my father finally got his audience, the Governor told him slavery was against the king's law – and because it was illegal, it could not possibly exist, anywhere on Rovian soil."

She let out a little snort of disgust.

"By then, my father had learned the slaves were being sold to a man named Roger Pembroke, to work in the silver mine on Sunrise Island. He told the Governor this. But the Governor demanded proof. He said the word of a Native was not enough – he needed witnesses, Rovian citizens who would come forward and testify the slavery existed.

"My father had made some friends among the Rovians in Edgartown. He asked them to help him find witnesses. At first, they tried to be helpful. Then they became frightened. They told my father Roger Pembroke had learned who he was, and what he was trying to do, and that his life was in danger.

"I didn't know any of that at the time. I was only ten years old, and I spent my days with the tutor, Mr Dalrymple. We went out one day to the meadows above Edgartown. I remember he was teaching me all the names for the different wildflowers.

"When we came home, we found my father's body. Mr Dalrymple tried to keep me from seeing it. But I did."

Her voice was flat and steady, without any emotion at all. Somehow, that made the horror of what she was saying even worse.

"Then I had to run and hide, because Pembroke's men would have killed me too if they could. For a week, I hid in the cellar of a man Mr Dalrymple knew. Then in the middle of the night, he took me to a small boat, and we sailed to a secret port, hidden in a cove. There were smugglers there. Mr Dalrymple paid them to take me to Pella Nonna. When I got to Pella, I met a Fingu woman who helped me find work washing clothes for a Cartager family. The family's father worked for *Li Homaya*. When he learned I was good with languages, he brought me to the palace, and I became a translator."

It was silent for a moment.

"I'm sorry. That was much more than you'd asked," she said.

"No! Fine," whispered Guts. "'S'all right. Good. I mean, not, y'know –"

"Is she really his daughter?" Kira asked.

I wondered if Millicent had been awake to hear the story. Her breathing sounded deep and regular.

"Yes," I said.

"We have to leave her. She can't travel with us."

"No," I said. "She's on our side."

"That's not possible."

"It's true."

Kira's voice was hardening. "She comes from great evil. It must be a part of her."

"It isn't," I insisted. "She's good. And smart, and strong –"

"He killed my father."

135

"He killed mine, too," I told her. "*And* my brother and sister. And I'd still trust her with my life."

Silence.

"Guts, tell her Millicent's all right," I said.

I couldn't see his face, but I could practically hear it twitching.

"She's all right," he grunted. "She's a *pudda bada glulo*. But she ain't evil."

"You can't say that," Kira said.

"She ain't, tho'. Ye can trust her."

"No, I mean the curses."

"Sorry. Got a bad mouth sometimes."

"It's not that – you're saying them wrong. You can't *glulo* a *bada*. It makes no sense. You can call her a *billi glulo*. But to a girl, it's not a big insult. Unless it's *billi glulo domamora*."

"Wot's that mean?"

"She's a — —."

Hearing such foul words come out of Kira's mouth was a bit of a shock. But Guts ate it up.

"Good one . . . ! Ain't wot I meant, tho'."

"You can say *bada maya*. But I don't think you mean that, either."

"Wot's *bada maya*? She's a — —?"

"Exactly."

"Nah, that's not right. Wanted to call her a — — —."

"Oh . . . That's *pudda hula saca*."

"*Pudda hula saca* . . ." Guts whispered in a dreamy voice. If there was any question he'd gone head over heels for Kira, the swearing lesson pretty much finished it. And it made me think they might have enough in common for the feeling to be mutual.

"Teach me more like that?" he asked her.

"In the morning." Kira raised herself up on one elbow to look at me. "What did Pembroke do to your family?" she asked.

I told her the whole story, making sure I stressed the parts where Millicent had helped us against her father and his men.

By the time I finished, Guts had fallen asleep, and Kira didn't say anything except "I'm sorry".

"Me too," I said. Then I drifted off, not knowing whether I'd changed her mind about Millicent, but too tired to spend any more time worrying about it.

I WOKE UP AT dawn to a strange muttering somewhere above me. It was Kira – she'd climbed the rock we were sheltered behind and was performing the same ritual she'd gone through at sunset, whispering an Okalu prayer as she slowly lowered herself flat, her hands stretched out on either side of the firebird necklace in the direction of the sunrise.

Guts and Millicent were both awake and watching Kira as well. When she hopped down off the rock, Guts motioned to the firebird pendant in her hand.

"Is he real?"

"Who?"

"Whoyecallim. Ka. Sun god."

"Of course," Kira said. "Ka is more real than you or me."

"An' that's him?" Guts asked, pointing towards the rising sun.

"Yes. But so is this." She held up one of the rocks she'd gathered as ammunition for her sling. Then she pointed to a tree. "And so is that. And so am I, and so are you. Ka is everything."

"What about the Fist?" I asked.

"What about it?"

"What is it? I mean, exactly?"

"It's a ring that goes across all four fingers." Kira raised her right fist and pointed at the base of each finger, just above the knuckle. "Made of gold, like the sun."

"What's it do? Why's it so powerful?"

"It is the hand of Ka, sent to earth to be his instrument. It has all his power. To give life and to take it. To heal and to kill. To burn and to build."

"And whoever has the Fist of Ka – they have these powers, too?" I asked.

"Yes," she said. "For a thousand years, it was held by the Fire Kings. And with it, they ruled the world."

"Not the whole world," I said.

"Yes. The world. *This* world." She swept her hand in a wide arc across the hillside and the valley below. "If my people had not lost the Fist, they would rule it still. And whoever finds the Fist will rule again."

"Wot if they're evil?" Guts asked.

"Then so will be the world," Kira said.

I heard a noise like a pained sigh. I looked to my left, where it came from. Millicent was staring at the ground with her eyebrows crumpled together like she might cry.

Looking at her, I felt awful all over again.

"Are you all right?" I asked her.

"Fine." She shook her head, and just like that, the sorrowful look was gone.

"Let's get moving," she said.

"We should eat first," said Kira. "We'll go faster with food in our stomachs."

"We've hardly got any left," said Millicent. "Be wiser to save it."

Kira shook her head. "There's food in the valley."

"How can you be so sure?"

"The Flut live there. They're farmers. They'll have food. One way or another, we'll eat."

"What do you mean, 'one way or another'?" I asked.

"We have money and weapons. One of them will get us food."

I watched Kira hand out the last bit of our rations, thinking that she scared me a little, but I was glad she was on our side.

Guts finished his portion in seconds. As the rest of us nibbled slowly, trying to convince our stomachs it was an actual meal, he started fidgeting with his hook, unstrapping it from his stump and shaking out the cowl before he strapped it back on.

"Everything okay with Lucy?" I asked.

Kira gave me a curious look. "Who's Lucy?"

"His hook," I said.

"Nobody!" Guts barked, talking over me.

The girls both looked amused.

"You *named* your hook?" Millicent snorted.

"Didn't!" Guts protested, turning red in the face. "He's a liar!"

I might have covered for him if he hadn't called me a liar. But after I'd just been branded a pig and a coward by Millicent, I wasn't in the mood to take any more abuse. Especially when I didn't deserve it.

"Come off it!" I said. "You named her –"

"Shut up!"

"– the day you got her!"

"Pack o' lies!"

"'Thunk aw'll cawl 'er Luuucy,'" I said, imitating Guts's voice in a way that made him sound even more deranged than he actually was.

Big mistake.

Guts leaped on me, which caught me so off guard I didn't have time to get my hands up, and we toppled backwards off the fallen tree I'd been sitting on.

He pinned my shoulders with his knees and started swinging. I managed to get both my hands on the wrist of his hook arm so he couldn't stab me, but that left his good fist free, and he kept slugging me in the side of the head with it. I tried to twist away, but my legs were still up over the side of the fallen tree, and I couldn't get any leverage to buck him off.

"Get off!"

"— you, ye – *porsamora!*"

Kira and Millicent were both on him, trying to pull him off me by his upper arms, when we heard a shout that froze us all in place.

"FOUND 'EM!"

I turned my head to the sound of the voice. On the crest of a nearby rock, about a hundred feet along the hilltop from us, was a beefy Rovian man with a shock of red hair and a rifle in his hand.

For an endless second, we stared at each other.

"OVER HERE!" he yelled. Then he started off the rock after us.

By the time we were up and running, answering shouts were echoing off the rocks.

CHAPTER 11

FLUT

I tore down the hillside. It was so steep that moving fast was easy.

The hard part was staying on my feet.

Trees and branches and roots and holes zoomed by in a blur.

FASTER.

One wrong step, and I'd break an ankle.

That wouldn't be the worst of it. If I fell, they'd catch me.

I could hear branches snapping behind me.

The others were up ahead. I couldn't raise my eyes from the ground long enough to get a fix on them, but I knew Guts and Millicent had got a head start on me.

I caught a glimpse of Kira's pack, bouncing on her shoulders.

That meant the noise behind me was a slaver.

FASTER –

I hit the side of a hole with my foot and nearly went down.

It hurt.

I tried to take shorter steps so I wasn't landing so hard.

My shoulder caught the side of a tree.

That hurt more.

I could still hear the slaver. He was gaining on me.

The ground began to flatten out. We were almost at the bottom of the hill.

The trees grew thicker – and then, almost in an instant, they were gone.

We were on the valley floor. Open land in every direction.

RUN FASTER.

The soil was loose and spongy now, mixed with the dry stubble of dead plants – at every step, my foot either sank into the ground or got spiked on a sharp stalk.

FASTER.

Gravity wasn't pulling me along any more. I had to pump my legs hard to keep them churning over the soft ground.

My lungs started to burn.

My thigh muscles were getting shaky.

I couldn't hear the slaver behind me any more. But I knew he was still there.

RUN FASTER.

A quarter of a mile ahead was a line of tall plants rising to the height of a man's head. They grew in what looked like a perfectly straight row.

Tall and straight and evenly spaced.

Nature hadn't grown them that way.

And nature hadn't made the soil under my feet this loose.

We were running over cropland.

Crops meant people.

I saw the first of them without realizing what I was looking at. Up ahead to the right, at the edge of the plantings, was a single crooked spire that rose thirty feet straight into the air.

At first, I thought it was the skinny trunk of a dead tree.

But there was a clump of something on top of it.

The clump was moving, shinnying down the spire.

It wasn't a tree. It was a lookout post. The moving clump was the lookout, climbing down from a Y-shaped joint at the top.

He vanished into the tall plantings.

They'd know we were coming.

I hoped they were friendly.

But they couldn't be any worse than the slavers chasing us.

FASTER.

Guts and Millicent were tiring. I was gaining on them. Just a few feet behind.

Was the slaver gaining on me?

I didn't know. And I didn't dare to look back.

Kira was twenty yards ahead, outrunning us even with the pack on her shoulders.

She looked back as she ran – first over her left shoulder, then her right.

When she looked the second time, her face showed alarm.

I turned my head in the direction she'd looked. A man was running towards us on a diagonal, about two hundred yards away. He was in Continental clothes, but he must have been a Moku, because he was much darker-skinned than the big redhead.

He was carrying a rifle.

The redhead must be behind us.

There was a third man somewhere. Maybe a fourth. They'd all have rifles.

RUN FASTER.

My lungs were on fire, and my legs felt limp. But there was nothing to do except keep going.

They weren't firing at us. Why? We were easy targets.

Because they needed us alive.

They needed *me* alive. For the map. The others . . .

FASTER.

I didn't have much left in me.

Neither did Millicent. I was dead even with her.

I made sure I didn't pull ahead. After everything that had happened, I was going to stick by her no matter what.

The tall plants were close now – close enough that I could see there wasn't just a line of them but a whole field, row upon row stretching back into the distance.

The rows were just wide enough to run between. Kira reached them first and disappeared.

Then Guts.

Then me and Millicent. We ran down adjoining rows, our arms slapping the long, yellow-tinged leaves as we went.

The ground was even softer now, and the damp soil sucked at my feet.

I heard noise behind me. The slaver was crashing through the plants behind us.

Up ahead, Kira made a sharp left turn and vanished.

A moment later, Millicent and I reached the spot where she'd turned. A three-foot-wide path lay crosswise to the direction we'd been running. We followed Kira down the path.

Kira stopped short.

As we reached her, we saw why she'd stopped – and we did, too.

Half a dozen Flut warriors – I'd spent enough time around the Natives in Pella to recognize the tribe by their long, thin faces – were blocking the path in front of us.

They were shirtless, dressed only in Native breeches. The first two were crouched on one knee, aiming rifles at us.

Behind the riflemen, the other four all had long wooden spears raised over their shoulders.

The spearheads were pointed at our chests.

The lead spear carrier yelled something at us. He was speaking Cartager – I recognized the slippery sound of the words, even though I didn't know what they meant.

Kira answered, her voice rising in a question. She was asking for help.

The leader answered. His tone was hostile.

The answer was no.

I could hear the redheaded slaver crashing through the plants behind us.

Millicent spoke up, in urgent, plaintive Cartager.

Kira turned to stare at her with a look of surprise.

Millicent had just finished speaking when the crashing noise behind us suddenly stopped.

We all turned to see the redheaded slaver standing in the pathway, panting and sweaty, his rifle in his hands.

He was gaping at the Flut, dumbfounded.

I heard a Flut yell something that sounded like, *"Hio!"*

"DUCK!" screamed Millicent and Kira together.

We all hit the ground as the Flut rifles roared over our heads. When I looked up, the plants were still rustling from where the slaver had dived back into cover.

The Flut leader issued a quick series of orders. The two riflemen and the other spear carriers vanished into the plants. A moment later, I heard a faint rustling off to my left as they headed for the spot where the slaver had taken cover.

The path was empty now except for us and the leader. He gestured to us: *come with me.*

Then he turned and started down the path at a run.

We followed him.

THE FLUT LEADER kept up a fast pace, his back muscles rippling under his long black hair as he ran down a series of pathways through the tall crops. None of us spoke – it took all our energy just to keep him in sight.

Twice, gunfire rang out in the field behind us. Whatever Millicent had said, it must have worked, because the Flut were fighting our battle for us.

We emerged onto open land. Still running, the leader took us down a worn path over a wide plain of low grass, dotted with the occasional shade tree. After half a mile or so, we reached a shallow, six-foot-wide stream.

The Flut leader splashed across the calf deep water, then crouched at the far bank to drink with his hands from the stream. The four of us did the same, grateful for the chance to catch our breath and drink. Kira pulled the two empty water skins from her rucksack. She handed one to me, and we both filled them.

A minute later, the Flut set off again, this time at a brisk walk.

As we followed him along another path through an open meadow, I fell into step behind Millicent.

"What did you say to him back there?" I asked.

"Nothing special. He didn't seem to care for Crazy Knife Girl much. I don't think their tribes get along."

"Where's he leading us?"

"I haven't the slightest idea. For all I know, he's going to kill us all."

"Seriously?"

"I said I don't know. Quit asking stupid questions."

She was still angry. That much was obvious.

"Millicent, I really am sorry –"

"And stop apologizing! It's pathetic."

After that, I fell to the back of the group and tried not to collapse in a heap. I was exhausted and starving, and all of a sudden, the whole thing seemed pointless.

Men with guns are chasing me. For what? The map to a treasure that's probably nonsense anyway. All that stuff Kira said about the Fist – power to heal and kill, burn and build, blah blah blah – seems awfully hard to swallow.

And if it does exist, I've got no business going near it.

I don't want that kind of power.

I just want a sandwich.

And some jelly bread.

Starving . . .

And the only people I care about have turned on me.

Millicent's furious.

Worse than that – she's in love with someone else.

Why I ever thought she and I . . .

I'm a fool.

And Guts attacked me! My ear's so swollen from his fist I can feel it throb without even touching it.

They're the whole reason I'm here.

I could've gone down to the Barkers. I would've been safe there.

But I came here. I didn't want to let them down.

And they turned on me.

And Kira . . . She doesn't care a thing for me. All I am to her is the map.

She'd probably kill me as quick as Pembroke's men if it got her what she wanted.

I don't even want the stupid map.

I'd trade the whole thing for a sandwich.

I'd give it away if I could. It's nothing but trouble.

I don't want any more trouble.

I just want a sandwich.

And some jelly bread . . .

I was half asleep on my feet, dreaming about jelly bread, when we came upon the sheep. There was a flock of a hundred or more, tended by a few shirtless young boys with long sticks.

The boys gawked at us as we passed.

"It's not polite to stare," Millicent told one of them.

When she spoke, he flinched in surprise and skittered backwards. But he didn't stop staring.

We left the little shepherds and their flock behind and started up a wide, easy hill. At the top of it, we came upon a village of a few dozen thatched huts, bustling with people.

The Flut warrior led us through the settlement, past women

who gossiped with each other as they ground corn in giant bowls; stone-eyed men who smoked long clay pipes and whittled blocks of wood with Continental-made knives; and packs of noisy, happy kids who darted among the huts, trailed by barking dogs so skinny you could count their ribs.

As we went by, everyone stopped to stare at us, and not in a friendly way. A couple of the men made a point of reaching their hands out to rest on the rifles they had lying nearby.

In the centre of the village, a ring of huts circled a small commons with a fire pit in the middle of it. The Flut warrior motioned for us to wait in the commons, spoke a few sentences of Cartager to the girls, then disappeared into a hut that was twice the size of the others.

"Let me do the talking," Millicent said to Kira.

Kira's lip curled in a snarl. "You know nothing of these people."

"I've seen enough to know they're not keen on you."

Kira shrugged. "Flut and Okalu are not allies. My people used to rule these lands."

"And this bunch doesn't seem to have forgotten it."

Just then, an older man – broad-shouldered but paunchy, his face wrinkled and his long hair more grey than black – stepped out of the big hut. He was followed by the warrior who'd led us to the village and a third, much younger Flut.

When the three Flut approached, Millicent stepped forward. So did Kira.

They both bowed deep to the elder Flut. Guts and I did the same.

The elder spoke a few sentences in Cartager.

149

Millicent and Kira both tried to answer at once.

He raised a hand to silence them. Then he looked past the girls to me and Guts, addressing us directly.

Millicent said something in Cartager. The Flut elder ignored her, looking me in the eye as he spoke again.

I didn't understand a word.

Millicent turned her head to look back at us. "They only want to talk to men," she said. She was careful to keep the annoyance out of her voice, but she rolled her eyes – which, since her head was turned away from them, the Flut couldn't see.

"Do they speak Rovian?" I asked.

"Of course not. They barely speak Cartager."

"I talk Cartager," Guts offered.

"Only swear words," I said.

"Stuff it!" Guts growled at me.

"If you want this to go well, you'll let me do the talking," said Millicent firmly.

The Flut were starting to look impatient. The elder addressed me and Guts again.

"What do we tell him?" I asked Millicent.

"Nothing. Just shrug your shoulders and look stupid."

I did as I was told.

"Both of you," she muttered, glaring at Guts.

He scowled and twitched, but offered a halfhearted shrug as he stared at the ground.

The elder looked annoyed. But when Millicent offered an explanation in her softest, most soothing voice, and added another deep bow on top of it, he grudgingly began a dialogue with her.

Kira tried to break in at first, but the hostile stares of all three

Flut persuaded her to keep her mouth shut and let Millicent handle things.

The conversation went on for some time. The Flut elder kept asking questions, and Millicent kept answering them.

His tone occasionally turned sharp, but even when it did, she kept her voice calm and steady. At one point, she lowered it nearly to a whisper, and it quavered with emotion.

I couldn't tell whether the emotion was real or just an act. But either way, it worked its magic on her audience. The Flut elder's brow knitted with concern, and although the other two Flut stayed motionless and square-shouldered, the eyes of the younger one seemed to melt into puddles as he stared at Millicent.

At first, I felt a pang of jealousy. But as I thought about it some more, I started to wonder whether I shouldn't try to warn the poor Flut warrior – who by now was looking positively moony as he listened to Millicent spin her tale – that she was nothing but trouble and he shouldn't get his hopes up.

I was still thinking about it when Millicent turned to Kira and asked in an undertone, "How much money do you have?"

"About two hundred," Kira replied.

"Gold or silver?"

"Neither. Shells."

"*Shells?* That's absurd!"

"Not to a Flut. They're more valuable than silver. Should I get the bag out?"

"Not until we've set a price."

Millicent went back to talking with the elder, and the tone of the conversation shifted – the back-and-forth got much faster, and Millicent's sentences turned short and businesslike.

I wasn't sure what they were haggling over, but I hoped it was food.

Finally, she sighed, gave a deep bow, and turned away from the Flut.

"Walk with me," she told us. "Don't look back."

She started off in the direction we'd come from, and the three of us had to scurry to fall in line behind her.

Kira was aghast. "Are you mad?"

"I'm negotiating. Keep your voice down," Millicent said, without turning her head or slowing down.

"We can't walk away! We're starving!"

"I'd rather starve than pay those prices," Millicent declared.

We'd almost reached the far edge of the commons. "Please don't walk away from food," I begged her.

"Should have thought about that before you tossed away all our silver."

"You were going to drown!"

"And now we're going to starve if we don't get the price down."

Fortunately, just then we heard the elder's voice, calling Millicent back. She returned, and within a minute, they'd come to some kind of agreement.

As Kira pulled out her sack of shells and counted out a handful to give to the Flut, Millicent explained the situation to me and Guts.

"They're going to feed us," she said, "then show us the best route across the valley and vouch for us with the other villages. We can buy the food we need along the way, and they'll keep an eye out for the men from the boat."

Almost as soon as the elder had his shells in hand, three

tribeswomen appeared with a bowl of corn pancakes, a pitcher of goat's milk and – I almost passed out from happiness at the sight – a long skewer with two full racks of cooked mutton.

They spread the food out on a blanket next to the fire pit. Then the Flut retreated to the porch in front of the main hut, leaving us to dine by ourselves. Only Millicent's warning that we should eat politely kept us from attacking the food like starving dogs. Even so, we tore through it with fierce speed.

The last of the mutton ribs had been spoken for and we were down to our final two pancakes before anyone stopped chewing long enough to talk.

"Is it true, what you said?" Kira asked Millicent.

Millicent didn't answer.

"How much of what you told them –"

"There's nothing to talk about," Millicent said sharply.

"But are the slavers –"

"Use that word in front of me, there's going to be trouble," Millicent warned her.

A tense silence followed. Millicent's eyes stayed fixed on the mutton rib she was gnawing. Kira's nostrils flared as she studied her own food.

Guts and I traded puzzled glances. I had no idea what the girls were talking about, but it seemed like a bad idea to ask.

Kira took a bite of mutton. Chewed it slowly. Swallowed. Then tried again.

"Why did you say –"

"I said what I said to get us what we needed," Millicent snapped. "And so help me – if you so much as move your tongue to slander my father, I'll cut it from your mouth."

Kira looked too shocked to answer. Millicent tossed the rib bone into the fire pit and stood up, flicking her fingers clean.

"I'm going to see about getting a bath. Sick to death of being filthy."

Millicent strode across the commons to speak with the Flut. We all watched as she bowed low to the Flut elder, sitting on a woven chair in front of his hut. He nodded and smiled, clearly won over by her.

"I don't understand your friend," Kira said.

"What did she say to them?" I asked.

"That Rovian soldiers are coming to invade the New Lands and make slaves of us all. And the four of us are on a mission to stop them." Kira turned to look at me. "Is it true? Or was she lying?"

"I have no idea," was all I could think to say.

CHAPTER 12

COMING CLEAN

My stomach was full for the first time in days, and for the moment we seemed safe from Pembroke's slavers. But now I had something new to worry about.

Why would Rovian soldiers invade the New Lands?

Rovia and Cartage were enemies, but not like the Moku and Okalu. They weren't dead set on wiping each other out. They only fought occasionally, and the Barker War five years back had seemed to settle things between them, at least as far as the New Lands went. When it was over, Cartage controlled the mainland, and Rovia ruled the islands. And that was that.

Or so I thought.

And this business about making slaves of everyone – how could that be? Rovia wasn't in the slave trade. The king had outlawed it. Roger Pembroke was a slaver, and a Rovian . . . but the only soldiers he had any control over were the hundred or so in the garrison on Sunrise, and that was just because according to Millicent, he paid their salaries.

Surely you couldn't invade a whole continent with a hundred soldiers. You'd need thousands. And warships, too. Roger Pembroke didn't have that kind of power.

Or did he?

I watched Millicent walk back to us from the elder's hut.

"What's this about Rovian soldiers invading the New Lands?" I asked her.

"Doesn't matter," she said, shaking her head.

"How can it not matter?!"

"There's a stream nearby," she said, ignoring the question. "They'll take us there if we want to wash up. Three shells a person, and they'll wash our clothes. I recommend it – you look like a pack of animals, and you smell even worse."

Two teenage Flut girls were approaching. One of them called out in Cartager, and Millicent turned to greet them.

"Fine," I said. "But what about the soldiers –"

She talked over me, directing a comment to Kira in Cartager. Then she and Kira began to follow the two Flut girls.

"Go with the boys when they show up," Millicent said over her shoulder as she walked off. "And don't waste time. We've got a long walk ahead of us."

"What about the soldiers?!" I called out, exasperated.

She didn't even turn round.

"Girlie ain't changed a bit," Guts muttered as he watched her go. "Still a *pudda saca*."

"Don't call her that."

"*Pudo la*, ye *billi glulo porsamora*."

156

"You sure you're saying it right?"

"Shut up."

A moment later, two boys a few years younger than us arrived and led us to a secluded spot on the bank of a slow-moving stream. They motioned for us to give them our clothes. We stripped down, and they began to rinse the clothes as we plonked ourselves down in the stream.

The water was chilly, but I forced myself to stay in it until I'd scrubbed myself clean, especially my hair. Then I sat down on the riverbank, shivering and wet, and watched the boys beat our clothes against some rocks. It was late morning, the sun was hot, and pretty quickly I stopped shivering.

Guts sat down next to me. "Wot ye make of this soldier business?" he asked.

I just glared at him, my teeth clenched together. And not from the cold.

"Wot's yer problem?" he asked.

"What'd you attack me for?" I yelled at him.

"Tryin' to make me look stupid! Nosin' in on her!" he yelled back.

The two kids stopped beating out our clothes and turned to watch us argue.

"I wasn't!" I told him. "I don't even like her!"

"Tell the other one!"

"I don't!"

"Prove it!"

"Oh, come on!" I lowered my voice. "You know how I feel about Millicent. I don't care about anybody else."

He thought about that. "Promise?"

"I swear it."

We were both quiet for a minute. The kids went back to beating out our clothes.

"Right then," Guts said finally. "We're square."

"Aren't you going to apologize?"

"Fer wot?"

"Beating me on the head!"

"Had it comin'! Shouldn'ta made me look stupid."

"I was telling the truth! I *told* you not to name that hook!"

"Still."

"You're out of your mind."

There was another minute of silence while I tried to tamp down my anger. I felt like the whole thing was his fault. But Millicent was still mad at me, and I didn't know what to make of Kira. So if I wasn't at least on good terms with Guts, I wouldn't have anybody.

"Sorry I made you look stupid," I said, trying not to sound resentful.

Guts nodded. "Sorry I beat yer head."

That was a start, I guess.

"She says she's marrying someone else," I told him.

He shot bolt upright. "Who is he?! I'll strangle 'im!"

"Not Kira! Millicent!"

"Oh." He relaxed again. "How'd *that* happen?"

I told him what I knew about this Cyril fellow. Guts considered the situation as he used the side of his hook to scratch a bug bite on his arm.

"No worry. Get out o' this mess, ye can go kill 'im."

I sighed. "I'm not going to kill him."

Guts shrugged. "Fine. I'll kill 'im for ye."

It was a ridiculous thing to say, but it made me feel good about Guts again.

WHEN THE BOYS returned our clothes, they were damp but clean. We put them on and walked back to the middle of the village. Kira and Millicent were waiting, looking clean-scrubbed and fresh. They'd both swapped their dirty clothes for Native cotton leggings and tunics, and Millicent's still-wet hair was tucked behind her ears.

She was so pretty it hurt a little to look at her.

There was a long final conversation between Millicent and the village elder. At one point, he took out a stick and scratched a map in the dirt. The girls nodded their heads like they understood, but I couldn't make any sense of what he'd drawn.

Then the elder presented Millicent with a thin strand of rope that one of his warriors had been busy knotting in dozens of places along its length.

At Millicent's direction, we all bowed to the Flut. They returned the bows. Then the same warrior who'd taken us to the village led us out in the opposite direction.

"Wot's with the rope?" Guts asked as we walked.

"It's a message," said Millicent. "To give to the other Flut villages. So they'll let us pass through, and sell us food."

Guts looked skeptical. "Can't say all that with a piece o' rope."

"Yes, you can," said Kira. "It's how the Flut write. With knots on string."

"Stupid," said Guts.

"No," Millicent told him. "Stupid is not writing at all."

159

"Shut up, ye *saca*!" Guts snapped at her.

"I wasn't talking about you," said Millicent.

There was an awkward silence after that. When I glanced over at Guts, he was red-faced and twitching.

I felt sad for him. Until just then, it hadn't occurred to me that he might not know how to write. But now that I thought about it, considering what little I knew about his past, it made sense.

The Flut warrior led us to a trailhead just outside the village. He left us there with a few final instructions in Cartager, and we set off down the trail, which led west along the bank of the stream where we'd bathed.

"So what about these soldiers?" I asked Millicent.

Once again, she didn't answer.

"Is it true? Why on earth would Rovia invade the New Lands?"

She was walking in front of me, and I couldn't see her face, but I heard her utter a short sigh.

"You've got to tell us what you know, Millicent," I said.

"There's some kind of plan afoot," she said reluctantly. "I don't know anything specific. But, yes. It's going to happen."

"Is your father involved?" I asked.

"How else would I know about it?"

"But how could he get the troops to –"

"That's all I know," she said sharply. "I've no idea how, or where, or when – just that they're planning it."

"If Rovians invade the New Lands, it will start a war with Cartage," said Kira.

Millicent shrugged. "I suppose so."

"Wot's this mean for us?" asked Guts.

"It doesn't change a thing," said Millicent. "Still got to get that map translated. And we've still got to find the Fist."

"What do *you* want with the Fist?" Kira asked her.

"Who says I want it?"

"If you don't, why are you here?"

"Because I fancy the outdoors," said Millicent.

I figured that would set Kira off, but she let it go. Something seemed to have changed between her and Millicent. I wouldn't go so far as to say they liked each other. But between her bartering with the Flut and her new willingness to threaten Kira with violence of her own, Millicent seemed to have earned Kira's respect.

I waited until we'd been walking for a while and were spread out along the trail before I fell in close to Millicent and quietly pressed her for more information.

"Tell me more about this invasion."

"There's nothing more to tell."

"You've got to know more than that," I insisted.

"Well, I don't! And it doesn't matter. We've still got to find this stupid tribe and figure out what that map says." She looked back at me with narrowed eyes. "You haven't forgotten any of it, have you?"

I felt a little pang of worry.

Dash dot feather cup two dash dot firebird . . .

"No! Course not!"

"Well, don't. It's the least you can do," she said bitterly.

"You know, I really am –"

"Quit saying you're sorry!"

161

"I wasn't going to!"

I was, actually. I couldn't help it. I still *felt* sorry.

Not that it was doing me any good with her.

THE VALLEY WAS ENORMOUS. We spent the rest of the day walking, and judging by the position of the mountains to the north, by sunset we hardly seemed to have made any progress at all. Partly that was because of the route we were taking. The Flut had told Millicent and Kira that the easiest way across the mountains was over a pass on the far western shoulder of the Gran, the tallest peak in the range.

The Gran looked almost as wide as it was tall, and it stood well to the west of where we'd started. So the route the Flut had sketched out sent us nearly as far west as north.

All of it was through farmland and pastures held by the Flut, who kept a close eye on their territory. Every few miles, we came upon another tall, slender lookout post. By the time we saw them, they were usually empty because their sentry had spotted us first and scrambled down to spread the news.

Within minutes, a hostile clutch of Flut warriors would approach us. They didn't always speak Cartager, but they all recognized the knotted rope Millicent carried. After examining it, one of the warriors would escort us through his fields before sending us off in the direction of the next territory.

After the time we'd spent running from the slavers, the sentries were a comfort. As long as we stayed in Flut territory and minded our manners, we didn't seem to have much to fear other than sunburn and sore feet.

In the late afternoon, we reached another village, twice as big

162

but otherwise identical to the first one. We bought a day's worth of food from them after an epic negotiation, during which Millicent made us pretend to walk away three times.

This time, we took the food with us. Half an hour before sunset, we came upon a lightly wooded stretch of high ground that some Flut shepherds must have used for camping themselves, because there was a pit already dug with the charred leftovers of multiple fires. We gathered some wood, then built a fire using the flints Kira had brought with her. After watching her pray to the sunset, we ate a quick dinner and fell asleep around the fire.

I woke up in the middle of the night to muffled sounds that at first I thought were coming from a wounded animal. I looked around the smouldering rim of the fire and saw just two bodies asleep on the ground.

I got up and walked towards the noise. About twenty yards away, I came upon Millicent, sitting hunched over on the hillside with her knees tucked to her chest, sobbing into her arms.

When she heard me coming, she tried to pull herself together.

"Leave me alone," she said in a scratchy whisper.

"What's the matter?"

"I said leave me alone!"

I sat down next to her.

"No," I said.

She started sobbing again.

"I don't want the others to see me like this," she said miserably.

I put a hand on her back, figuring she'd pull away. But she did the opposite, shifting closer and pressing her head against my chest. I put an arm round her and ran my hand back and forth across her shoulder until it grew warm from the touch.

Eventually, she stopped crying. She nuzzled my chest a little, but I wasn't sure if she meant it, or if she was just wiping her runny nose on me.

Then she sat up straight and stared out at the moonlit pasture with a wrung-out look in her eyes.

"It just gets worse," she said. "Every time, I think, 'That's it. It can't get any worse.' But then it does. It never stops."

I wasn't sure what she was talking about. But opening my mouth hadn't been working out too well for me lately, so I kept it shut.

She started to cry again. "The whole silver mine," she whispered, her voice quavering through the sobs. "They're all slaves up there. They always have been."

I gave her arm a gentle squeeze. "It's okay," I said.

"No, it's not." She buried her head in my chest and really let go. Her whole body shook with grief, and as I held her, I finally understood why she hadn't wanted to talk about the slavers, or even admit they existed.

She'd spent her whole life rich and happy and carefree. But all that happiness had been paid for with other people's pain. And knowing it was too much for her.

Eventually, she cried herself out. She straightened up and took a few deep breaths. Then she let out a long, shaky sigh.

"I'm not a bad person," she said.

"I know you're not," I told her.

"I had no idea! Nobody on Sunrise does. They say they're paying them. And it's not like anyone goes up there to see for themselves. Mother doesn't know, I'm sure of it. I mean, she's beastly, but she'd never put up with *that*."

Millicent sighed again, wiping her eyes. "And he's *such* a good liar . . . When I'm with him, and he looks me in the eye, and turns on all his charm . . . You should have heard Daddy on the way back from Deadweather. When we first got on that boat, I didn't even want to speak to him. But he was *so* kind, and he seemed so sorry about the whole mess . . .

"He told me it was all a terrible misunderstanding. That he'd just asked Birch to lean on you a bit, like businessmen do. But that Birch misunderstood. Daddy said it's because of the way he manages employees – he gives them too much leeway, and some of the more ruthless ones go overboard trying to impress him . . . He said the same thing happened with the lawyer, and the legal papers. And when Birch went over the cliff, he completely misread the situation, and didn't realize the truth till he got to Deadweather – but now that he knew it, he'd leave you be.

"And he *did* – I mean, first thing when we came back to Sunrise, he had all your wanted posters taken down, and I heard him tell Birch's brother and the garrison commander you were innocent, and not to be bothered if you showed up."

It was such obvious nonsense it made me burn a little to hear the way she talked about it, like there was any chance her father had ever been telling the truth.

"He admitted he'd bungled the whole thing, and never should have brought troops to your plantation, but he said he'd been too distracted by the Cartager problem to think it through. I asked him what he was talking about, and he told me Cartage was plotting against Rovia in the Blue Sea – and maybe even planning to invade Sunrise. And it was really the Cartage Navy, not the pirates, that attacked the *Earthly Pleasure*."

"That's ridiculous," I said. "I was on that boat – it was a pirate attack."

"I know! When Daddy first told me Cartagers were to blame, I thought it was absurd. But back on Sunrise, I kept hearing the same thing. Everybody was whispering that it must have been the Cartage Navy behind it. Even the refugees from the *Earthly Pleasure* – to hear them tell it, *all* the pirates were Short-Ears."

I thought about that. "It's true Ripper Jones is a Cartager . . . So are a few of his men. But not a lot – maybe five or six out of fifty."

Millicent shrugged. "People are sheep. If everyone around them says up is down, soon enough they'll start saying it, too. I remember once . . ."

As she went on, the memory of the Cartager pirates from Ripper's crew who'd harassed Guts back in Pella Nonna jumped into my head. For a moment, I tried to puzzle out whether their meeting with *Li Homaya* meant there was any truth to Pembroke's claim that Cartage was behind Ripper's attack on the *Earthly Pleasure*.

But Millicent was still talking, and I couldn't think and listen at the same time, so I had to quit trying to think.

"There was a lot of bluster about making Cartage pay for what they'd done. One morning, I came down to breakfast, and Daddy was talking to Lord Winterbottom. As I walked in, I heard Daddy say, 'One stroke, and we'll own the whole continent.' He wouldn't tell me what he meant by that. But later, Cyril came over. He and I talked it through, and we pieced together that they were talking about invading the New Lands."

At the mention of Cyril, my heart sank. I'd been hoping he didn't really exist, and she'd just invented him to get back at me for not being nicer to her when she first showed up.

"Then the night before I was supposed to leave for Rovia, Cyril came –"

"Wait – 'leave for Rovia'?"

"Oh. Right . . . A couple of days after I got back from Dead-weather, my parents sat me down and said they thought it'd be a good idea if I went across the Maw to school. There's a famous boarding school for girls, called Winthrop. All the Rovian noblemen's daughters go there, and I'd been itching to go for years. But Daddy had always said no. And now suddenly, he was practically begging me to get on a boat.

"So I agreed. I mean, I knew he was just doing it to get rid of me after I'd caused so much trouble running off to help you. But even so, going to Winthrop was a dream come true. There was a ship coming down from the Fish Islands to pick up the *Earthly Pleasure* refugees and bring them back to Rovia, and they got me a ticket, and the ship came in, and I was all set to leave.

"Then Cyril came over the night before I left, full of news. He'd eavesdropped on a meeting his father held at their house. His father works for Daddy – I mean, Cyril would tell you they're partners, but it's nonsense, Daddy's the one who calls all the shots. Mr Whitmore's just a glorified bookkeeper . . ."

It was strange how Millicent could manage to be completely disgusted by her father and still not be able to resist bragging about how important he was.

"Anyway, the meeting was all about some attack they were planning – lots of talk about troops, and ships, and bombarding something from the sea –"

"How can your father *do* all that? He's just a businessman."

"Daddy's not just any businessman. And this wasn't just him.

He'd somehow got the approval of the Governor-General in Edgartown. That's why it was so important for people to think the *Earthly Pleasure* was attacked by Cartagers. Because then it wasn't a pirate attack – it was an act of war. And Rovia had to fight back."

There was so much to keep straight that my head was starting to hurt from it. And Millicent was still talking.

"At one point in the meeting, someone mentioned Birch – not the dead one, but his brother. They said he was leaving for the New Lands in two days.

"Someone else said, 'What's he up to?' And the answer was, 'He's off on Pembroke's errand.' 'What errand?' they asked. The man said, 'The one he advertised all over town,' and they all laughed. And right away, Cyril figured out they were talking about your wanted posters, and Birch was coming after you."

I didn't much like hearing that a room full of evil rich men was laughing about Birch coming to kidnap me. And I was even less keen on hearing this Cyril fellow had relayed the news to Millicent.

"I knew I had to help you if I could. But they were putting me on the ship for Rovia the next day, and if I ran off, Daddy would tear the island apart looking for me. So Cyril and I went to see Etsy Featherton."

"You mean that girl who cuts her hair exactly like yours?" I'd met Etsy once while I was staying with the Pembrokes. Millicent and I had run into her in Blisstown, and even though Millicent wasn't exactly nice to her, Etsy had spent hours tagging along after us like a hungry puppy.

"That's the one. Complete prat. But she's always been desperate for attention, and she positively *hates* her family, so when I offered to pay her to stow away on the ship to Rovia and pretend to be me, she jumped at the chance. Didn't even have to pay her that much. But that's the thing about most people – dangle a few coins in front of them and they fall all over themselves. It's sad, really.

"Anyway, the next day, right after I boarded the ship and said goodbye to Mother and Daddy, Cyril paid a couple of deckhands to start a fight on the dock. During the commotion, we snuck Etsy on board and into my cabin. We traded clothes – she was *thrilled* about that – and I told her to pretend she was seasick and stay in the cabin the whole trip. That way, no one would see her except the crew when they brought her meals. And none of the crew knew what I looked like, so nobody'd be the wiser until the ship got to Rovia.

"When we sailed out past North Point, I jumped from the porthole window and swam to shore. Cyril met me there, and we waited until the middle of the night, then went to the cove – Daddy's secret port, where you and I got the boat to Deadweather. I understand why it's there now, and why Daddy made me promise never to tell anyone about it. He always said it was so he could come and go without being bothered. But the truth is, that's how they get the slaves up to the mine without anyone in Blisstown knowing about it."

She paused, and for a moment I thought she might start to cry again. But she didn't.

"Birch's ship was anchored there, and I snuck on board and hid down in the hold. The next day, it set sail for the New Lands. The whole thing went off beautifully, except I didn't bring enough food and water. And I couldn't have managed any of it without

Cyril – he thought the whole idea was mad, and he never stopped trying to persuade me not to go through with it. But he came through for me. I really owe him for that."

I guess I did, too. Which was annoying, because it made me feel guilty for hating his guts.

"Thanks for doing all that," I said.

Millicent shrugged. "You would have done the same for me."

I still had my arm round her, and as we sat in the silence, I started to wonder whether it might be a good idea to try and kiss her.

I turned my head towards her. She met my eye with a pained look.

"I'm sorry for what I said about marrying Cyril. I know it was cruel."

I smiled at her. "That's okay. Long as it's not true."

I waited for her tell me it wasn't. Instead, she turned her head away to stare glumly into the distance.

My stomach started to sink.

"It's not true, is it?"

She shook her head and made a noise that was somewhere between a sigh and a huff. "It doesn't matter. Not at a time like this . . . I understand why Daddy wants the Fist now. You heard Kira – you know what kind of power it's got. He's going to use it to take over this whole continent. And he'll make slaves of them all. Every one."

"He doesn't need *that* many slaves to run a silver mine."

"The silver mine's just a drop in the ocean. Daddy wants an empire."

"You really think the Fist is that powerful?"

Millicent nodded. "Whatever else my father is, he's no fool. He's been searching for the Fist of Ka my whole life. If it wasn't that powerful, he wouldn't be trying so hard to find it."

Her eyes met mine again. The pained look was gone, replaced by a fierce one.

"And we've got to make sure he doesn't get it."

CHAPTER 13

THE CLUTCH

It took us three more days to reach the foothills, and aside from the nagging sense of dread I could never quite shake, it turned out to be a wonderful trip. The weather was sunny but not too hot, the Flut croplands were easy on our feet, and we all did our best not to mention any subject that might get one of the others riled up.

That was a long list: military invasions, nervous twitches, slavery, murdered parents, evil parents, missing limbs, illiteracy and people named Cyril were all off limits.

Partly because everyone was so careful not to bring up the more serious stuff, we wound up spending a lot of time teasing each other about little things – like Millicent's bossiness, or my embarrassing inability to fart silently after meals, or Kira's talent for spying cute little furry animals and killing them dead with her sling.

They were mostly gophers, and to be fair they were usually so far away it was hard to tell how cute they really were. Kira walked with her sling at the ready, collecting stones as she went, and she had such sharp eyes that the first glimpse we usually got of her prey was a puff of red mist, followed a second later by a distant, dark streak as the little corpse returned to earth.

Kira shrugged off our half-amused, half-horrified catcalls. "They eat the crops," she said. "The Flut would thank me. So should you. If I have to hit something tomorrow, it's better I practise today."

Of the four of us, Guts was the easiest to wind up. I tried to avoid rattling his cage because I didn't want to get a hook in the neck, but the girls were rightly confident he'd never attack them, and they thought his spluttering rages were so hilarious that they couldn't resist. Kira kept a running tally of the number of words he could speak in a row without cursing (he broke ten a few times, but never reached twenty), and one night around the campfire, Millicent did an extended impression of Guts as the Governor-General, dispensing justice ("kill 'im, kill 'im, kill 'im, kill 'im . . . wot, already dead? Kill 'im again!") that made Kira and me laugh until our sides hurt.

It sent Guts into such a fury that he threatened to kill us all, which only made the girls laugh harder. Then he jumped up and declared he was leaving us for good. But Kira reached up and grabbed him by his good hand.

"Oh, stay," she said with a smile. "The sharpest knives are for the closest friends."

"Wot's that mean?"

"It means we laugh because we like you," she said as she yanked him down off his feet. Then she wrapped him up in a hug and planted a kiss on his cheek.

His face glowed as red as the embers in the fire. He didn't say a word for the rest of the night, but it wasn't because he was angry. And the next morning, right after Kira teased him again for not being able to put a sentence together without a curse in it, I caught him smiling when he didn't think anyone was looking.

We all did a lot of smiling over those three days, me especially. Just being able to spend hours on end with Millicent, listening to her stories, laughing at her jokes and arguing with her about books we'd both read, was a real gift. If you asked me to imagine a perfect day, a long walk through a sunny field with Millicent would be one of the highlights. And I got to do it all day long for three days in a row.

Having Guts and Kira along made it that much better. By the time we left the valley, we were all getting on so well that I'd started to think of them as the brother and sister I'd always wished I had. Strangely enough, thinking that way made me wistful for my real brother and sister, and I found myself ransacking my memories for moments when Adonis and Venus hadn't been completely horrible to me.

The fact that I couldn't seem to come up with any made me appreciate Guts and Kira all the more.

The deeper we travelled into Flut territory, the more we had to pay for food, and the harder it got for Millicent to haggle over the price. Not only were the northern Flut much less likely to speak Cartager, but even the ones who did weren't thrilled about negotiating with a girl.

In one village, they refused to speak to her at all, and I had to buy our food. I did my best, but we wound up paying five shells each for a single meal, and I never heard the end of it.

In the middle of the third day, we reached the last Flut village before the foothills.

"We need to buy all we can," Kira warned us. "The only settlements between here and the Cat's Teeth are Moku. And all they sell are humans."

The Flut village was larger than most, and we were relieved to find out we weren't the only outsiders. A Cartager had arrived just ahead of us, a journeyman trader with a beard that nearly reached his stomach and a pack mule piled high with goods. When we showed up, he was finishing his business with the tribal elders. Since none of them spoke Cartager, the trader offered to translate for us.

We were happy to accept the offer. Millicent quickly settled on a week's worth of food and two blankets, which Kira told her we'd need at night in the mountains.

By then, we'd spent almost all of our shells, and I figured we'd got everything we needed. We traded farewell bows with the Flut elders, but as we were packing up the food, Millicent and the trader started a fresh conversation.

Kira jumped in, and judging by the tone of her voice, she had a very strong opinion about whatever it was they were discussing.

A moment later, the trader beckoned the girls over to his mule, and Guts and I followed them.

"What's going on?" I asked Millicent.

"Tell you in a minute."

The trader pulled a beat-up tin box from one of his packs and opened it to show the girls what was inside. I looked over Millicent's shoulder and saw a few dried clumps of a fuzzy, greenish-blue substance that looked like dead tree moss.

Kira scoffed at it, and an argument began to brew between her and Millicent. The trader chimed in, seeming to take Millicent's side, and an exasperated Kira switched to Rovian to cut him out of the discussion.

"We don't need it!" Kira insisted.

"If it's true what he's saying –"

"It's not. He just wants our money."

"But I've heard the stories," said Millicent. "What happened to the Cartager Army back in –"

"It was the Judgement of Ka! No plant can stop that. And our cause is just – it'll never touch us."

"That's what you think."

"I *know* it."

"What are you talking about?" I asked.

"Nothing important," snapped Kira.

"Not to *you* – you grew up there, you'll be fine," said Millicent.

"We *all* will. Our cause is just –"

"That's just religious nons–" Millicent saw the flash of anger in Kira's eyes and stopped herself.

"Wot ye talkin' about?"

"According to Marko here –" Millicent pointed to the bushy-bearded trader – "there's a sickness that strikes almost every stranger who enters the Valley of Ka –"

"Not everyone!" insisted Kira. "Only the wicked."

"That's not what he says –"

"He just wants our money!"

"What kind of sickness?" I asked.

"A stomach thing. They call it the . . . what is it in Rovian . . . ?"

"The Judgement of Ka," said Kira through clenched teeth.

"He didn't call it that! Called it . . . I guess it's the Stranger Clutch. Marko says it kills people dead. And it makes sense, because if you think about the legend of what happened the first time the Cartagers invaded –"

"What killed the first Cartagers was the will of Ka!" Kira interrupted. "It is Ka's Valley, and Ka's power protects it from the wicked."

Millicent snorted. "Then how did the Moku run you off it?"

Kira looked like she might slap Millicent in the face. But the trader turned away just then, along with his tin of whatever it was, and Millicent broke away from Kira to speak to him again in Cartager.

After a short exchange, the trader shrugged and raised his hands as if to say, *You two work it out.*

"What is it he wants to sell us?" I asked.

"A cure," said Millicent.

"So he says," scoffed Kira. "But it's only a dead plant he scraped from a tree. And he wants thirty shells for it! We only have six left."

"I can get the price down," said Millicent. "And if we give up one of the blankets –"

"Then half of us will freeze to death in the mountains."

"But if our cause is just, won't Ka keep us warm?" Millicent asked with a sting in her voice.

Kira drew her hand back in anger, and I had to step between the two of them.

"Stop it!" I told them. "Look, we're not going to need more money where we're going, right? I mean, there's nowhere to spend it after this."

"So?"

177

"So if we've got six shells left . . . why can't Millicent spend them on as much of this cure as she can buy with it?"

"It's a waste of money," said Kira.

"It won't be enough," said Millicent.

"Better than nothing. And we can't give up the blankets or the food. So what choice have we got?"

We went back and forth for a while, but eventually they both gave in. The trader wrapped a clump of the greenish-blue moss in a scrap of cotton and handed it to Millicent in exchange for the rest of our shells. A few minutes later, we'd left the village and were headed for the foothills.

WHATEVER FRETTING I might have done about the Stranger Clutch, or the Judgement of Ka, or whatever it was called, quickly got overwhelmed by the more immediate worry that we were heading into Moku territory. About half a mile before we started to climb out of the Valley of the Flut, we came upon a magnificent road, paved with wide, flat stones that must have weighed hundreds of pounds each. It snaked up into the hills, through a dense forest, and I was thinking it'd be no trick to get over the mountains on a road like this when Kira told us we had to leave it.

"Wot, and break trail through them trees?" Guts looked at her like she was nuts.

"The Moku hold this road," said Kira. "If we stay on it, they'll capture us before we reach the pass."

"Go round it, then."

"We can't. Look –"

Kira sat down on a paving stone by the side of the road and used a stick to sketch a map in the dirt.

She drew a large oval. "That's the Valley of Ka," she said. "On the other side of these mountains. And it's all Moku territory. We've got to cross it one way or another."

At the bottom of the oval, she placed an X. "That's the Gran," she said. "The south side of the valley. The pass is here." She pointed to a spot to the left of the X. "And we're down here, on the far side of the Gran." She moved the stick below the X, just outside the circle.

Then she drew four X's in a row at the top of the oval, furthest from the Gran.

"These are the Cat's Teeth. The Okalu camp is on the other side of them. That's where we need to go. The Moku control the whole valley, so the best way to avoid them is to stay on the high ground, along the ridge of the mountains here." She traced a wide arc along the left half of the oval.

"Don't the Moku control the mountains, too?" asked Millicent.

"Yes. But their settlements are either in the valley or further west, across the range. They travel in the mountains and hunt there, but if we move quickly, we can hopefully get through without being seen.

"But we can't use the road, or any trails," Kira insisted. "And if we *do* run into Moku, we've got to make sure they don't tell others."

In case we didn't understand what she meant by that, she opened her pack and started handing out weapons.

Kira kept her sling. Millicent got one of the knives. I took the other one. Guts complained about being left out, but he had his hook, and if he carried a weapon, he wouldn't have a hand free to steady himself if he tripped on something.

And there was a lot to trip on in those woods. The vegetation wasn't so thick that we had to hack through it like we did on the edge of the swamp, but the hills were steep, and the trees that covered them were gnarled and ancient, with root systems so tangled you had to keep your eyes on the ground if you didn't want to go sprawling.

When night fell, we quickly figured out the knotty ground wasn't much good for sleeping. What it *was* good for, though, was breeding small armies of bugs that made themselves at home all over us, and tried to sneak under our clothes, and were all the more creepy for the fact that we couldn't see them because we didn't dare build a fire.

Nobody slept much, and by the time we got under way the next morning, it no longer mattered that we couldn't speak for fear of the Moku hearing us, because we were all too grumpy to talk.

Our second day in the hills was worse all around until mid-afternoon, when we finally reached the top of the pass. The Flut who'd told us to take this route had given us good advice – we were on the upper edge of a saddle between the Gran and the mountain range that ringed the Valley of Ka to the west, and both sides sported endless craggy stretches of almost vertical rock that walled off the valley from the south and west, and looked to be impassable everywhere except the saddle we were in.

The valley itself couldn't have been more different from the one we'd just left. It was less one big valley than a series of little ones that snaked in and out of a jumble of hills, most of them carpeted in a thick green canopy that looked more jungle than forest.

Kira pointed to the middle of the valley, at a flat-topped hill that was taller than most of its neighbours. In the middle of its crown, I could make out a grey triangle poking up over the tree-tops. The fact that we could see it from such a distance made me realize it must be enormous up close.

"That's Mata Kalun," she said. "The Temple of the Sunset. I grew up at its feet. Now Moku live there."

No one said anything. A moment later, Kira turned towards the ridge that led to the mountain range on the west side of the valley. She led us along the ridge just below the tree line, where we couldn't be seen as easily. At that elevation, there was an eerie quiet in the woods, and every snapped twig seemed to echo off the mountains above and ahead of us.

We crossed the first ridge and then quickly dropped a few hundred feet in elevation. Down lower, the forest sounds were more comforting, but it was also a lot buggier, and I had bites on both arms and my neck by the time we started up the side of the next ridge.

We were halfway across the second ridge when the sun set. Kira said her evening prayer silently, mouthing the words, and we ate without talking. The moon was getting skinny, and under the trees the night turned so black I could barely see my hand in front of my face. It was cold, too – we huddled together for warmth under the blankets, and I was glad we'd listened to Kira and bought them.

We started moving again as soon as it was light enough to see. As we started down the far side of the ridge into another hollow, we heard running water. Everyone picked up their pace – we hadn't crossed water since we'd left the last Flut village, and our skins were getting thin.

At the bottom of the hollow, we found a fast-moving stream.

Millicent and I drained the rest of our skins into our mouths while Kira and Guts drank directly from the stream. Then we re-filled the skins and started moving again.

About an hour later, the trouble started.

Guts had been lagging at the back of the group, and Millicent and I were taking the lead when we heard a *Ssst!* behind us. We turned to see Kira about fifty feet back, motioning to us. Guts was nowhere in sight.

I hurried back to her, and as I got close, I saw Guts on his knees behind a nearby tree. He looked like he was going to be sick.

And then he was, with a retch so loud I wanted to poke him with my foot to be quiet. He puked three more times, one after the other, his whole body convulsing each time.

He lifted his arm to wipe his mouth on his sleeve. Then he stood up, holding the tree for support, and turned to face us.

He was pale as a ghost. The morning air was still cool, but beads of sweat glistened on his forehead. Kira reached out to help him, but he shook it off and stepped past us to take the lead.

He started off at a good clip, I guess to prove that he was okay. But he wasn't. About twenty strides up the hill, he went to his knees again.

When we reached him, he was curled up on his side, face twisted in pain. Kira and Millicent knelt down on either side, trying to comfort him.

I was watching Guts clutch helplessly at his stomach when the realization hit me.

That's why they call it the Clutch.

CHAPTER 14

BROUGHT LOW

Guts didn't want to stay down. Even though the girls pleaded with him to lie still and rest, he got up three more times and tried to keep going. But he couldn't make it more than a few steps without doubling over again, and eventually he gave up.

He lay on his side and retched a few more times, but there was nothing left in his stomach. Then he asked for water. Millicent held up the skin she was carrying so he could drink from it.

Half a minute later, he threw it up.

"Sorry," he said to no one in particular.

"It's okay. Just let us know what we can do for you," Millicent said.

"Jus' need a minute," he said through gritted teeth. Beads of sweat were rising on his forehead.

"Think you might need more than that."

"Couple, then."

I nudged Millicent. "What about the trader's cure?" I whispered.

"I'd give it to him if I thought he could keep it down. We've just got the one clump. If he heaves it up, where's that leave us?"

"How's he going to stop throwing up if he doesn't take it in the first place?"

"Give it a bit. See if he can keep some water down."

I looked over at Kira to get her opinion. She was kneeling a few feet away from us, her face pointed in the direction of the rising sun. The firebird pendant was pressed between her hands, and she was whispering a prayer to it with her eyes closed.

Watching Kira, Millicent pursed her lips but didn't say anything.

"How long does it last?" I asked Millicent.

"How would I know?"

"What did the trader say?"

"He didn't. Just that . . ." She lowered her voice even further so Guts couldn't hear. "It kills people."

"Everyone?"

She shook her head. "I don't know. Most of them, it sounded like."

"What causes it?"

"Something in the valley."

"We're barely in the valley. We're above it. And the rest of us aren't sick."

"Kira wouldn't get it. She's from here. It only gets the strangers."

"So why don't you and I have it?"

Millicent shook her head again. "I don't know."

"How soon would it . . . you know –?"

184

"I don't *know*, Egg!"

"A day," I heard Kira say over my shoulder. Her prayer finished, she came back to sit next to Guts. "Two at most. It goes quickly."

"How do you know?" Millicent asked.

"I saw it. When I was young. If it's the Judgement, he will get a fever. The pain will get worse . . . It helps if he can hold water down."

Guts was on his side with his eyes squeezed shut in a grimace. Kira moved closer to him. She placed the firebird pendant against his side with one hand and put her other hand gently on his head.

His body tensed at her touch, and his hand jerked up to shove her away. But when he realized it was Kira, he relaxed and let her stroke his forehead.

"It's not any 'judgement'," Millicent said in an irritated voice. "It's just a sickness."

Kira glared at her.

"What does it matter?" I asked.

"A sickness has a cure." Millicent dug into the pocket of her tunic and produced the little cotton packet. As she unwrapped it, Kira looked away, shaking her head and turning her attention back to Guts.

The clump of dried moss looked pitifully small in Millicent's hand. "So give it to him," I said.

Millicent sighed. "Let's wait a bit. See if he can keep water down."

HE COULDN'T. After a couple of hours of watching Guts take in mouthfuls of water, only to retch them up again, nothing had changed except his temperature. His whole body was hot to the touch, he was drenched in sweat, and even wrapped in both blankets, he couldn't stop shivering.

He was going downhill fast, and his answers to our questions were starting to get loopy and confused. Kira prayed over him nonstop, but it didn't seem to be doing any good.

Finally, Millicent and I decided to chance the cure. She knelt beside Guts with the dried moss in her hand.

"Guts, I have medicine –"

"— —!"

Millicent looked at Kira for help. Kira frowned, but she bent her head and spoke softly into Guts's ear.

"Listen to her," she said. "Just try it."

Guts stared up at Kira. The only colour on his face came from the heavy dark circles under his eyes.

"Awright," he croaked.

Millicent showed him the clump of moss. "You have to chew this. As long as you can. Then swallow it. And whatever you do, *don't throw it up*. It's all we've got. Okay?"

Guts's head moved in what looked like a nod. He opened his mouth just wide enough for Millicent to place the moss inside. Then he closed his teeth over it.

We watched him chew, his jaw slowly rising and falling.

Then his lower cheeks bulged as his jaw clamped down hard. A second later, his whole upper body jerked in a retch.

"Don'throwitupdon'throwitup!" Millicent begged him.

He fought it as hard as I'd ever seen him fight anything, through one convulsion after another as his body tried to reject the cure. It must have hurt like a demon, but he kept his jaw clamped down and his lips pressed white, and eventually his body began to settle down.

His jaw started to move again. A minute later, he stopped chewing.

"Are you going to try and swallow it now?"

His eyes were still shut.

"Just did."

She exhaled with relief. Then, just as quickly, she looked worried again.

"Don't throw it up!"

"Shut up."

There were a few more convulsions after that. But he managed to keep it down. For the next couple of hours, nothing about his condition seemed to change.

Then his face gradually started to relax.

"Not hurtin' so much," he said.

Ten minutes after that, he said, "Think it's better."

Pretty soon, the shivering had stopped, and his skin wasn't nearly as hot. He asked for water, and for the first time since he'd eaten the moss, we decided to risk giving him some.

He drank a hefty amount, and this time he kept it down. Then he drifted off to sleep.

Millicent looked at Kira with a smirk. "Must have been the prayers."

Kira scowled a little, but she was too relieved to really get angry.

WHILE GUTS SLEPT, we gathered brush for camouflage. The blankets we'd bought were chequered in bright blue and red, and to any Moku travelling through the forest, they would have stuck out like a signal fire.

As we gathered the brush and arranged it in a thin layer over Guts and the blankets, I couldn't stop thinking about how thirsty I was. It was late afternoon, and the rest of us hadn't allowed ourselves any water since Guts had taken ill, reckoning we were at least an hour's round trip from the stream we'd passed.

We still had one full skin, but Guts had gone through a fair amount of the second one. I held up the half-empty skin.

"Think we can drink this now?"

Kira nodded, but Millicent looked skeptical. "Rather we wait a bit," she said.

"What if I run back to that stream and refill it before dark?"

Millicent didn't like the idea of our splitting up, but it was a straight shot downhill and back, and Kira didn't have a problem with it, so she reluctantly agreed.

Before I left – and so I wouldn't feel guilty when I drank it myself – I offered them what was left in the skin. Millicent declined, which seemed crazy to me.

"Aren't you thirsty?"

"Some. But . . ."

I watched Kira drink from the skin. "But what?"

"What if it was the water that made him sick?"

That didn't make sense to me. "Water's just water," I said. "And Guts didn't drink from this until *after* he got sick."

Kira finished her drink and offered the skin to Millicent again. "I'll wait," said Millicent.

More for me, I thought as I drained the skin.

I could feel the water slosh in my belly as I trotted down the hill to get more.

I can still remember how delicious that water tasted – clean, crisp and still cold even though hours had passed since we'd drawn it from the stream.

And I remember laughing to myself at the idea that something so good could possibly hurt me.

I was halfway to the stream and moving at a good clip when my stomach started to feel quivery. I figured it was because I was going too fast with all that water in my belly, so I slowed my pace.

When the quivery feeling didn't go away, I chalked it up to hunger and tried to take my mind off it by focusing on the forest around me. The sun hadn't quite sunk over the mountains looming to my right, and scattered shafts of light filtered through the trees, dappling the woods in shimmery white patches. Birds chattered here and there, and if I listened carefully, I could hear the hum of insects.

I didn't know much of religion, but right then the forest struck me as something more than beautiful. It was almost holy.

The Valley of Ka. The Sun God . . .

Those shimmery patches were part of the thing Kira worshiped, and they were everywhere, all around me. I marvelled at that, thinking it was just possible that Ka really existed, and was watching over us, and that was why we hadn't come across any Moku, and that only Guts had got sick, and when he did, we had just enough of the cure to fix him.

And now he was on the mend, and soon we'd be on our way again, none the worse for wear.

We were blessed. And the forest was a temple, and I was grateful for it, and everything was fine.

Except for the rumbling in my stomach.

But dinner would fix that.

I was close enough to hear the stream below me when the first pains arrived, little needles in my gut that came and went. Then they started coming faster, and staying longer, and the water wasn't sloshing around in me any more, so I was sure it must be hunger, and there was nothing to do but wait it out.

By the time I reached the stream, the pain had built to a steady ache in my gut. I figured the best thing was to drown it with the clear water, so I knelt down along the spongy bank and took up a mouthful in my cupped hands.

It was so cold it froze my fingers and made my teeth hurt. I counted the handfuls as I slurped them down. Four . . . five . . . six . . . My hands turned numb from the cold.

Seven . . . eight . . .

Then there was a bolt of pain like a hammer to my gut, and it hit me so hard I felt my forehead go clammy.

I've got to get back to the others.

I filled the skin with fumbling, cold-stiff fingers and turned back up the hill.

There was another bolt of pain, so bad it stopped me in my tracks. When it faded, I started to run, straight uphill as fast as I could.

Almost from the first step, I was shaky and weak. All the energy had been sucked out of me.

I did my best. I stumbled up the hill.

Then I fell.

I didn't get back up.

I hadn't gone far. I could still hear the stream behind me.

The next wave of pain hit me so hard I nearly cried out.

I rolled onto my side and vomited.

Once I started to puke, I couldn't stop. My stomach squeezed into a knot and tried to force its way out through my teeth.

It went on for a while. My body was strangling itself to get rid of something that wasn't even there any more.

I'd been sick before. But never like this. I'd never felt this kind of pain.

Got to get back to the others.

I got up and tried to walk. I didn't get far.

I curled up on the ground.

Just like Guts . . .

I wanted to yell out for my friends, but I knew I couldn't because there might be Moku nearby.

The pain kept coming.

I started to shiver.

I was going to freeze to death.

The light in the forest was fading. The pain was only getting worse.

I prayed I'd pass out so I didn't have to feel it any more.

Time seemed to stop. Everything stopped. I might have passed out.

But if I did, the pain followed me.

"SHHH . . ."

I heard Millicent's voice in my ear, floating above the fog.

"Shhh . . ."

I was shivering and wet, and the pain was like a burning rod running through my gut.

I opened my eyes. It was night. I couldn't see a thing. But I could feel Millicent lying beside me, her body pressed against my back, one arm moving rapidly across my chest, trying to keep me warm.

"Shhh . . ."

She wanted me to be quiet.

I didn't even know I'd been making noise.

I shut my eyes again. I just wanted the pain to stop.

I OPENED MY EYES. It was light now. I could hear the sound of the stream.

I was alone. There was a blanket on me. I couldn't move. Or didn't want to. I wasn't sure which.

I was still shivering. The pain was different now. Deeper and heavier. And it was spreading. Like it was swallowing me.

I didn't want to be alone. I tried to raise my head to look around, but it took too much effort.

In the corner of my eye, there was a tree.

Something big and red was in the tree.

The thing that was red moved.

I tried to shift a little to get a better look at it. It hurt just to move my eyeballs.

The red thing was a bird. Huge and terrible, with a long, sharp yellow beak.

It was staring at me.

Then it swivelled its head away, looking back over its shoulder.

It unfolded its giant wings and flapped off.

I heard footsteps.

They grew louder. Someone dropped to their knees in front of me.

It was Kira. She was holding something green and dank-smelling in front of my nose.

"Can you eat this?"

The smell made me retch.

"Please."

She held it in front of my mouth. I opened it and let her stuff a piece inside.

I tried to chew. I gagged.

She had more of the stuff. And water in a skin. She gave me both.

I threw it all up.

She stood up fast. Then I felt her pull me from behind, moving me away from the sick I'd left on the ground. It hurt to be moved like that, and right away, the cold shot through me and I started to shiver. I felt her adjust the blanket.

It was so cold.

More footsteps.

"How is he?"

"I gave him this."

"Ain't it. Too green. Gotta be more blue."

"Did you find anything?"

"Nah. Gonna go lower."

"That way."

"Ye'll stay with 'im?"

"I should look also. There's not much time."

Then they were gone, and I was alone again.

"C'MON!"

"Please!"

"Egg, you've *got* to!"

They were begging me to do something, but I couldn't understand what. Their voices sounded like they were under water.

Something kept brushing against my lips. I shook it off.

I just wanted to be left alone.

Someone pulled my jaw down, forcing my mouth open. Then they stuffed something inside and pressed my mouth shut.

I wouldn't chew.

They moved my jaw for me.

I retched.

They held my jaw shut.

"Hold it in. Please!"

"Please, Egg!"

I tried. I even managed to swallow it.

Then I threw it all up.

We did the whole thing over again.

Then again.

Finally, I kept it down.

They gave me water, and I slept.

I woke a little before dawn, just as the forest birds were beginning to stir. The pain was gone and the fever had finally broken – under the blanket, my clothes were damp with sweat, but I wasn't shivering, or even all that cold.

Lying on my side, I didn't see anyone in front of me, but I

194

could feel a body through the blanket, nestled against my back. I rolled over. It was Millicent. She was sharing the second blanket with Guts and Kira, who were huddled beside her.

Millicent stirred. She smiled at me, then nodded her head in the direction of a water skin just above my head.

"It's okay to drink?"

"It is now. You got the cure."

I got up on my elbows and drank from the skin. She took it from me and drank some herself.

"Did you get sick, too?"

"Just a bit. Not like you and Guts. I took the cure before I had any water."

"How'd you get it?"

"It grows down in the valley. On the bark of some of the trees. Took some doing to find it."

She reached out and combed back the hair on my forehead with her fingers. "Try to sleep some more."

I closed my eyes and drifted off again.

SOMETHING PRODDED ME in the head, startling me awake.

"*Da lata.*"

It was a man's voice, deep and rough. I opened my eyes to see a pair of copper-skinned legs right in front of me, the calf muscles thick and ropy. I followed his legs upwards with my eyes.

He wore just a loincloth on his lower half. A thin rope circled his waist, a knife dangling from it in a sheath. The rest of him was draped in a jaguar skin, complete with a hood made of the animal's head, its upper teeth sticking out above his painted face.

The black hole of his rifle barrel looked straight down at me.

He lifted his bare foot and shoved me in the forehead with his heel.

"Da lata!"

I stumbled to my feet along with Guts and the girls. Half a dozen warriors with rifles surrounded us. They'd already taken all our weapons except Guts's hook.

Soon enough, they had that, too.

CHAPTER 15

MOKU

One of the Moku warriors barked an order.

"Put your hands on your heads," Kira translated as she raised her arms. We all copied her except Guts. Bright red blood streamed from his mouth, where he'd been clocked with a rifle butt for not giving up his hook fast enough.

"Nuts to that," he spat, along with a fair amount of blood.

"Don't be stupid. They'll shoot you."

If it had been anyone but Kira telling him, he probably wouldn't have done it. But he put his arms up, grabbing his stump with his good hand to hold it over his head.

The Moku who must have been their leader – he looked older than the others, had thick scars across both cheeks, and was doing all the talking – gave an order to the man next to him. The man knelt down and began to empty the contents of Kira's pack onto one of our blankets.

As he did, the leader stepped over to stand in front of Kira.

"Da gi Okalu?" His voice was sharp and cruel.

"Ke, Okalu." Her voice was flat, but she stared back at him with hate in her eyes.

The leader took a step back and handed his rifle to one of the others.

Then he drew a black stone knife from a sheath at his waist.

My heart started thumping hard in my chest. I turned my shoulders towards Kira, the muscles tensing in my arms and legs. On the other side of her, I saw Guts lower his head like a bull about to charge.

The other warriors raised their rifles a little higher, ready to shoot any of us if we moved to help her.

Just then, the warrior searching Kira's pack spoke up. Everyone turned to look at him.

He was holding up the firebird necklace.

The leader's eyes widened in surprise. He lowered the knife.

Then he took the necklace. He held it up in front of Kira as he asked her a question.

She answered. This time – even as he faced her with a knife in his hand – she couldn't quite get the hate out of her voice.

The leader glared at her for a long moment. Then he lowered his eyes, putting the knife back in its sheath so he could examine the necklace with both hands.

He traded a few words with the man who was searching Kira's pack.

After that, he asked Kira a series of questions. At first, her voice rose at the end of her sentences, like she didn't quite understand what he was asking her. But pretty soon, her tone turned flat again.

Finally, the leader reached some kind of conclusion. He carefully put the necklace in a small leather sack that hung from a cord round his waist. Then he issued several orders to his men. Two warriors with machetes headed off into the trees while the others herded us into a tight cluster and sat us down.

Then they ate our food as they kept their rifles trained on us.

"What's happening?" Millicent whispered to Kira.

Kira shook her head. She looked a little bewildered. "Possibly I don't understand Moku. But I think he believes we fell from the sky."

"That's crazy." Guts had his mouth pressed to the tail of his shirt, sopping the blood.

"Yes. But it stopped him cutting my heart out. So I think it is better if he believes it."

The leader barked at us, gesturing with his knife. We didn't need a translator to understand we had to quit talking.

HALF AN HOUR LATER, the two warriors returned with a ten-foot length of tree trunk, newly cut, its branches hacked off. The Moku stood us up in a line, placed the trunk across our right shoulders, and used long strips cut from one of our blankets to tie us to the trunk by the wrists.

Then they marched us straight downhill. It was a steep slope with a lot of brush, and tied together like that, it was hard going. Guts was in the lead, and I was last, just behind Millicent. Without our hands free to keep our balance, we were constantly pitching over, and whenever someone fell, they dragged the others down with them.

Worse, whenever Guts quickened his pace or leaped over

something, the trunk would jerk the rest of us forward, and we'd all topple to the ground face-first.

Even after he got it through his head that he had to keep a steady pace, Guts didn't seem to understand that if he veered to one side, the trunk swung around and pushed me in the opposite direction, which usually meant I caught a branch to the face.

And whenever I yelled to Guts to be more careful, the Moku bringing up the rear would smash a rifle butt against my back as a warning not to talk.

We were on the hill for a miserable hour or two, and the whole time it took every bit of my concentration just to keep moving forward. When we finally reached the valley floor, it got easier.

A while after that, we met up with the stone-paved road that we'd avoided back on the pass.

Once we were on the road, it was no trick to keep moving, although the Moku forced us to double our pace, and it was hot and muggy on the valley floor, so it wasn't exactly pleasant. Even so, now that I wasn't preoccupied with just staying on my feet, I had a chance to think things over for the first time since I'd fallen ill with the Clutch.

The situation was bleak. These Moku were different from any other Natives I'd encountered, either in Pella or the wilderness. They were harsh and humourless, both with us and each other – even watching them talk among themselves, I hadn't seen any of them so much as crack a smile or speak in a warm tone of voice. They doled out violence casually and with no warning, in a way that made me think it came as naturally to them as haggling did to the Flut.

I found myself thinking back to what the crew of the *Thrush*

200

had told us on our first night at sea – that there were Natives who'd cut our hearts out and eat them while they were still beating. With all the other tribes I'd encountered, the idea seemed laughable. But with this bunch, it was all too easy to imagine. Kira's comment about not getting her heart cut out just confirmed it – and I was terrified that although they'd spared her for the moment, sooner or later that'd be her fate.

It might be true of the rest of us as well.

Even if it wasn't, I knew enough about the Moku's recent history to be pretty sure the rifles they were carrying – identical to the flintlocks used by the Rovian soldiers who'd marched on my plantation – had come from Roger Pembroke, or someone connected to him.

The men who were marching us down this road were allies of my enemy.

How often did they speak to him? How much did they know about who we were?

Did they have anything to do with the invasion Millicent said was coming?

And what would be worse – if they knew how valuable the map in my head was, or if they didn't?

Either way, it wasn't good.

If I'd only listened to Millicent and hadn't drunk that water, we wouldn't have got stuck in one place for so long, and the Moku never would have found us. I'd doomed us all by being an idiot.

The afternoon sun was brutal, and the thick air on the valley floor was as stifling as a bad day back on Deadweather. I watched my friends stagger along in front of me, wilting from the heat and the lack of food and water. Tied up like animals.

Or slaves.

I got a sick feeling in my stomach that had nothing to do with the Clutch, or even the lack of food and water.

I got them into this. It's my fault we got captured.

I've got to make it right. I've got to get us out of this.

Maybe I can bargain with the Moku. Offer them the map for our lives.

But who knows if they even care about the Fist of Ka?

More likely, they'll just pass it on to the man who buys slaves from them.

Millicent stumbled and fell, bringing us all down. I hit the stone paving with my elbow, and a burst of pain shot up my arm.

The Moku leader barked something at his men. Two of them opened up our water skins and forced us to drink. The one who fed me did it so roughly that half of what came out of the skin wound up dribbling down my neck. Then they shoved pieces of cured meat in our mouths, raised the log to force us to our feet, and prodded us to get moving again.

The road snaked through a pair of hills. On the far side, the forest gave way to cropland. Most of the fields were untended and overgrown with weeds, except for a few orchards of skinny trees heavy with a kind of yellow-brown gourd I'd never seen before. In one orchard, we passed a group of Moku women and children picking the gourds and stacking them by the side of the road in big, messy piles.

Then we rounded another hill and got a view of the valley ahead. In the distance was an anvil-shaped hill, and above its thick cover of trees rose the upper reaches of what Kira called Mata Kalun, the Temple of the Sunset. It was the shape of a cropped pyramid, its smooth sides tapering up to end at a perfectly flat platform with a big square box perched on top of it.

Even from miles away, it was awesome. I couldn't believe human beings had built something that enormous.

The road was headed straight for the temple. We continued on through the wasted cropland for several miles, until we approached the base of the temple hill and another forest swallowed us. We were seeing more and more Moku on the road now, mostly older women bent at the waist from the weight of large woven containers strapped across their backs, or clusters of male warriors carrying dead game strapped to poles, just like we were.

The road wound up the hillside in a series of switchbacks. When we turned one corner, we came upon a group of young boys shouting skywards at two of their friends who seemed to be in a race to the top of a pair of tall trees by the side of the road. The lead warrior called out to them, and several of the boys split off from their friends to run full speed up the road, quickly disappearing round a turn.

At the top of the hill, we came upon a wide, six-foot wall of stone that at one point must have been gated to keep out intruders. But there was no gate now, and for several feet on the right side of the road, the wall had been reduced to a pile of rubble. It was still intact on the left side, and a lone sentry stood atop that section of wall with a rifle. When we appeared, he turned, cupped his hands to his mouth and shouted an announcement to the settlement behind him.

We crossed the ruined wall and entered the town. Ancient-looking trees lined both sides of the paved road. Between the trees and down the cross streets were low stone buildings of varying sizes. A lot of them had collapsed, many more were scorched black from fire damage and the handful of undamaged ones all looked abandoned.

I had the eerie feeling that we weren't walking through a city, but a graveyard.

After a hundred yards or so, people began to appear, and the buildings started to look more lived in. But as often as not, the low stone structures had been used as a platform on which the Moku had built little thatched huts like the ones we'd seen in the Flut villages, leaving the original stone buildings to their snuffling pigs and rib-skinny dogs.

It no longer felt like a graveyard, but it didn't quite seem like a city, either. It was as if the Moku, having driven off the Okalu, weren't living in their enemies' city so much as camping out there.

We neared the city centre, and up ahead I got a glimpse of a giant, open square, with the massive base of the temple visible on the left. Then our captors stopped us, and when I craned my neck to look past the others, I saw why.

A group of ten Moku was striding down the avenue towards us. Up in front were two men who couldn't have looked more different from each other.

One was the size of an ox – the Moku who captured us were all a good six feet tall, and the two Moku who'd kidnapped us in Pella were even bigger than that, but the ox made them all look puny. He wore a jaguar cape like the other warriors, and underneath it his bare chest looked like it was made from slabs of rock the size of the ones that paved the road.

The man next to him was old and shrivelled, and while he had longish limbs, age had made them sort of fold in on themselves, so the effect was like looking at a wrinkled grasshopper. He wore a chest piece made of bleached-out bones strung together, and atop his head was a teetering headdress of feathers in such bright reds, blues and greens that they almost glowed with colour.

The other Moku treated him like royalty. As he spoke to the lead warrior, even the ox hung on the old grasshopper's every word.

The warrior gave the grasshopper the firebird necklace, and the old man held it up to the late afternoon sun for a better look.

Then the whole group made a slow circle around us, squinting at our faces and bodies like we were livestock for sale.

On his way back around, the grasshopper stopped in front of Kira and asked her a question. She answered in her flat, emotionless voice. As he asked a second question, he raised a bony finger and jabbed it at the sky overhead.

Kira nodded. *"Ke. Ka mol."*

He snorted, like she was a trader who'd just quoted him a ridiculous price on something.

He took a few steps back and took us all in with his watery eyes.

Then he looked again at the firebird necklace in his hand. He gave a curt order, turned and started back towards the city centre. The ox and the rest of their party followed him, along with the warrior leader and one of his men.

Four warriors stayed with us. One of them took hold of the front end of the tree trunk and yanked it sharply round, forcing us to stagger backwards and sideways as he reversed course and started back down the road in the direction we'd come.

Three-fourths of the way back to the ruined wall, the warriors led us off the main road, down an unpaved side street with just a couple of scattered buildings. When we turned down the street, I heard Kira sigh, like she knew where we were going and wasn't happy about it.

We followed the road past the last of the buildings, to a wide patch of rocky dirt surrounded by trees. In the middle of it was a gaping, twenty-foot-wide hole in the ground. At the near edge of the patch, a bored-looking Moku warrior lounged on a rock. One of the warriors called out to him, and he stood up.

The five of them guided us over to the open pit, past several lengths of knotted rope that lay in sloppy coils on the ground. A couple of the ropes had big woven baskets tied to them.

They stopped Guts right at the edge of the pit. I was the furthest from it, and from that angle I couldn't see anything in the pit but a dark chasm.

One of the warriors pulled a black stone knife from its sheath, and with a few quick sawing motions, he cut Guts free from the trunk.

Then he shoved him into the pit.

It wasn't as deep as it looked – right away, I heard Guts hit the bottom with a *thud* and an *oof*. Then there were muffled voices of surprise from inside the pit, but I couldn't focus on them because I was getting jerked nearly off my feet as the warriors pulled Kira up to the edge.

They cut her free and shoved her in.

Millicent was next.

Then me.

MY FEET CAME DOWN partly on Millicent's back, and she yelled as we tumbled together onto the smooth-worn rock of the pit. It stank of human waste and sweat down there, and it was so dark and gloomy that at first I could barely see anything. There was a confused jumble of voices, not just the four of us but a man bellowing in Moku.

"*Fola batakay! Fola batakay!*"

"Sorry! You all right?"

"I think –"

"*Fola batakay!*"

"*Tuma pa!*" That was Kira, warning off the Moku.

"Back off!" That came from Guts.

Then there was another voice, so familiar I felt an instant jolt of recognition.

"Watch 'im! Got a shank, he'll stick ye!"

I knew that voice.

But it was impossible –

"*Fola batakay!*"

"Back off!"

"Ay! AY! Yer Rovian?! So's me!"

I couldn't believe what I was hearing. I blinked hard, trying to get a look at him through the gloom. He was big and hulking, I could see that much.

"Wot ye – *EGBERT*?! *Wot the deuce . . . ?!*"

He stepped over to me, and I finally saw his face. He'd lost a fair bit of weight, making him look hollow and drawn. A ragged beard was growing in patches around his jaw.

We stared at each other, dumbfounded. A thick lump of emotion started to swell up in my throat.

Which was strange, because I hated him.

The others went quiet. Even the skinny, crazed-looking Moku quieted down – he kept growling *"fola batakay"*, but with much less energy.

Guts finally spoke. "Who are you?"

When Adonis didn't answer, I spoke up for him.

"He's my brother."

CHAPTER 16

REUNION

Adonis stared at me like he was seeing a ghost. "Ye come lookin' fer us?"

I shook my head. "I had no idea –"

"Where to look!" Millicent broke in, talking over me. "At first. But thank heavens we found you. Egg was worried sick!"

We both turned to stare at Millicent. I had no idea what she was talking about. My brother scrunched up his face and squinted, trying to figure out why she looked so familiar. Then he remembered.

"Yer that Sunrise girlie! Come to get yer balloon back?"

"Of course not! We came to rescue you! Egg insisted on it!"

"No, I di–" I started to say.

She kicked me hard in the foot. I shut my mouth.

What she was saying made no sense. But at the moment, nothing did.

"Fer true? Ye really come to rescue us?" For the first time in my life, Adonis was looking at me with something besides a scowl.

Did he say "us"?

"Dad and Venus are here?"

"Course! Didn't ye see 'em?" He jerked his head skywards. "Dad'll be by soon. Brings me dinner round now."

My head felt like it was floating up off my shoulders.

My family's alive. All of them.

"Fola batakay!" The crazy-seeming Moku was pacing back and forth against the far wall, yelling at us.

"Tuma pa!" Kira yelled back at him.

Adonis stared at her, then at Guts.

"Who's these two?"

"I am Kira Zamorazol."

"Name's Guts."

Adonis's lip curled up in a sneer. "Kind o' name izzat?"

"Pudo la, ye billi glulo."

"They're friends of mine," I managed to say.

Adonis looked confused.

"Since when ye got friends?"

"Since . . . uh . . ." I was having a hard time making my brain work. "How did you *get* here?"

"Landed. Didn't have no choice. Can't steer a balloon. How'd *you* get here?"

"Walked."

"Across the Blue Sea?!"

"Oh . . . That part was a boat."

"Still got it?"

"Got what? The map?"

Millicent kicked me again. But Adonis didn't even blink at the word. He had other things on his mind.

"The boat, stupid!"

"Oh . . . No."

"How ye gonna rescue us with no boat?! Crimey, Egbert! Can't do nothin' right."

"Can I sit down?" I was starting to think I might pass out.

"Yeh. On them rocks. Keep yer back to the wall – otherwise, that lot'll shank ye." He nodded in the direction of the crazy-seeming Moku, who'd retreated to a dark corner to mutter *"fola batakay!"* at us.

We all sat down on some big rocks at the far end of the pit.

It was a relief to get off my feet. My whole body ached from the day's forced march. And my head was spinning like a top.

"How'd ye know where to find us?"

"Just lucky, I suppose," said Millicent. "We've been scouring the countryside."

Adonis scrunched up his face again. Thinking didn't come easy to him.

"Ain't *too* lucky, if yer in the pit," he finally said.

"How come you're down here, and Dad and Venus aren't?"

"'Cause Venus is a — —," he said, using two of Guts's favourite words. "Tryin' to get me killed, she is! And Dad can't keep her in line. She was *my* daughter, I'd smack her silly 'fore I'd let her go on like that with them savages."

"Go on like what? What did they do to her?"

He snorted. "*Do* to her? Made her queen's wot they did!"

"*What?!*"

"Lives inna palace! Runs the whole show!"

What he was saying was so crazy I must have misunderstood him.

"You can't be . . . what?"

"Yells 'boo', they all jump! Look wot she did t'me! Had 'em toss me in here –"

"Adonis!" The unmistakable growl of my father's voice boomed down from the mouth of the pit. "Heads up! Dinner comin'!"

I looked up. One of the big woven baskets I'd seen lying near the pit was dangling above us on a rope. Just past it, I could see Dad standing at the pit's edge, feeding the rope through his hands.

"Dad!!" I yelled.

He stopped lowering the basket and craned his neck out over the hole. "Izzat . . . ?"

"It's Egbert!" Adonis yelled to him.

"WOT?!"

"It's me," I said. "Egbert."

The light was behind him, hiding his face in a shadow as he stared down at us.

"How the blazes . . . ?"

"Came to find us, them savages tossed him in here," Adonis explained. "Drop the food, will ye? Starvin'!"

"Is it really you, Egbert?"

His tone of voice wasn't at all like the Dad I remembered – it was husky and low, almost tender. I felt another big lump swell in my throat.

"It's me," I croaked.

"Saviour's sake . . . Saw 'em bringin' in prisoners, but I never woulda –"

"Dad! The food!" Adonis wasn't about to let our reunion get in the way of his dinner.

"Right." Dad began to feed the rope again, and a moment later the basket bumped to the ground. There was a small corked jug and a leg of what looked like either a big chicken or a little turkey, charred black from a cooking fire. Adonis snatched them up and hurried back to his rock, turning away from us as he tore into the bird leg.

"Would you mind sharing that?" I asked him. "We haven't eaten in a while."

"Ai'm muff fu fare!" Adonis protested through a mouth stuffed with meat.

"Think I might jump him fer it," Guts muttered to me as he licked his lips.

Dad spoke up again. "Ye really come all this way, Egbert? Just to find us?"

Millicent kicked me in the side of the foot again.

"Will you stop!?" I hissed at her. Then I called up to Dad.

"We, uh . . . sure did," I said. I must not have sounded too convincing, because Millicent gave an annoyed snort.

But it was good enough for Dad. "That's sumpin' . . . Sure is . . ."

He started to hoist the empty basket back up.

"Gimme a few. See 'bout gettin' ye outta there."

"Wait! I brought friends. There's four of us."

His head swivelled from side to side as he peered down into the pit. "How'd ye get friends?"

"Just . . . did."

"Mm . . . See wot I can do. Dunno wot kind o' mood she's in."

"Who?"

"Yer sister."

"Is it true? Did they really make Venus queen?"

His shoulders slumped a little. "Sumpin' like it. Yeh."

Then he started off. "Back soon."

"Wait!"

"Wot?! Gettin' dark!"

"We're awfully hungry. Thirsty, too."

"Awright. See wot I can do."

DAD WAS GONE until after sunset had taken our last bit of light. By that point, it was clear to me that Adonis wasn't himself. He was still generally horrible – I'd had to stop both Guts and Kira from getting into fistfights with him after he made some ugly comments about both Guts's missing hand and Kira's sundown prayer to Ka. But in the hour or so we spent together, he didn't slug me once, or even take a swing at me, which was some kind of record for him. And the handful of insults he lobbed at me were halfhearted at best. I wasn't sure if it was because he knew he was outnumbered, or if he'd genuinely changed how he felt about me.

The Moku might have had something to do with it. It was clear he was terrified of them. "Stone killers . . ." he kept saying. "Treat ye rough . . . Ye'll see."

"But why on earth did they make Venus queen?" My sister was the last person I could imagine inspiring a bunch of strangers, let alone the Moku. She was vicious enough for them, I guess, but they seemed like a pretty clever bunch, and Venus was dumb as a post, and lazy on top of it – back home, she didn't even like to cut her own food if she could get somebody to do it for her.

"Dunno," was about as much as Adonis had to say about it – he repeated that about twenty times in response to my questions, along with "can't figger it" and "stone crazy, it is".

And he had a thousand questions of his own, some of which were tough to answer – especially with Millicent sitting next to me with her foot at the ready.

"Why do you keep kicking me?" I muttered, quiet enough that Adonis couldn't hear.

"Because you can't tell him the truth!"

"Why not?"

"What do you want them to think – that you're a hero? Or a treasure hunter?"

"I'm neither," I protested.

"You'll be one or the other to them. And we need their help."

And it wasn't just hard explaining things to Adonis because I couldn't tell him the truth about the treasure. My brother wasn't exactly quick-witted, and he had a hard time getting his head around even simple concepts, like the fact that Roger Pembroke had tried to murder our whole family.

"I'd want to kill a bloke, too, if 'e lost my balloon."

"You didn't lose his balloon – he had his men cut the tethers so you'd drown in the ocean!"

"Stuff! Who'd waste a balloon like that? 'Sides, if 'e wanted to kill us, why'd 'e buy us lunch?"

"To butter you up!"

"Wot fer? Coulda plugged us on the spot . . . Fine meal, too. *Still* thinkin' 'bout that jelly bread."

"Adonis – he's *evil*."

"Says you. Bought us lunch and gave us a balloon ride, says me."

"You know the silver mine on Sunrise? He owns it – and all the people he's got working there are slaves."

"So?"

"So?! He's a *slaver*. He buys human beings and works them to death."

"Smart move if ye can pull it off. Beats payin' 'em . . . Dad oughta do that. Get slaves fer the plantation. Be a sight easier to manage than 'em lazy field pirates."

After that, I gave up on trying to talk to Adonis. I figured Dad would tell me what I wanted to know.

Meanwhile, Kira managed to start a conversation with the surly Moku, but she had a hard time getting anything useful out of him, either.

"Did you ask about my sister?" I whispered to her after they'd been talking awhile.

"I am trying. First, he only wanted to talk about why he was innocent."

"Innocent of what?"

"Stealing. That's why he's here. And now he won't stop talking about how much he hates your brother. But I will keep trying."

Once darkness fell, their conversation died out, too.

"Did you learn anything?" Millicent asked Kira.

"Not much. He is very afraid he will be put to death soon. He wants to sleep now. But he says we can talk more when morning comes."

WE MOSTLY FELL SILENT ourselves after that. I was so wiped out, I was starting to doze off by the time Dad came back, along with a middle-aged Moku warrior. They both carried burning torches, and after ordering us to stand back, Dad dropped his torch into the middle of the pit.

"Here! Give ye light to see the food."

He lowered a basket with food and water for us. The empty basket went back up, and before I'd had time to take more than a few sips of water, Dad tossed the end of a knotted rope into the pit.

"Climb up, Egbert. Just you."

Adonis didn't like that. "Dad! Wot the deuce?!"

"Watch yer mouth! Know where ye stand with her. Doin' me best, but it takes time. Now, c'mon, Egbert. Get up that rope."

"What about my friends?" I asked Dad.

"Tried. Nothin' doin'. Maybe tomorrow."

I didn't want us to get separated – it made me worry for both them and me – but there didn't seem to be any choice.

"Sorry about this," I said to the others. "I'll get you out. I promise."

"Be careful," said Kira.

"See about gettin' my hook back," said Guts.

I turned to Millicent, and to my surprise she wrapped her arms round me in a fierce hug. I hugged her back just as hard.

Then she pulled away, just far enough to take my head in her hands with her fingers nestled in my hair, and stared into my eyes.

I stared back, mesmerized by that inner furnace I could see glowing behind her eyes even in the dim flicker of the torch near our feet.

For a moment, time seemed to stop. Or at least my heart did. First, I thought she might kiss me. Then I thought maybe I was supposed to kiss her.

Then I realized if things went badly, I might never have another moment with her like this one, and I should tell her I loved her so I'd never have to regret not having said it.

The words were on my lips when she spoke first.

"Don't say anything stupid," she said. "You came here to rescue them."

"I *know* that." The last thing I wanted just then was a lecture.

Then she smirked, and the whole moment was ruined.

"C'mon, boy!" Dad was getting impatient.

She dropped her hands to my chest and pushed me gently towards the rope.

"Be smart. Get us out of here."

I turned away and grabbed the rope. My hands tightened on the knots, ready to start climbing.

Then I stopped. I was annoyed – no, mad – no, furious with her, for being such a condescending snot.

And I loved her like nothing else in the world. And I didn't want to leave feeling just the anger and not the rest of it.

I turned round. They were all watching me in the torchlight. She still had that infuriating smirk on her face. I marched over to her. As I got closer, she started to open her mouth to say something clever and probably insulting, but before she could do it, I pulled her to me and kissed her hard on the lips.

I broke it off first. Her eyes were still closed when I pulled back. They fluttered open. The smirk was gone.

"I love you," I said. It came out sounding angry.

Her eyes got wider. She looked shocked. Or maybe it was scared.

"I love you, too," she said in a quiet voice.

As I turned back towards the rope, I heard Adonis mutter something, but I didn't catch it. All I could think was that I had to get out of there before I botched something. I grabbed the rope and climbed as fast as I could.

WHEN I REACHED the top and dropped the rope, my arms and legs started shaking, and there was nowhere to sit except the ground, so that's what I did.

"Ye awright?" Dad asked.

I looked up. He was staring down at me with a look of concern. The grim older Moku with the torch was standing to one side of him. In the flickering torchlight, Dad's nose cast a jumpy shadow across the side of his face. There was a surprising amount of grey in his beard.

Even with all the time I'd had to get used to the idea that he was still alive, seeing him up close was a shock.

"Just need a second," I said. My limbs were shaking hard – getting up the rope had been tougher than I'd expected, and with so little food in me, I guess my muscles just couldn't take it.

And my head was swimming.

She said she loved me . . .

"Is there more food?" I heard myself ask.

"Plenty where we're goin'. C'mon."

I thought I might pass out if I stood up, but I managed to get to my feet. Dad put one of his meaty hands on my upper arm. When I looked at him, he had a strange kind of nervous look on his face that I'd never seen before.

He raised his other arm, and at first I thought he was going to hug me. Then the arm sort of hung there for a moment, until finally he used it to pat me awkwardly on the shoulder.

"Good seein' ye."

He dropped both arms and turned away with an uncomfortable grimace.

"C'mon."

He and the Moku with the torch started towards the road.

I followed them, still woozy.

Did he just . . . Was he going to hug me?

He'd never hugged me before in his life. It just wasn't something he did.

The ground felt like it was tilting away from me. I realized I was about to pass out. There was a big rock a couple of steps ahead, and I lurched over and sat down on it. I pressed my hands to my forehead. When I shut my eyes, I saw little explosions of light behind my eyelids.

A moment later, I heard Dad's voice in front of me.

"Wot's wrong, boy?"

I took a deep breath, and my whole chest shuddered. I felt like I might start crying, and that was the last thing I wanted.

"Just . . . need a minute." My voice was all wobbly. "Haven't eaten much . . . Kind of a strange day."

"Get ye more food. Oughta do it."

"Yeah. Must be it."

I kept gulping air until I could take a breath without shuddering. Then I stood up again, much more carefully this time.

"Right. Let's go."

Dad and I walked slowly, side by side a few steps behind

the Moku holding the torch. Nobody spoke until we were on the paved road, headed to the centre of the city. On either side of the road, small cooking fires burned in front of the makeshift huts and stone buildings, and I caught the occasional glimpse of a person moving ghostlike around them.

"How the blazes did ye get here?"

"Captain Racker gave us a ride to Pella Nonna. Then . . . mostly, we walked." I left out the part about getting kidnapped, because it would have meant explaining about the map. And even though I wasn't sure I agreed with Millicent that I should lie about why we were here, I didn't have the energy to explain everything right then.

"Ye got the harvest in? Ship sailed full?"

"Pretty much."

He clapped me on the back. "Good work, boy." Then he sighed with relief. "That's a load off. Could barely sleep for worryin' they'd all slack, and we'd end up bust."

Even brain-fogged as I was, it seemed a little queer that Dad could find himself stranded in the wilderness with a tribe of deadly Natives, only to lose sleep worrying about who was going to get the ugly fruit harvest in.

"Field pirates give ye trouble? Did ye need to get on 'em much?"

"A bit." It had been more than a bit. If I hadn't sold the plantation to the field pirates in exchange for their help against Pembroke, they would have let the harvest rot in the fields.

But that was another thing I didn't have the energy to explain.

"Who's watchin' the place fer ye? Not Percy!" His eyes widened at the thought of our fat, lazy and treacherous former tutor in charge of the plantation.

"No. Percy's gone. It's Otto, mostly. Him and Quint."

"An' ye trust 'em? Achh . . ." He scratched at his beard and grimaced. "Almost rather ye stayed on Deadweather, kept the place runnin' 'stead o' comin' after us . . ."

"I'm sorry," I said, half sarcastically. Even though I hadn't actually gone looking for them, it was still irritating to hear him tell me I should have stayed home to watch the plantation instead.

At the same time, I got a little twinge in my gut at the thought of how he was going to react when I told him I'd sold most of the place.

Maybe lying was a good idea after all.

"'S awright." He clapped me on the back again. "Good yer here." He shook his head and sighed. "It's a bloody mess, I'll tell ye. Can't make heads or tails of it."

He gave me a little nudge and jerked his head towards the Moku with the torch.

"Take this feller. Spends half his time followin' me round. Don't speak a word. Couldn't understand 'im if he did. And wot I can't figure – is he s'posed to be servin' me? Or guardin' me?"

"How on earth did they make Venus queen?"

"Dunno wot she is, tell ye straight. Some ways, seems like she's queen. Other ways . . . dunno. See fer yerself, I guess."

We reached the end of the avenue and stepped into the main square of the city. The scope of it was breathtaking – it was easily three times as big as the palace courtyard in Pella Nonna. The left half was dominated by the Temple of the Sunset, its tapered sides as smooth as hammered steel except for a wide set of oversized steps leading from the middle of the square up to the cropped platform where a rectangular structure the size of a small palace perched atop the pyramid. At the top of the steps, a pair of fires burned in large urns on either side of the entrance to the rectangular palace.

Facing the temple on the opposite side of the square was another temple-like monument, this one much lower and flatter but almost as wide, with a similar set of steps that led up its base and fires burning in urns atop the steps.

"Wow," I said.

"Yeh. It's sumpin', awright."

We followed the Moku with the torch towards the steps at the base of the Temple of the Sunset. Looking out over the vast square, I saw a few Moku here and there, most of them in a hurry to get wherever they were going. But otherwise, the place was deserted.

"Mind yer tongue round yer sister," Dad warned me. "Way they been puttin' her on, it's gone to her head. Best ye don't get on the wrong side of her."

We were at the foot of the temple now. The bottom step was nearly as high as my waist.

"Where is she?" I asked.

He tilted his chin skywards, nodding towards the palace atop the giant pyramid of stone that loomed above us.

"Straight up."

CHAPTER 17

QUEEN

The temple steps were almost too high to climb. To get up each one, I had to raise my knee practically to my chest, and by the time we were a third of the way to the top, my legs were shaking so badly that I had to stop and rest. A few minutes later, when I stopped a second time, I caught the Moku with the torch giving me a look of contempt.

"Sorry," I said to Dad, because he was the only one of them I knew how to apologize to. "Haven't eaten much lately. And I was sick the past couple of days."

"Pain in yer belly? Made ye puke?"

I nodded. "Did you have it, too?"

"We all did, at the start. Natives had us eat some plant, cleared it right up."

"I think it's something in the water."

"Could be."

When we reached the top, it was surprisingly cluttered. There were gnawed-over animal bones and cores of fruit strewn about, and sloppy piles of firewood were stacked on either side of the burning urns. At the corners of the platform were big Continental-style cannon on wheels. Their equipment – steel worms, thick cotton swabs on poles, crates that I guessed held cannonballs – was scattered around them.

The giant stone columns that fronted the palace were carved with figures. I recognized a lot of them from the map in my head – firebirds and snakes, fists and spears, faces and skulls.

As we passed between the urns, a pair of warriors with rifles stepped out of the shadows. They exchanged a few words with the Moku who carried the torch before they let us proceed through the thick columns on either side of the entrance.

We walked down a wide corridor, and the first thing I noticed was the smell – smoky and sickly sweet, like someone had doused a pile of burning wood with some kind of heavy perfume.

The corridor opened up into an enormous hall, so wide and high I couldn't see the ceiling or the side walls through the nighttime gloom. It was lit by torch sconces along the central columns that ran down the length of the room. Food scraps littered the floor, flies buzzing around them, along with dirty plates and bowls, broken cups, little piles of fabric that I guessed were clothes –

"WHAT TOOK YOU SO LONG?"

There was no mistaking the snotty whine of my sister's voice. But as I peered down the length of the room, all I could make out in the dim light was a handful of figures standing around a giant, lumpy pile of something.

"Takes time! Bit of a hike, innit?" Dad yelled back.

"I'VE BEEN WAITING FOR-EV-ER!"

Something began to stir in the middle of the giant lump. As a couple of the figures rushed towards the lump, what looked like a giant feathered plume rose up and began to sway. Even though the plume of feathers looked nearly weightless, it was making a terrible racket, all jangly and metallic-sounding.

As we moved closer, the first two people I made out in any detail were Moku warriors, dressed in loincloths and holding feather-trimmed spears as they stood to a sort of attention in front of the group. Beyond them were three older Moku women in simple frocks. They stood together to one side of the giant lump, hands by their sides, like they were waiting for orders. Two more Moku women were making a fuss around the lump, trying to pull something up from just below the feathers – and I realized all that plumage was just an attachment, stuck to the top of a big heavy thing that was making all the noise.

The lump turned out to be pillows – a humongous pile of them, stacked around some kind of stone altar in the middle of the room.

And the big heavy thing was my sister, struggling to her feet under the weight of what looked like a hundred pounds of rattling jewellery, and crowned by a feathered headdress as tall as she was and twice as wide.

The headdress lurched to one side, threatening to topple over. One of the women helping Venus gave a little gasp and rescued it just in the nick of time. Venus elbowed her out of the way and staggered towards us, grunting from the effort it took to raise her bracelet-heavy right arm and hold out a hand covered with rings stacked all the way to the nails of every finger.

Her hand rattled as she wriggled it at me.

"Kiss it!" she demanded.

"Kiss it, boy," Dad muttered out of the corner of his mouth.

I stepped forward and started to bend over to kiss her hand – or actually her jewellery, because I couldn't find any hand under all that metal and stone.

"No, no! On your *knees*! Crimey, Egbert – I'm a *queen*!"

Her eyes bugged out as she said it, which was actually helpful, because until then I'd been having trouble locating them. She was wearing about six different colours of heavy makeup, plastered over every inch of her cheeks, mouth and eyelids. Between the jewellery and the makeup and the enormous headdress, it was hard to figure out where the outfit ended and Venus began.

The "on your knees" business seemed a bit much, but it was pretty clear she was going to raise a fuss if I didn't do it. So I got on my knees on the hard stone floor and kissed a hunk of rock on her index finger that I think might have been a diamond.

When I looked up at her, she was grinning from ear to ear, although it's possible the smile was drawn on with makeup.

"Isn't it *amazing*? I mean, can you *believe* it? I'm *queen*!" The headdress was fixed with a strap that ran under her chin, and the whole thing wobbled dangerously every time she opened her mouth.

"It's really something," I said. "Can I get up now?" My knees were already hurting from the stone floor.

She ignored the question. "I always knew I'd be a princess someday! But now I'm a queen, too! I'm both. I think. Can you do that? I mean, is it – *eegh*!"

The headdress had started to topple backwards, momentarily threatening to strangle her. Two servants rushed in to lift it upright, but Venus wrestled the strap off her chin and let it fall.

"Ugh! Done!" She seemed to lose patience with the whole outfit – as the servants slunk away with the headdress, she started yanking off necklaces, tossing them every which way.

"Done!"

More servants swooped in and started harvesting necklaces off her. Venus shook out her hands, spraying a shower of rings over everything, including me.

I turned my head away so I wouldn't get a ring in the face. When I did, I saw Dad had taken a seat just behind me, on a little stool that was too small for him. He was averting his eyes from the jewellery storm, too.

Finally, Venus got down to a manageable weight of riches and plopped down on a big stack of cushions. Now that I had a better look at her, I realized she'd gained quite a bit of weight.

"So, can I?" she asked.

"Can you what?" I'd forgotten what we were talking about.

"Can I be a queen and a princess both?"

"Oh . . . I'm not sure."

"Not sure?! What good are all those stupid books you read, if they can't tell you that?"

I searched my brain for an answer. It was hard to think clearly. The whole situation was making me woozy.

"Well . . . usually a queen's a princess first," I said. "Like Queen Madeleine. She started out as Princess Madeleine, but then –"

"Who am I like?"

"What?"

"Which queen's the most like me? In your books?"

Mad Queen Minerva instantly popped into my head, but I didn't think it was a good idea to tell Venus that.

"I think you're . . . really . . . quite original –"

"Who's got the biggest palace? Is mine the biggest?"

"Oh, yeah." I nodded. "By a long shot." No reason not to agree with that. It might even be true, for all I knew. Venus looked thrilled.

"And what do the other queens do all day? Like, should I be going to war or something? Or do they all just sit around drinking chocolate, too?"

"Drinking what?"

"Chocolate! Don't you know?" Her eyes popped open wide. "Oh, you've *got* to try this!"

She turned to the line of servants and yelled, *"Drink!"*

Two servants shot off into the darkness.

"Just wait. You're not going to *believe* these things. They're like those chocolates they sell in Blisstown, only all melted, so you can quaff them right down. I have like twenty a day. Sometimes more."

That explained the weight gain.

"They just bring them to me," she went on. "Because I'm like their favourite queen ever. It's *very* sweet."

She frowned. "But it's hard, too. Because they're dreadful stupid. They only know like three words. And those took *forever* to teach them. The rest they don't get at all. Not even if I yell. Watch this."

She turned to the three remaining women, opened her mouth, and bellowed, *"Raise your hands!"*

The women all gave Venus hasty bows.

"Hop on one leg!" she yelled.

They bowed nervously a few more times. Venus sighed and shook her head.

"See? They just bow. It doesn't even matter how loud I yell. They still don't understand. It's *very* sad. I'm thinking of getting them a tutor."

The two servants returned with three clay flagons of thick brown liquid. One of the flagons was twice the size of the other two, and Venus got that one. The servants gave the smaller ones to me and Dad.

"Drink it!" Venus ordered me.

I didn't need much encouragement. And she was right – it tasted like liquid chocolate, and I couldn't believe how delicious it was. I took a few long sips, momentarily forgetting everything but the drink in my hands, until a loud, aggressive belch brought me back.

"Buuuuurrrp!" Venus tossed her empty flagon over her shoulder, and it bounced across the floor. I heard Dad exhale hard through his nose, and when I glanced back, I saw he had his lips pressed together so tight they were almost white. He'd always had a quick temper, and it must have been a real struggle for him to keep still and not smack Venus for her awful manners.

"More drink!" Venus barked. As another pair of servants scattered to do her bidding, she beckoned to me with her hand.

"Ugh. They take forever. Give me yours."

I hesitated. "But I only had –"

"Give it to me or I'll kill you."

Her eyes narrowed. I knew that look. It was the one she used to get right before she threw a tantrum.

I handed over my drink. As she guzzled it, Dad gave his flagon to me.

"Drink it quick," he whispered.

I did.

"Yer brother's right hungry," he told Venus once she'd downed the second glass and uttered another belch that echoed off the distant walls. "Wot d'ye say to –"

"Food!" More servants took off.

"Thank you," I said.

She shrugged. "You're lucky they know that word."

Then her eyes went wide and excited as she remembered something.

"Did Daddy tell you about the pony?"

"I don't think so." Venus had always wanted a pony.

"My king's getting me one! Well, he's not my king yet – I don't think – but I'm pretty sure we're going to have a big wedding soon, and it'll be *amazing* – anyway, he promised me a pony. It might actually be a very big dog. But I'm *almost* sure it's a pony. It was hard figuring out what he was saying, because he's just as dumb as the rest of them. But he's very tall and handsome, and he has reeeeally huge muscles, and he'll kill you if I tell him to. So watch yourself."

The food arrived – two big piles of fruit and some kind of cooked bird on a long wooden slab.

"Ugh. Not even hungry. Maybe just a little." She took one of the legs and tore off a bite. As she chewed with her mouth open,

I selected a piece of meat, watching Venus carefully in case I took the wrong one and she pitched a fit.

We ate in silence, except for the smacking of Venus's gums. After a few more bites, she pressed her hand to her stomach and made a face.

She turned to one of her servants and pointed to her full mouth. The servant shuffled over and held out her cupped hands. Venus spat the half-chewed food into them.

"It's hard sometimes," she sighed. "I can only fit so much in my tummy." Then she threw the leg of meat over my head. I heard it land somewhere behind us.

She sank back into her giant mound of pillows and let her chin drop to her chest, making her look like a painted frog. She sighed again.

I ate as fast as I could, thinking I'd better wolf it down in case she decided to take the food away.

"So here's what you're going to do, Egbert: you're going to write my book."

"Wrrph?" It was hard to talk with my mouth stuffed full and my jaws working at double speed.

"People write books about queens, yeah? So you're going to write mine. And then send it out, so everybody knows what a great queen I am."

"I'm not sure –"

"Don't talk! Just do it!" Her eyes narrowed again. "If you don't, I'll kill you. I'm having Adonis killed, you know."

That set Dad off. "*He's apologized!* I told ye! If ye jus' give 'im another –"

"Shut *up*, Daddy! *I'm* the queen! *My* kingdom!"

I braced myself for Dad to explode. But he stayed on his little stool, gripping his knees while his face turned red.

It made me queasy to see him like that. Growing up, the rules had always been clear. If you mouthed off, you got smacked.

Now the rules had been turned upside down, and somehow that was more unsettling than watching my sister act like a monster.

She turned her attention back to me. "So what's it going to be, Egbert? You going to write my book? Or do you want to get killed, too?"

"I'd love to write your book," I said. "I'm sure it'll be a big hit."

It was a little scary how easily that came out of my mouth. But I guess after all I'd been through to stay alive, lying to my fool sister wasn't much of a hurdle.

And it brought a smile to her face, so wide I knew it wasn't just the makeup. "I know! People will love it. I'm an *amazing* queen." The sour look had vanished, and her eyes gleamed with pride.

I wondered if this was the right time to bring up the others. She seemed to be in a good mood again, and I had no idea how long it would last. So I decided to chance it.

"I know a few other people who'd like to help with the book," I said.

"Really? Who's that?"

"Friends of mine. They're –"

"*Friends??* HA! How'd you get those? Everybody hates you."

"Just . . . sort of happened. Anyway, there's three of them. One you've met already, Millicent. We played croquet with her."

"Oooh, I know her. She liked my dress!"

"She did! Very much. And there's another girl, and a boy –"

"Another girl? Maybe they could be my servants! I'd love someone younger than these old hags. And not so stupid."

"Well, if you could just get them out of the pit –"

"Maybe tomorrow." She yawned. "Leave me alone now. I'm tired, and I need to make a poop."

"But if –"

"Out! And start writing my book!"

"A BLOODY MESS, is wot it is."

Dad and I were lying in the darkness in the little stone building he'd been given for a home, down a side street off the main avenue. I was on a straw pallet that Adonis had slept on until Venus banished him to the pit.

After Venus ordered us out of the temple, I'd tried to go back to the pit to tell the others what I'd seen, but the Moku with the torch had made it pretty clear with his body language that the only place I was welcome to go was Dad's house. Now he seemed to be hanging around somewhere outside the door.

I thought about waiting him out and then trying to sneak back to the pit. But Dad promised me the others would still be in one piece in the morning, and I was exhausted. So I lay down on the straw, thinking I'd take a short rest and get my head straight about the situation before I decided what to do.

But when I tried to wrap my mind around everything that had gone on that day, I drew a blank. My whole head felt hollowed out, like so many crazy things had happened that they'd made my brain explode out of the back of my skull.

"A right bloody mess," Dad repeated.

"Still don't get why they made her queen."

"Dunno she's queen," Dad said.

"Sure seems like it."

"Yeh. But . . . dunno. Whole tribe fussed over her at first. Hopped to pretty good. But she ain't done herself no favours, way she carries on. Seems to me she's worn hard on 'em. Big chief used to come see her every day. Been a while now since he even went up there. An' she don't go out none herself. Spends all day lyin' round, stuffin' her face. Venus bein' Venus, maybe she's just lazy. Or maybe they don't let her out. Can't tell which."

I heard him sigh. "Get some sleep now, boy. Come mornin', ye can help me figger out wot to do. Get us all out of this madness. Back to the plantation where we belong."

Except that I'd sold off the plantation.

"Dad?"

"Wot?"

". . . Nothing."

Sleep was tugging hard at me, so hard I let go of the nagging fear that time was precious, and if I didn't act fast, whatever chance we had to escape would slip away.

I should have listened to that fear. If I had it to do over again, I never would have slept.

CHAPTER 18

NEWS

I must have been out for a good ten hours, because the sun was over the trees by the time I woke up. There was a bucket of fresh water and a cloth by my bed, and I used them to wash up before I stepped outside.

Dad was sitting by the side of the building, watching his Moku shadow roast a side of pork over a small cooking fire.

"See wot I mean?" Dad said, nodding to the Moku. "Sometimes he's guardin' me. Sometimes he's servin' me. Can't figger it."

"Ever try talking to him?"

"Early on, yeh. Wouldn't speak a word, in his language or mine. Tried signin', too. Shrugs me off."

"I'd like to get some food to the others."

"Gotta ask yer sister fer it. We'll head up once we've eaten."

I sat down beside Dad and watched the Moku cook our breakfast.

"We've got to get them out of that pit." I figured the Moku didn't understand Rovian, but I kept my voice low just in case.

Dad nodded. "Yer brother 'specially. Been in there ten days now. Don't end well fer them wot stays that long."

I didn't ask what he meant by that.

"Think the Moku would let them go if Venus ordered it?"

Dad scratched his face through his beard. "Think so. Hard to say."

"Otherwise, we'll have to sneak them out. Is the guard there all night?"

"Far's I know. Still have to get yer sister on board, tho' – can't leave without her."

"Doesn't seem like she wants to go anywhere."

"Even so. Been thinkin' – once she gets this pony she's on about, starts takin' it fer rides . . . might be the time to make a move."

"How on earth is she going to get a pony?"

"Got it in her head some men with horses are comin'. Gonna give her one."

My stomach dropped when I heard that.

Men with horses sounded like Pembroke's slavers. They bought slaves from the Moku. Was it these Moku? Or were there others, somewhere else? Did the slavers come here?

"What kind of men?"

Before Dad could answer, a rising commotion reached us, coming from the main avenue. The second he heard it, Dad stood up with an alarmed look and ran down to the avenue.

I followed him. A cluster of Moku warriors were headed up the road. Two of them were dragging along the crazed Moku from the pit. His wrists were tied, and he was yelling in protest with every step.

A warrior at the front of the group bellowed *"Chala Tulo-Ma!"*

whenever he passed a building. Moku villagers were leaving their homes and putting down their work to follow the group towards the city centre.

When he saw who they were dragging along, Dad's shoulders sagged with relief. "That's a mercy. Thought they was takin' yer brother."

We stepped aside to let the throng pass. When I got a look at the wild-eyed fear in the captive Moku's eyes, a chill went through me.

"What's happening to him?" I asked.

Dad grimaced as he watched them drag the man towards the square. "Gonna do him rough," he said in a quiet voice.

Then he turned and went back to his house. I followed him.

Dad's Moku shadow was still cooking the meat. We sat down again to wait for breakfast. A few villagers passed by from up the street, headed for the main square. It seemed like everyone was going there.

"Should we go, too?" I asked Dad.

He shook his head. "Don't."

I could hear the rising hum of the crowd gathering in the nearby square, along with the steady *"Chala Tulo-Ma!"* call of the crier and the angry, increasingly hoarse yells of the condemned man.

Then the noise of the crowd faded away. It was replaced by a single voice, chanting out some kind of song, or maybe it was a prayer.

Every once in a while, the crowd piped up, chanting a few syllables along with the leader.

"What are they doing?" I asked Dad.

He just shook his head.

Dad's Moku shadow pulled the meat out of the fire, split the side with a stone knife and put the pieces on a pair of wooden trays. He gave us each a tray. Then he rushed off towards the square.

The meat was unseasoned but delicious, and so hot I burned my tongue on the first bite. I was blowing on it, trying to get it to cool faster, when the chanting voice rose to a climax.

The crowd joined in a final burst of noise.

Then it was silent.

For a moment, the only sound I heard was Dad chewing his meat.

He nodded his head at the food on my lap. "Eat," he said.

I took another bite, trying to chew with my mouth open so I wouldn't burn my tongue again.

I was on my second bite when I heard the scream.

It lasted for several seconds.

Then it was silent again.

I looked at Dad. He was staring down at his half-eaten breakfast.

"We've got to get out of here," I said.

He nodded.

"Soon . . . Eat yer food."

I did my best. I didn't have much of an appetite. The chanting had started again – first the lone voice, then the crowd.

It went on for another minute or so. Then it was all over.

By the time the Moku villagers began to reappear, I'd managed to force down most of the pork. I watched them walk past us. Just another day.

We've got to get out of here.

Dad stood up, brushing his hands clean. "Go and see 'bout gettin' food to the others."

We were halfway to the main avenue when a group of four warriors turned up the road from the direction of the main square. Dad's Moku shadow was with them.

Their eyes were all on me. My heart started to race.

I told myself I was just imagining that they were staring at me.

But I wasn't. They stopped right in front of us, blocking our path.

With his eyes on me, Dad's shadow gestured towards the main square. Then he said something to me in Moku.

The meaning was clear. He wanted me to follow them.

My insides started to quiver. I shot Dad a panicky look.

He shook his head. "They ain't gonna. I'll make sure of it."

"How?"

He didn't answer. "We'll go. See wot they want."

He stayed close by me as we started towards the square. The four warriors took up positions on either side of us. They didn't touch me, or glower at me, or point their rifles at me.

But I was terrified just the same.

When we reached the square, it was still emptying out. What was left of the crowd was walking away from the low, wide monument that faced the temple. There was movement at the top of its steps, but I tried not to look at it.

The soldiers led us over to the base of the Temple of the Sunset. Then they all stopped. So did Dad and I.

Two of the warriors sat down on the temple steps. Dad's shadow did the same. Then the lot of them started a conversation, in a bored, passing-the-time sort of way.

The terror that had been building in me started to settle a bit. But only a bit.

"Why'd they bring me here?" I asked Dad.

"Dunno. Venus wants ye, I guess."

We waited there, under a sun that was getting so hot I had to keep pulling up my shirt to wipe sweat from my face. Once the last of the crowd had left, the square stood nearly as empty as it had been the night before.

There was still movement atop the steps of the monument on the opposite side of the plaza. For the first time, I looked closely at it.

Its big twin urns still held the blazing fires I'd seen during the night. In between them was an altar of some kind. Something bright and colourful was moving around on top of the altar, but the shimmer and ripple of heat distortion from the fires made it hard to figure out at first just what I was looking at.

It was a group of birds – massive ones, all bright red with streaks of blue and green. Their heads were crowned with plumes of feathers. There were three in all. They were eating.

My mind flashed back to the ruby-red firebird necklace, and the similar-looking hieroglyphs in the map and on the temple walls. I pointed the birds out to Dad.

"Are those firebirds?"

He shrugged. "Dunno wot they call 'em."

I tried not to watch them, but I couldn't help myself. They looked strangely familiar, and not just because of the map and the necklace.

Then I realized why. I'd seen one in the forest, staring down at me when I was sick with the Clutch. I'd been so feverish then that until now, I thought I might have just imagined such a strange and terrible-looking creature.

I was still watching the firebirds when one of the warriors spoke up, pointing in the direction of the avenue. We all turned to look.

Another small group of warriors was leading Kira, Guts and Millicent into the square. I was glad to see they were walking under their own power, their hands free. Nobody looked too much the worse for wear.

As they came near, Millicent caught my eye and gave me a hopeful smile. I smiled back, wondering if she'd heard the ceremony and hoping she hadn't.

When the group reached us, the warriors turned my friends up the steps and nudged me along with them. Dad started to follow. His shadow stopped him.

I turned my head to look at Dad, and he nodded to me.

"Be waitin' here fer ye," he said.

I nodded back and started up the steps with the others. It was a much easier climb after a meal and a good night's sleep.

"Where are we going?" Millicent whispered to me.

"To see my sister."

I wanted to warn them about what to expect from Venus, but one of the warriors barked something at me, and I figured it was better not to talk.

Kira was in front of me. When we reached the top of the steps and she saw all the clutter, I heard her give a little sigh. It occurred to me that she wasn't going to appreciate Venus's making a pigsty of the temple.

Kira's tribe used to worship their god here, and my sister had turned the place into a trash heap.

Then I remembered what a hard time Kira had disguising her hatred when she spoke to the Moku, and I got worried enough to risk whispering, "Don't make her angry!" as we entered the temple.

One of the warriors shot me a warning look, but no one said anything.

It was surprisingly bright inside – there were wide openings in the upper walls and ceiling, so sunlight was coming in from several angles. Unfortunately, the bright light didn't do the place any favours – it was much more vast than it had seemed in the shadows the night before, but it also looked even filthier. For Kira's sake, I wished the Moku would put some effort into cleaning up after my sister.

"FINALLY!" yelled Venus when we came into view at the end of the long, columned hall. She had on her six-foot headdress and a face full of fresh paint, although she'd shed most of the jewellery, so she managed to get to her feet without help.

Half a dozen Moku servants were still clustered around her pillow-smothered altar, but she wasn't the only centre of power in the temple.

Off to one side, about twenty feet towards us from Venus's crew, was a slightly larger group surrounding the big ox of a chief. He was lounging in a thronelike wooden chair they must have dragged out specially for him, because it hadn't been there the night before.

The way everyone, even Venus's servants, stood in relation to him made it clear – to probably everybody but my sister – that even though his seat was tucked between a pair of columns, sideways to the altar, he was the one calling the shots.

We crossed the long, rubbish-strewn hall, and as we approached the spot where the chief was sitting, we all hesitated, not sure whether to turn towards him instead of continuing on to Venus.

That seemed to annoy her.

"Hurry *up!*"

The chief smirked, waving us along with a bored flick of one of his massive hands.

We continued on towards Venus.

"On your knees!"

We did as we were told, forming a straight line in front of her. Millicent was on the far end, and Venus tottered over to her, a servant following right behind in case the swaying headpiece toppled over again.

Venus held her hand out for Millicent to kiss. This time, the stack of rings only went as high as her middle knuckle.

"Kiss it if you love your queen!"

Millicent kissed Venus's rings, doing an outstanding job of looking meek.

Venus waddled sideways, over to me.

"Now you!"

When I looked up at her as I kissed one of her rings, I saw she was wearing just a single necklace.

It was the firebird pendant.

Venus moved on to Kira, waggling her fingers as she held them out. I prayed Kira wouldn't notice the pendant round my sister's neck.

To my surprise, Kira managed to kiss the hand without a protest or a dirty look.

Guts was last. He managed a halfhearted peck. His face was twitching worse than usual.

As Venus drew her hand back, her lip curled under the makeup. "Why do you blink like that?"

"Just do."

"Stop it! It's creepy."

I held my breath. This could go bad in a hurry.

But to my relief, Venus turned away from him and tottered back to sink into her pillows. Her headdress wobbled, but a little nudge from Venus's servant steadied it.

"So I'm your queen," Venus announced, pursing her lips in what I imagine she figured was a very queenly expression. "And everybody loves me. And Egbert's writing a book about it."

She pointed to the chief. "Over there's your king. We're going to be married. There's going to be a *huge* party. If you're very, very good, and you serve me well, you can come to it. Otherwise, you can't. And you'll have to stay in the pit while everybody else goes to the party. And also you might get dead."

She gave a happy little sigh. "Now. Who likes my headdress?"

"I was just thinking about how gorgeous it is," said Millicent. "It frames your face perfectly. And it *really* sets off your eyes – you're quite beautiful!"

Venus beamed. "I know! Right?"

Then she looked at the rest of us. It took a second for us to realize we were supposed to chime in, too.

"Yeah! Beautiful! I love it, I really do."

"It's wonderful. You are a beautiful queen."

"Nice, yeh. Like it!"

Her smile faded a little. She didn't seem to think our answers were quite up to snuff. "So. You're living in a hole in the ground. Right?"

"Yes. Thank you!" said Millicent.

We all nodded. Venus looked a little confused. I think she wasn't sure if the "thank you" was sarcastic or not.

Then she frowned. "If I take you out of the hole. And I make you my servants. How will you serve your queen? Egbert wants you to help with the book, but I think he's just being lazy."

There was a pause as everybody thought about the question.

"How would you like us to serve you?" Millicent finally asked in a sweet voice.

That seemed to stump Venus. She scrunched her eyebrows together, making the thick smears of orange and blue makeup above her eyes bend in on themselves.

Finally, the orange and blue smears sprang up. She'd thought of something.

"I want my pony," she demanded.

"Perhaps we could find one for you," suggested Millicent. "Of course, we'd have to travel out of the city to –"

"No, no, no," said Venus impatiently. "*They're* supposed to get me one, and they haven't." She pointed behind us, in the direction of the chief. "I want *that* one. The one they promised."

I heard the deep, gruff voice of the chief, his voice rising in a question. Out of the corner of my eye, I saw Kira turn her head in his direction. She answered him in what must have been Moku.

"Don't you go talking to my king!" Venus shrieked. She started to lurch to her feet, but the sudden movement sent her headpiece

careening wildly to one side, and while Venus and her servants were trying to keep her from choking on the strap, the chief answered Kira.

I risked looking over my shoulder. He was leaning forward in his chair, his eyes wide with interest. By the time Venus freed herself from the headdress and got to her feet, Kira and the chief were well into a conversation.

Dumb as she was, it must have dawned on Venus that this could work to her advantage.

"You actually understand him? You talk that gobbledygook, too?" she asked Kira.

Kira turned back to look at her. "Yes."

"Don't just sit there nodding! Ask him where my pony is!"

As Kira turned back to the chief, something caught Venus's eye, and she suddenly screamed in horror.

"AAAAAAH! WHERE IS THAT BOY'S HAND?"

She pointed a shaking finger at Guts, whose stump was up near his face, where he must have raised it to scratch his nose. He quickly lowered it, his lip curling in a snarl.

"He lost it," I said quickly. "Trying to serve you!"

Venus turned to glower at me.

"It's disgusting! Get him out of here, Egbert! Right this minute! Don't go bringing me one-handed subjects! *Eeew!*"

I scrambled to my feet and practically dragged Guts towards the exit.

"Gimme hook back, won't have to see it," he growled.

Venus didn't hear him. She was too busy yelling, *"Eeew! Eeew! Eeew!"*

The chief watched us pass, his eyes crinkling with amusement.

The warriors who escorted us into the room were coming forward to intercept me and Guts.

"MAKE EGBERT COME BACK ONCE THAT FREAK'S GONE!" I heard Venus yell, followed by a slightly quieter "Tell them that!"

The last line must have been directed at Kira, because I heard her call out in Moku. When she did, the warriors heading towards us looked at each other, unsure of themselves.

Then the chief said something, and all but two of them stepped back.

As the two warriors escorted Guts and me to the exit, I could hear the chief and Kira start talking again.

"Some family ye got," he muttered.

"Tell me about it."

I went with him as far as the corridor that led outside. "Don't worry," I said. "We're going to get out of this."

"Get my hook back!" he yelled as he left with the two warriors.

By the time I returned to the group, both Kira and the chief were on their feet. He was halfway to Venus, words tumbling out of him as Kira stood between them, listening intently. He finished, and Kira turned to Venus and offered a translation in a voice too low for me to hear.

Whatever Kira said, it made Venus screech with fury.

"LIAR! LIAR!"

I quickened my pace as Kira answered her. The response seemed to just make things worse.

"PUNISH! PUNISH! PUNISH!" Venus screamed, pointing a shaking finger at Kira.

The warriors ran past me towards Kira and Millicent, who were already retreating towards us in the face of Venus's fury.

The chief was laughing. The blind rage of his bride-to-be, or whatever she was, was hilarious to him.

By the time the girls and I reached each other, the warriors had formed a wedge in front of them, and I had to quickly step aside or the men would've flattened me as they passed.

Kira and Millicent both looked frightened.

"What happened?" I called out.

"Rovians are coming! Any minute!" said Kira.

"There's no time!" Millicent yelled over her shoulder at me as the warriors hustled them out of the temple.

"EGBERRRRRT!"

I turned away from the girls and back towards my sister. Her servants were flocking around her, trying helplessly to soothe her fury.

As I started towards Venus, the chief turned in my direction and headed for the exit, his stone-faced attendants following in his wake.

He was still laughing. As we passed each other, he said something to me that sounded like it was Moku for "good luck with *that*".

When I got to Venus, I hit my knees without even being asked. She fixed me with a venomous look.

"You're not to speak to those people any more or I'll kill you," she hissed. "That savage girl especially. She told the most *disgusting* lies."

"What kind of lies?" I asked, trying to sound meek.

"Not even repeating them, they're so horrid. Ugh!"

Venus plopped down on her pillows.

"Drink!"

One of the servants took off like she'd been shot from a cannon.

"Are some . . . men coming . . . ?" I asked.

"Yes!" She brightened a little. "That's the *only* true thing that witch said. They're bringing my pony!"

"And it's . . . Rovians bringing it?"

"Yes! Tons of them. All on horses. Maybe *they* can translate all this babble without lying like filthy pigs."

"Venus . . ."

"Queen!"

"My queen . . ."

"What is it? Don't be a prat. Spit it out."

"Those Rovians are very bad men –"

"Don't you start, too!" she hissed.

"I know you want a pony. And I want you to have one. But the men who are coming aren't friends of ours. They make slaves of the Natives. And –"

"Don't!"

"– they're the same ones who tried to kill you! All of –"

"AAAAAAAAH!" She pressed her hands to her ears and screamed, just like she used to back at home whenever someone told her something she didn't want to hear.

"GET OUT!"

I got out of there so fast the warrior escorts had to trot to keep up with me. Time was precious, and the help I needed wasn't going to come from my sister.

CHAPTER 19

ESCAPE

Dad was waiting at the bottom of the temple steps.

"Wot's she on about? I heard the yellin'."

"I've got to talk to the others." I started off in the direction of the pit.

"Can't," he said. "Only let ye near it if yer bringin' food."

I glanced back at the two warriors who'd followed me out of the temple. They stared back at me with blank faces.

I figured Dad was right. I went back to the temple steps, where I could sit and think. Dad followed me.

"We've got to get them out. We've got to leave here. Right away."

"Wot fer?"

"Rovians are coming."

"That's great! Ticket out."

"No. It couldn't be worse."

"How ye figger?"

There was no telling him what the problem was without

coming clean about the map. So I did. I didn't know if Millicent would have approved, but she was in a hole in the ground, and I had to trust my own judgement.

It came as a real shock to Dad that the balloon accident was no accident, but he didn't have trouble believing it the way Adonis did.

"Figgered it was a map," Dad said. "Sumpin' to do with that legend." He shook his head. "Never shoulda trusted that weasel lawyer."

I suddenly remembered I wasn't the only person with a copy of the writing on the wall of the Fire King's tomb.

"Do you still have the map?" I asked him.

He nodded, patting the pocket of his trousers. "Good thing, too – cut us a break with the savages."

"What do you mean?"

"First we landed, seemed like as not they was gonna kill us. Then I showed 'em the parchment, and all a sudden we was honoured guests."

"They could read it?"

"Course. Same marks as wot's on their walls." He pointed to the temple.

I shook my head. "They're from a different tribe." I nodded at the warriors, lounging around with Dad's shadow a short distance away from us. "These men are Moku. But they captured this city from the Okalu – the Fire King's people. They're blood enemies."

"Huh." He mulled that over. "Now ye mention it . . . dunno they read it or not. Passed it around a good bit. Looked confused, lot of 'em. But I put it to just havin' part of it."

252

"Part of what?"

"The map. Only copied the beginnin'. Get a flavour of it so's I could take the measure of whoever was gonna read it fer me. Didn't want to write down all of it, case 'ey'd steal it fer themselves. Frightful long to copy, anyhow. Ye really fit the whole thing in yer brain?"

I nodded. "I think so. I *hope* so. Had to wreck the original so Pembroke couldn't get it."

Dad stiffened. "Bloke better not've gone messin' near me plantation," he growled.

"He did more than that – he took it over for a while," I said.

"*Wot?! — —!*" he bellowed.

I nodded. "First he sent a whole squad of soldiers. Paid off Percy to help them. They moved into the house, dug up half the plantation looking for the treasure. When I got back, we had to run them off. Then Pembroke came back with a hundred men, and we had to stand them down, too."

Dad was staring at me, his mouth open. I could feel the pride swell up in my chest. After all those years of getting ignored, smacked around and picked on, he was finally figuring out it was me, not my fool siblings, who'd come through for him when the chips were down.

Growing up, I used to dream about a moment like this – when all the unfairness and stupidity of my family got turned around and made right in a heartbeat. In spite of all the danger we were in, I couldn't help smiling.

Except I was dead wrong. He wasn't gaping at me because he was impressed. He was just trying to do the maths in his head.

"Four o' ye? Run off a hundred soldiers?"

"Three, actually. And the field pirates helped. Sort of. Most of them skipped out when it got hot, to be honest."

"They didn't stab ye in the back? Not even the smart ones?"

"Not at first."

"Don't sound like 'em."

"I think they were loyal enough to –"

"Ain't no field pirate's loyal."

"Well, they certainly didn't want Rovian soldiers on their land."

"Ain't their land. It's mine. An' why'd they let 'em in to begin with?"

"What?" I was starting to feel a little panicky.

"Said the soldiers moved in! Dug up half the plantation. Who let 'em do it?"

"Wasn't me. I wasn't there –"

"Field pirates were. Let 'em waltz right in! Then ye come back, an' they flip to backin' yer lot? Jus' like that?"

"Well, kind of –"

"Wot'd ye pay 'em?"

"A share of the treasure –"

"Weren't no treasure yet. An 'em Rovians hadn't cut a better deal? That Pembroke richy weren't smart enough to line some thin pockets?"

It went on like that for a while. Dad kept getting more and more angry and suspicious, and I got so flustered, I could barely stammer out answers. I knew if I admitted the truth, he was going to explode. But I wasn't clever enough to come up with a lie that made sense.

And we were wasting valuable time. So finally, I gave it up.

"Don't make no sense! Wot'd ye give 'em to flip?"

"A share of the plantation."

"*WOT?!*" He bellowed so loud that a pair of Moku women a hundred yards from us on the far side of the plaza whipped their heads round to see what was happening.

"Not all of it! Just a share."

"Wot kind o' share?!"

"Equal."

"Equal fer who?!"

"All of them."

"*There's FIFTY of 'em!*"

"I didn't have a choice! I had to give them –"

"*It weren't yours to give!*" He was standing over me now, purple-faced with fury.

"I thought you were dead! I –"

"*It's all we have!*"

He raised his arm to hit me. I squeezed my eyes shut and waited for it.

But he didn't lay a hand on me.

He kept yelling, his rage mixing with grief.

"I built it from *nothin'*! With me bloody bare hands! Me life's work! An' the day I go – ye *give it away*? Like it was *nothin'* to ye?!"

I couldn't look at him. He sounded like he was about to cry.

He was quiet for a second. When he spoke up again, the words hurt more than his fists ever could.

"Knew ye was a curse on me from the day ye killed yer mum."

For all the times my brother and sister had accused me of

murdering my mother just by being born, I'd never once heard it come from Dad himself. He might have thought it plenty. But until then, he'd never said it out loud.

And it broke me. I put my head in my hands so he couldn't see the tears.

Then I heard the scrape of his boot as he turned and left me.

BY THE TIME I put myself back together enough to look up, I was alone. Dad had disappeared, and his shadow must have followed him. The two warriors were gone, too. I guess the Moku didn't think I was worth keeping an eye on.

I went to the pit, hoping I could talk to the others. As I walked there, passing the occasional Moku who eyed me with the kind of wary look you'd give a stray dog, I told myself it didn't matter what had happened with Dad. No matter how awful I felt, or how bad things seemed, I still had to get my friends out of that pit.

I figured if I could just talk to them, they'd have ideas about what to do. But when I got near the pit, the guard chased me off, waving me back to the avenue with his rifle.

I stood in the road for a while, trying to work out a plan in my head.

All I could think was to wait until the middle of the night, sneak over to the pit, knock out the guard and pull them up.

But it was barely midday, and as far as I knew, the Rovians might show up any minute.

And even if I got them out of the pit, how were we going to leave the city without being seen?

I walked back to the ruined wall where we'd first entered, to see if it was still guarded, and whether we could somehow get out that way.

There was a sentry with a rifle in the same place as before – to the left of the road, atop the intact side of the wall. He barely looked at me, even when I passed the wall and started down the road. For a moment, the thought crossed my mind that no one was stopping me, and I could leave right then if I wanted to.

Except I couldn't, because everyone I cared about was still back inside the city, and anyway I had no idea where to go even if I did abandon them.

I turned back round and picked my way over the pile of rubble on the far side of the road until I reached the intact section of the wall, which I managed to climb from the top of the heap.

From the top of the wall, I could see the road snake across the valley for a few miles until it disappeared between the forested hills.

There was no sign of men on horseback. Not yet, anyway.

The sentry yelled something at me from across the road. I had no idea what the words meant, but his tone was pleasant enough – and when I looked at him, he was grinning. I managed a smile back and gave him a sort of wave, and he chuckled and said something else in a friendly voice before he went back to ignoring me.

It didn't make any sense. We were prisoners, marched in at gunpoint with our hands tied, but I was free to leave.

They tossed us in a pit, but they cooked us breakfast.

They did unspeakable things to their own people, and then they laughed and joked with me.

And they made my fool sister into a queen, or something like it.

Maybe they'd let the others go if I just knew how to ask.

But then why wouldn't they let me near the pit?

I wished I could talk to Kira. She understood Moku, and she might be able to explain things.

I watched the horizon for a while, looking for any sign of men on horses.

Then it occurred to me they might be coming from a different direction, and I needed to scout other possible exits anyway, so I started to walk the length of the wall.

It was ten feet high and maybe two feet wide, and over the next few hours I walked the whole thing, all the way around the perimeter of the city.

I didn't learn much. Most of the buildings near the wall were abandoned, and one whole section had been fenced off and given over to pigs and chickens. There was a second gate on the far side of the city from the ruined one, with a paved road leading away down the hillside. That gate was intact, its heavy wooden doors shut with a massive bolt that looked like it'd take several men just to lift.

The wall was too high and smooth to climb. The best option I found for getting over it was a spot west of the temple, not far from Dad's house, where a couple of big trees looked just close enough to the wall that I could jump to it from one of the lower branches. It'd be tricky, especially in the dark, but I studied the location of the spot carefully so I could lead the others there.

When I came back round and the sentry saw me approach from the opposite direction, he laughed and said something.

I smiled at him and shrugged. Then I jumped off the wall, nearly spraining an ankle, and spent the next hour scouring ruined buildings for a rock the right size and shape to use as a weapon.

Eventually, I found a long, narrow stone about ten inches long that fit my hand pretty well and felt like it could do some damage at close quarters. I paired that up with a fist-sized rock that was good for throwing.

By then, it was late afternoon. I was getting hungry, so I went back to the middle of town to look for food I could eat and maybe bring to the others.

I didn't see Dad anywhere, but his Moku shadow was outside the house, cooking meat over the fire. I put the rocks down, then pointed to my mouth with what I hoped was a polite look. He nodded and gestured for me to sit.

I sat down in the shade of the house. Then I pulled out a smaller rock I'd picked up to use as a chisel and started to chip away at one end of the long stone, trying to give it a sharper edge.

A few minutes later, Dad came back. He was frowning.

"Where ye been?"

"Looking around. Thinking."

"Been thinkin', too." He sat down next to me, his back against the wall of the house.

"I'm sorry about the plantation," I said.

"Yeh." He rested his forearms on his bent knees and stared at his hands.

I was about to apologize a second time when he spoke up.

"Lookin' at it from yer angle . . . makes sense. I know ye was

259

hard up against it, and thinkin' we was dead besides. Talked to yer friends some when I took 'em food just now –"

"You did? Can we go back? So I can talk to them?"

Dad grimaced. "Best not. Don't want them savages gettin' suspicious."

"Of what?" I asked.

"In a minute. Gotta say this first . . ." He took a deep breath, then let it out slowly through his nose. He studied the line of dirt under the nail of his grimy index finger.

"Seem like good kids ye hooked up with. That blondie got a knife fer a tongue. Reminds me of yer mum."

He raised his head and stared at the sky with the same achingly sad look he used to get back on Deadweather, when he'd sit on our porch and stare out past the shoulder of the volcano, in the direction of my mother's grave. I'd seen that heartbroken look on his face a thousand times, but until that moment, I don't think I'd ever really understood what it meant: that after all these years, he was still in love with my mother, and grieving her loss.

And if the fact that she'd died having me meant that I was the person who'd taken her from him . . .

My eyes were welling up. "I'm sorry –" I started to say.

"Nah," he said, stopping me. "Got nothin' to be sorry fer. On me, it is. Ain't been much of a dad to ye. I know it."

My throat was thick, and it was hard to talk. "You've been all right," I managed.

He shook his head. "Nah, I ain't. But there's time yet. Gonna do right by ye."

He lowered his voice. "Cooked a plan with yer friends to get ye all out. Adonis, too. But ye gotta promise me sumpin'."

"What's that?"

"Gonna help me get that plantation back."

I nodded.

"Not just fer me. Fer you, too. 'S'all we got in this world. Be sunk without it."

I wiped the wetness from my eyes. "We'll get it back. I promise."

"Told Adonis the same. Gonna have to work together, I said. Told 'im yer his brother. He's gotta treat ye like it."

That seemed like a pretty tall order where Adonis was concerned. But I nodded again.

"Right, then. Here's wot we'll do."

Dad's plan was basically the same as mine – to wait until dark, sneak over to the pit, knock out the guard and pull the others up with the available ropes. Kira had told Dad she knew a way out of the city and could lead us to it even in the dark.

In the meantime, we just had to hope the Rovians didn't show up before we could take our shot.

And Dad added one more complication.

"Gotta make it look like ye did it without me. Can't let on I helped ye."

"Aren't you coming with us?"

He shook his head. "Gotta stay with yer sister. Get her out, too. Gonna take time. Might help matters havin' them Rovians come round, tho'. 'Specially if they speak savage."

"What about Roger Pembroke?"

"Wot of 'im? Far as he knows, I still think that business with the balloon was an accident. Map on Deadweather's busted, wot else he want from me? Long's I play dumb 'bout you and yers, man's got no reason to trouble me.

"Same's true o' them Moku – long's they don't figger I helped ye cut out. I been square with this bunch. Do just fine with 'em till I can convince yer sister to give it up and go home."

I wasn't so sure about that. The Moku were friendly enough to him now, but I figured things would get pretty hot for Dad after we'd escaped, especially once Pembroke's men showed up.

But when I tried to persuade him to come with us, he shrugged it off.

"No point in chewin' on it. I'm stayin'."

THE NEXT FEW HOURS were tense and endless. Until well after sunset, I kept jumping at random noises in the distance, thinking they were horses' hooves. And when I wasn't fretting over that, I was worrying about how we were going to pull off the escape, and what the Moku might do if they caught us.

We turned in early, pretending to go to sleep. Then we had to wait for what seemed like an eternity before Dad's shadow quit hanging around in front of the dying fire by our door and went off to sleep himself.

After that, we waited another hour to make sure the rest of the city had turned in for the night.

Finally, I felt Dad's hand shake me on the leg. I got up and followed him outside, carrying the two stones I'd planned to use as weapons.

We'd decided to travel to the pit separately so no one would spot Dad walking with me. Since he knew the city much better than I did, he sent me down the main avenue while he made his way along the smaller dirt roads behind it.

There wasn't much of a moon, and if it hadn't been for the

262

occasional cooking fires in front of the buildings off the main road, I would have had a hard time keeping my bearings. As it was, I missed the turn the first time and had to double back.

It felt odd to not even try to hide myself, but when we'd discussed it earlier, Dad had pointed out that I hadn't done anything wrong yet, so there was no reason to fear being seen. In any case, I didn't see a soul until I got near the pit and made out the hazy outline of the rock that the guard usually sat on.

I was surprised to see nobody was sitting on it, and for a moment I dared to hope the guard had left for the evening. But as I got closer, I saw the body of a Moku lying splayed on the ground, unconscious, beside the rock.

Dad had started without me.

I hurried past the guard, and the first person I saw was Adonis, watching Dad haul someone up out of the pit. Adonis glanced at me, and from what I could see in the dark, something looked out of kilter on his face – like his eye was swollen, or maybe his cheekbone.

I wondered if he'd had a run-in with one of my friends.

But I didn't have a chance to look closer, because just then Dad pulled Kira up. She stepped past him, and he quickly fed the rope down for the others.

"You know a way out of the city?" I whispered to her.

"There's a tunnel. Shhh. Stay quiet."

Millicent came up next, and she gave me a quick hug. Half a minute later, Guts joined us.

Just like that, we were done. Dad was breathing hard from the effort. He reached out and grabbed my shoulder with one of his big hands, then pulled Adonis to him with the other.

"Look out fer each other. And git that plantation back," he said in a low growl, squeezing my upper arm hard to make his point. "See ye there soon enuff."

Then he vanished into the night.

Kira beckoned us to follow her. We tiptoed past the still-unconscious guard and went to the main avenue. Kira led us across the road, between a pair of low stone buildings. A hundred feet further on, we reached a back road.

Kira started us down the back road in the direction of the temple, moving so fast it was hard to keep up with her and not make noise. Most of the buildings we passed were abandoned, so there wasn't any firelight, and when she turned a couple of times, I nearly lost her.

As we weaved our way closer to the temple, a few scattered cooking fires began to appear, and Kira slowed her pace so we could move more quietly.

We came upon a street that felt familiar even in the near-darkness. When she turned us down it, I realized why – it was the same street where Dad had his house. Kira led us right past his place, away from the main avenue and towards the city wall.

When she stopped us, we were close enough to the wall that I could make out its silhouette against the sky. There was a small stone building on either side of the road. The embers of a cooking fire smouldered in front of one.

Kira took a few tentative steps towards it, her neck craned as she stared at it.

Then she turned and led us to the second building, directly across the street. A few feet from the entrance, she held up her hand to stop us. She continued forward alone, peered into the open window, then cautiously stepped inside.

A moment later, she reappeared and beckoned us to follow her inside.

It was pitch-black in there, with just enough junk on the floor and people to bump into that it quickly started to get noisy.

"*Shhhhhh . . .*" Kira whispered.

I picked my way over to the back wall, where her voice had come from, until I bumped into someone I was pretty sure was Kira.

"What are we doing?" I whispered in the direction of her ear.

"There is a problem," she whispered back. "The tunnel is in the building across the street."

"Someone's living there."

"That's the problem."

CHAPTER 20

CHOICES

It was two hours past sunrise, and the old man who lived in the building across the road was still eating his breakfast.

I'd never seen such a slow chewer in my life.

Everything about him was slow – from the way he shuffled out of the little stone house just after dawn, to the way he carefully rebuilt his fire from a pile of kindling round the corner of his house, to the way he turned the stick he used to roast some kind of potato over the low flames.

Now he was savouring that potato like it was the last meal he'd ever eat. And judging by the dark scowl on Kira's face whenever she raised her head to check on him through the little window, if he didn't clear out of there soon, it might *be* his last meal.

Or it might be us who'd eaten our last, if the Moku found us. There was only one way out of the little one-room shack where we were holed up, and nowhere to hide among the bits of broken furniture littering the floor. If anyone showed up at the door, we'd be trapped, with no weapons except the stones I'd brought and the lengths of wood the others had scavenged from the floor.

We knew the Moku were looking for us. Once we realized someone was living inside the tunnel building, I'd told Kira about the tree I'd seen growing near the wall. It was nearby, and she had agreed it was worth trying to get out that way instead. We'd set out to find the tree, but we hadn't gone more than fifty feet from our hiding place when we heard voices shouting in the distance. It sounded to Kira like the guard at the pit had come to and raised the alarm, so we'd beat it back to the house in case the streets filled with warriors searching for us.

And they had. Within minutes, we'd seen torchlights flickering down the road by the main avenue. At first, they'd clustered near Dad's house, making me terrified that we'd doomed him. But soon, they'd left his place and fanned out through the city. Every time we'd poked our heads out, there were torches bobbing on the main avenue, and occasionally search parties would pass by on the path that ran beside the city wall, so close to us that their lights danced on the walls of our hiding place.

But they never came up our street, and when dawn had broken and the old man had first appeared, I started feeling hopeful that we might be able to make a dash for it soon.

But the old man never went any further than round the corner of his house, and when he did, it was only to pee or gather wood.

So we had no choice but to wait him out, praying all the while that no warriors would come down the street searching house-to-house for us.

With the sun up, the others all looked filthy and exhausted.

Adonis turned out to be sporting a nasty black eye, along with a pretty good cut near his chin, but under the circumstances I had to swallow my curiosity about who had slugged him. Nobody was talking, for fear of giving our position away.

At one point, I stuck my head out of the window to look down the street at Dad's house. Before Kira yanked me back, I got a glimpse of what looked like Dad's Moku shadow, cooking breakfast in front of the house.

That was a relief. If the Moku was cooking his breakfast, Dad must still be there. Which meant they hadn't hauled him off on suspicion of helping us.

After that, I tried not to move unless there was a good reason to do so. Time dragged on. As excruciating as yesterday's waiting had been, this was worse.

Finally, when Kira checked the window for what felt like the hundredth time, I saw her eyebrows jump. I leaped up to see what was happening.

The old man had finally finished his breakfast. He was standing up, stretching his legs like he might be getting ready to use them.

All around me, the others got to their feet, ready to run for it the moment the old man walked away.

Then he started tidying up.

It was endless. Just putting away the big roasting stick seemed to take him five minutes. One by one, we sat down again, dejected.

Then I felt Kira's hand tap my head. I stood up and looked out.

The old man was shuffling down the road towards the main avenue. Just before he passed out of our line of sight, I saw him turn down a side street.

We were all up now, clustering behind Kira by the door.

She poked her head out to survey the street.

Then she drew it back with a sharp intake of breath.

"Warriors," she whispered.

I stepped round her and took a look for myself. There were a dozen buildings on either side of the street between us and Dad's house. Three Moku warriors with rifles were coming up the road in our direction, halfway between the abandoned house next to Dad's and its closest neighbour.

As I watched, one of the soldiers approached the house and poked his head in the door while the others paused to wait for him.

They were searching every house, on both sides of the street. At the rate they were going, they'd reach us in a couple of minutes.

We had to make a choice. Should we run for it? Or stay and try to ambush them?

Either way, the odds were terrible.

Kira stepped to the far side of the doorway and raised the length of wood she'd taken from the floor. She wanted to fight.

I shook my head. She scowled at me.

"They've got guns," I whispered. "And they're spread out. We can't take all three of them."

"If we cross the road, they will see us," she said.

"What if we hide behind the house?" suggested Millicent.

"It's open to the road behind us. Anyone could see us."

Then, in the space of a second, Kira changed her mind.

"We have to run," she said decisively. She set down the piece of wood. "In the house, at the bottom left corner of the back wall, is a stone. This wide." She held her hands up, shoulder width apart.

"It slides out. That's the tunnel entrance. There is a ladder down and only one way to go at the bottom. Follow it to the end as fast as possible. Probably they will see us and give chase."

She took a deep breath. "Stay close."

She turned back to the door and was getting into a crouch when we heard the hoofbeats.

They grew louder by the second – a steady rumble of riders, dozens of them from the sound of it, moving into the city over the paving stones of the main avenue.

The Rovians had arrived.

Kira turned her head to peek down the road, then looked back at us. To my surprise, her face showed relief.

"They are turning away."

I poked my head out. The three Moku warriors had their backs to us as they walked together towards the avenue.

"Go!" I said.

Kira took off like a shot. The rest of us followed on her heels. The sound of hooves on the paved avenue was loud enough that we didn't need to worry about anyone hearing us. Whether they saw us, I couldn't say, because I was running too hard to turn my head.

The old man's house had an odd musty smell and no furniture. There was a straw sleeping pallet in the far left corner, where Kira had said the tunnel would be. By the time I entered, she'd already yanked it aside and was working to pull a heavy stone block from the wall just off the floor.

The stone looked like it weighed as much as she did. I would have offered to help, but she managed to pull it free in just a couple of seconds. I helped her push it to one side, revealing a wide, dark hole.

"Feet first. On your stomach. Go!"

Millicent was closest, and she dropped to the floor on her stomach and wriggled backwards into the hole. Guts followed her. Then Adonis.

"You go. I'll close it," Kira told me.

I lay down on my belly and shimmied backwards. When I got far enough in to drop my legs, my feet quickly found the rungs of the ladder. I climbed down into the darkness.

The tunnel wasn't far underground. Ten feet, maybe. When I reached bottom, I couldn't see a thing. But Kira was right – in the narrow space, there was only one way to go. I started off, one hand on the side of the dirt wall and the other out in front of me so I didn't plough into anything face-first.

I could hear the others moving up ahead. Right in front of me, Adonis let out a curse of surprise. A moment later, my head brushed the ceiling, and I realized he must have hit his head when it suddenly dropped. I bent my knees and kept going.

Pretty quickly, I bumped into Adonis. He growled at me.

Half a minute later, he came to a sudden halt, and I bumped into him again.

"Watch it!"

"Why'd you stop?"

"No place to go!"

"There's a ladder!" I heard Millicent say.

Kira's hand touched my back. She called out to Millicent. "When you reach the top, push hard on the ceiling!"

As we waited for Millicent to climb up and get the ceiling open, Kira gave a sigh that sounded like relief.

"We are close now."

It was good to be able to talk again. "I hope my dad's all right," I said.

"Why does he think the Rovians will save him?"

"Save him from what?"

"Being killed with your sister."

"*What?!*"

"It just pops off?" Millicent called out from up the ladder.

"Yes! Push hard!" Kira answered.

"Who's killing my sister?"

"The Moku. At the next thunderstorm. I thought you knew this."

"If they're going to kill her, why are they treating her like a queen?"

"They think she is a goddess. Of the Okalu. The Princess of the Dawn. Come from the sky to save my people. And your father serves her. They treat her well to make her happy until the next storm, when Ma comes to earth –"

"I can't budge it!" said Millicent.

"Lemme at it," said Adonis.

"Millicent, come down," said Kira. "Let him do it."

There was some jostling in the narrow space. Adonis elbowed me in the gut.

"When *who* comes to earth?" I asked Kira.

"Ma. Thunder God. Moku worship him. When there is a storm, with thunder and lightning, Ma is present. And they will offer your sister as a sacrifice, to increase Ma's power. Along with your father, and all her servants."

From somewhere up the ladder, I heard Adonis snort. "Says *her*. Them savages ain't killin' Dad. He's square with 'em."

"Your brother is a fool," Kira told me.

I felt woozy and sick. The darkness didn't help. "He doesn't know. I've got to tell him."

"Don't be stupid. It's too late for that." She raised her voice, calling out to Adonis. "Do you need help?"

"Almost got it," he grunted. "Stuck on sumpin'."

My mind was racing.

The tunnel's not long. He's right down the street. If all the Moku are distracted by the Rovians . . . off in the square . . . and Dad's in his house . . .

I pushed past Kira. "I'll be right back."

"NO!"

"I won't be long!"

I ran in a crouch down the tunnel, my arm stiff in front of me. They were calling out behind me, but I was too busy trying to work things out in my head to listen.

If he's not there, I can leave a message . . . Scrawl it in the dirt . . . What if the shadow's with him . . . ? I'll just peek out. Go right back to the tunnel if the coast isn't clear . . . It's not far . . . Fifty yards, there and back . . .

I was already at the top of the ladder. My body seemed to be moving without much input from my brain. I started to push the stone away, feeling the shudder through the earth as it rumbled across the floor. A square of light opened up round the corners of the stone.

"Don't . . . !" I heard Kira hiss from below me.

I didn't answer. I wasn't thinking about whether what I was

doing made any sense. I was thinking about how I was going to pull it off.

Still got the stones. In my pocket. The sharp one, and the one for throwing . . . Keep the throwing one in my right hand, just in case . . .

I shoved the stone back just far enough to squeeze through the opening. The old man's house was still empty. In the distance, I could hear the clop of hooves on stone. I went to the door and peered out.

The street was empty down to the avenue, where a double line of soldiers in Rovian blue were trotting past on horseback, headed for the main square.

Is that . . . ?

It was. Dad was standing in front of his house, his back to me, watching the troops go by. He was alone.

I looked behind me to make sure the street was empty that way, too.

Deserted. Not a Moku in sight.

Run.

I sprang forward, my head low and my legs pumping hard –

Then I was on the ground, colours exploding in my eyes and a hammer blow of pain across the top of my head. I'd run head-long into something that hadn't been there a second ago. Pieces of wood – *wood?* – were tumbling down on top of me.

I heard someone cry out.

I lurched to my feet, trying to make sense of what had happened.

The old man was sprawled on the ground in front of me, split wood lying all around him.

He must have come round the corner of his house with an armload at the exact moment I started my sprint, and I'd hit the wood head-on.

But I didn't figure that out in the moment. There was too much else to worry about.

Like what I was going to do next.

The old man was on his back, staring up at me in terror. His lower lip was trembling so much that the whole bottom half of his face quivered along with it, all saggy wattle and spit.

His mouth gaped and puckered, and I could see his Adam's apple bounce in the middle of his throat. He was trying to scream, but he couldn't make the sound come out.

The long, narrow stone was still in my left hand. I'd pulled it from my pocket before I started running, and somehow I hung on to it even as I dropped the other stone when I fell.

Kill him before he screams.

I had to do it. If he raised an alarm, I was doomed.

I switched the stone to my right hand and raised it up, closing in on him.

Do it quick.

His watery eyes were locked on mine, piteous as a broken-winged bird staring up at a cat.

Kill him.

He was old and feeble. He wasn't going to put up a fight. All I had to do was bring the stone down on his head.

Do it!

I was still clenching my upraised hand over the stone, trying to will myself to bring it down, when the scream came out of him in such an earsplitting shriek that it hardly sounded human.

"Shut up!" I fell on him, knees across his arms, and covered his mouth with my free hand.

He bit me hard on the fleshy part of my palm. When I drew my hand back, he screamed again.

I looked up. Down the road, Dad was staring at us, his mouth open in shock.

And two Moku warriors were running towards me, rifles in hand.

Where they came from, I don't know.

I leaped up. I knew if I went for the tunnel, they'd catch me there and find the others as well.

So I turned and sprinted in the other direction, towards the city wall.

Get to the tree.

I reached the path by the wall and turned left.

The tree was up ahead, its branches drooping over the wall.

If I can get there . . .

I could hear the Moku shouting behind me. I passed a side street and saw a blur of movement – *more Moku* – but paid them no mind.

The tree was close. A few more seconds.

How to climb it?

The lowest branch was at least a foot above my head. It was thick and sturdy, but I'd have to leap up just to reach it.

Jump!

I sprang into the air, fully extended. I managed to catch the branch with both hands, but my momentum carried me forward so hard I nearly lost my grip. I stiffened, trying to steady myself – and too late, I realized I should have tried to use my momentum to get my legs up onto the branch.

Now I was hanging there, dead weight. I swung my legs. Once, twice –

I got a leg up over the branch. I was going to –

Someone grabbed hold of my midsection, trying to pull me down.

I hung on with everything I had. I could feel the bark rip at the inside of my forearms.

Then someone else grabbed me round the legs, and that was it.

THERE WAS A WARRIOR on either side of me, marching me by the arms down the avenue towards the main square. There was a third one in front, and two more behind. I could see the horses up ahead in the square, and I wondered if Venus might actually get her pony.

It didn't matter. Eventually they'd kill her. Dad too.

I heard his voice behind us, out of breath.

"Wot happened, boy?"

One of the Moku barked a warning at him.

"You've got to leave while you can," I said. "They're going to kill you both."

One of the warriors grabbed me by the jaw and slammed it upwards, knocking my teeth together. They didn't want us talking.

"Wot ye mean?"

Dad was trotting alongside us. One of the Moku from the back stepped up to cut him off.

"They're going *tomph smrf* –" The Moku on the right grabbed my head and pulled it to him, yanking me forward in a headlock.

They marched me the rest of the way to the square like that – bent at the waist, my face smothered, tripping over my feet.

I wasn't an honoured guest any more.

I could hear Dad behind me, trying to argue his case to men who didn't understand a word of what he was saying.

We entered the square. I couldn't see a thing, but I could hear a clatter of voices in both Moku and Rovian, along with the clop and *pbbllth* of horses.

As they dragged me deeper into the square, the individual voices kept falling away as we passed, like people were stopping their conversations to stare at me.

By the time they quit dragging me forward, it was nearly silent. The warrior who'd been pulling me by the head let go with no warning, and I fell to the pavement.

There was a little ripple of laughter from the crowd.

I looked up. I was in front of the temple steps. Three men were staring down at me.

The first was the old grasshopper with the headdress.

The second was the big ox of a chief.

The third was Roger Pembroke.

CHAPTER 21

PEMBROKE

His clothes were dusty and grime-streaked from travelling, and there was a week's growth of beard on his sun-browned face. I'd never seen him like that – to me, he'd always been a creature of the frilly white shirts and velvet cushions of Sunrise Island.

But he seemed to thrive on it. As he stared down at me with his ice-blue eyes, he'd never looked more powerful or alive.

"Where is Millicent?"

"Gone away," I said.

"Gone away where?"

"Leave 'im be!" Dad's voice rang out. Getting to my feet, I turned towards the sound of it, and for the first time I got a look at the crowd.

It was much smaller than I'd expected. There were just twenty or so Rovian soldiers, and maybe twice that number of horses, all weighed down with provisions. There were about a hundred Moku, most of them armed warriors.

Several of the Moku surrounded Dad, their rifles trained on him as they waited for orders.

"Oh, my . . ." I heard Pembroke say. I turned back to him. He was looking at Dad with wide eyes and a hint of a smile. "*This* is rather curious."

Pembroke looked at the Moku chief. *"Ma le ba?"*

The chief gave him a long answer. Pembroke's Moku must have been pretty good, because he seemed to follow along with no trouble. Occasionally, he interrupted with a question.

Their tone and body language were casual, like they were speaking to each other as friends, or at least equals.

That struck me as a very bad thing.

Dad was trying to push his way towards us, but the Moku guarding him were having none of it.

Still explaining things to Pembroke, the Moku chief gestured to the top of the temple, where Venus lived.

"Aaaaah . . ." said Pembroke, nodding. He started to say something to the chief, but I broke in.

"They think my sister's an Okalu goddess," I told him. "And they're going to sacrifice her to their god. Please tell them –"

Something struck me hard in the back of the knees, knocking me to the ground.

As I scrambled to get back on my feet, I heard Pembroke say something in a sharp tone, like he was telling the Moku who'd just hit me to cut it out.

"Wot's this, boy?"

Dad was staring at me, confused.

"They're going to sacrifice you both!" I yelled to him. "At the next thunderstorm!"

I turned back to Pembroke. "Please don't let them do it."

Pembroke's eyebrows rose along with his shoulders, like he was helpless to do anything. "I'm afraid I'm just a guest here. It wouldn't be my place to question their religious practices."

"Look here!" Dad bellowed. "I got no quarrel with yer lot. This boy don't, neither. Leave us be, we'll make our way out with no harm done."

Pembroke pursed his lips and nodded thoughtfully, like he was considering the offer.

"The trouble of that is . . ." He gestured towards me. "This one's got something I need."

"Ye don't give us no trouble, I'll see he gives it to ye," Dad said.

"I do appreciate the offer," said Pembroke in a mild voice. "But I have to admit, I'm a trifle confused as to why *you're* dictating terms to *me.*"

Dad drew himself up straight, squaring his wide chest. He raised a meaty hand to point to the temple, just like the Moku chief had done.

"Me daughter's up in that temple. Wotever she is to this lot, fact is they do as she says. I say the word, she'll call this whole pack o' savages down on yer heads."

"Will she, now?" Pembroke was smiling so wide I could see his teeth.

"Dead certain," said Dad. He started towards me. "Come on, boy. We're leavin'."

The Moku warriors closed ranks, blocking Dad's way. He shoved the nearest one aside, grabbing the man's rifle barrel as he did. They began to struggle over it while Moku converged on Dad from all sides.

As I watched, terrified, I could hear Pembroke and the Moku chief behind me, exchanging words in low voices.

The warriors had just about overpowered Dad when the chief barked a command, and they all let go in an instant. Then they stepped back, leaving Dad alone with a rifle in his hand and a look of surprise on his face.

The chief gave another order.

"Move back. Give him room," Pembroke ordered his own men.

The Moku and Rovian soldiers standing between us melted away, leaving a clear path between me and Dad.

"Terribly sorry," Pembroke said to Dad. "Let my emotions get the best of me. It's a perfectly reasonable offer. So why don't you collect your daughter, and as soon as your boy gives me what I need, you can all be on your way?"

Dad looked wary. I had my doubts, too.

Pembroke called out to a Rovian soldier in the group. "Bring me a pen and ink. And some parchment. Should be on my pack-horse." Then he turned back to Dad.

"Go ahead and fetch your daughter. We'll still be here. The boy's got a bit of writing to do."

Pembroke said something to the chief and the grasshopper, and all three of them stepped aside, moving away from the temple steps.

Dad approached me, a bewildered look on his face and the Moku's rifle in his hand.

"If I give him the map," I whispered, "he'll find the Fist of Ka. We can't let him have it."

"Don't be a fool, boy. Give him wot he wants. Rest of it ain't yer concern."

Pembroke was still speaking in Moku with the chief and the grasshopper. Dad called to him.

"Me daughter's gonna need some convincin'. She ain't got a mind to leave."

"Don't worry about that," said Pembroke. He nodded to the chief. "Kala-Ma here will follow you up. He'll make things perfectly clear."

"I thought you weren't going to question their religion," I said.

Pembroke gave me an easy smile. "It's the prerogative of an educated man to change his mind." He waved Dad towards the steps. "Please, Mr Masterson – go and fetch your daughter. Before I change my mind again."

They were all watching Dad, waiting for him to start up the steps.

"I don't like this," I whispered to him.

"Be awright," he said. "Back in a few."

He gave me a pat on the shoulder and walked to the tall steps. He climbed the first three. Then he paused and looked back at the chief.

"Ye comin'?"

Pembroke said something to the chief. In response, the chief turned to his warriors and said, "*Krav.*"

The warriors raised their rifles as one and shot Dad from three sides at once.

CHAPTER 22

DARKNESS

Dad's body pitched forward. I screamed and ran to him, leaping over the lower steps.

He'd landed on his side on the third step. Blood was running fast out of the ragged holes in his back. I pulled him towards me and got one long, awful look at his glassy eyes before his body tumbled from the step and knocked me off my feet.

I landed hard, hitting my head on the bottom step.

I heard Pembroke curse.

"Mind his head! It's valuable!"

A pair of Rovian soldiers stood me up by the arms.

Pembroke stepped over to me. He lowered his chin and stared into my eyes.

"Once again – where is Millicent?"

I spat in his face.

His eyes flashed with anger. He took a few steps back, out of spitting range. Wiped his face with his hand. Wiped the hand on his trousers.

"You'll find that sort of behaviour is unhelpful to your interests."

The soldier he'd sent off for parchment and ink appeared at his side, holding a long wooden box and a ribbon-bound leather sheaf. Pembroke eyed them for a moment, then shook his head.

"Put them back. Bind him up for travel." He jerked his head towards me. The soldier ran off again towards the packhorses.

Pembroke walked back over to the Moku leaders and restarted their conversation. As I watched them, out of the corner of my eye I could see Dad's body lying crumpled on the steps. No one cared.

I tried to move to him, but the Rovian soldiers held my arms tight.

I was turning my head away so I wouldn't have to look when I heard Millicent's voice, choked with tears.

"Daddy!"

She was running towards him from the avenue, Moku warriors on all sides of her. Pembroke called out an order in Moku. The chief repeated it, and the warriors dropped back to give her space.

Pembroke began to stride forward to meet her, and as the space between them closed, Millicent began to beg through her sobs.

"Daddy, if you ever cared for me at all – if I ever meant anything to you as a daughter –"

He reached her just then, and struck her across the mouth so hard she fell.

"No daughter of mine would disrespect me this way," he said.

"You're going back to your mother. And if I ever see you again, you'll regret it."

He turned on his heel and left Millicent on the ground for the soldiers to pick up. I called out to her, but just then the soldier with the parchment came back and shoved a gag into my mouth.

Then the blindfold went on, and my world turned black.

THE BLINDFOLD STAYED ON for two days, all through the Rovians' quick departure from Mata Kalun and a hard ride broken by only a few hours' sleep. Late on the second day, we started up a hill thick with trees, and even with my hands tied to the saddle horn, stray branches kept knocking me off my horse. The soldiers must have got sick of having to stop and pick me up, and they finally took the blindfold off so I could duck the branches.

Until then, I didn't know where we were going or who was with us. I didn't know anything, except that Dad was dead and Millicent was caught and my sister was doomed and my friends were in a bad way and it was all my fault. And I was too sick and numb and tired and thirsty and hungry to think about anything. There was no point to it anyway, because all my thinking had done was wreck things for everybody, myself included.

When the blindfold came off and we topped the hill, I realized we were on the ridge that separated the Valley of the Flut from the lowlands where we'd first escaped the slave ship. At the bottom of the hill, we stopped to camp for the night – which struck me as odd, because we were close enough to make the ship with just another hour in the saddle, and I figured that was where we were headed.

When we camped, I discovered there were only a dozen

286

soldiers in the group, about half the total I'd seen in the city. Pembroke was with us, but Millicent wasn't. That might have been worth puzzling over, if I'd been able to see any point to puzzling over anything.

They kept me apart from the group, and I couldn't hear any of their conversations. One of the soldiers took my gag off and gave me hard biscuits and water, which I ate on the ground with my hands tied in front of me. Then I slept on my side, with my forearms over my cheek to try to keep the mosquitoes off my face.

We set off again at daybreak. I'd expected us to head into the swamps, where the slave ship had been anchored, but instead we turned inland.

After a few hours, I realized we were going to Pella Nonna.

That didn't make a whole lot of sense. According to what Angus Bon had said at the dinner party in the palace – looking back, it was hard to believe it hadn't been more than a week or two ago – Cartage had passed the Banishment Laws specifically to keep Pembroke and his slavers out of the New Lands, so I knew they wouldn't be welcome in the city.

But knowing we might be headed there set a faint light of hope in the darkness of my head. People knew me in Pella – and they liked me, even if it was only because I was Guts's friend. I might have a chance there.

But a chance of what? Staying alive? Stopping Pembroke? What did I even want any more?

I wanted Dad to be alive. And I wanted to be with Millicent. But one of those things was impossible now, and the other nearly so.

Pretty quickly, I had to force myself to stop thinking again. It hurt too much.

They'd left my blindfold off, and by now, the scenery was unfamiliar – we were going over ground that I'd last covered while blindfolded and trussed across the Moku slaver's horse.

It was pretty land, I suppose. Not that it mattered.

The sun set. We kept going. We were on a road now – not a paved one, like the road through the Valley of Ka, but a wagon-rutted dirt road, winding through low hills.

Then we came out onto some cropland, and after a few miles, I saw city walls up ahead in the moonlight. I thought it was Pella, but I'd never seen it from that side, so I wasn't sure until I got a glimpse of the palace roof peeking out over the wall.

One of the soldiers called out to the guards on the wall. To my surprise, they answered in Rovian.

The gates slowly swung open.

The city guards staring down at us from the wall wore Rovian uniforms.

Pella Nonna didn't belong to the Cartagers any more.

The courtyard was deserted, and the horses' hooves echoed against the walls as we crossed it. When we neared the far end, Pembroke and two of the soldiers split off and headed for the palace. The rest of us took the main street towards the port.

There was a burnt smell in the air, and several of the buildings along the main street had been reduced to nothing but stone chimneys rising out of a pile of ash. The streets were empty, and if it hadn't been for the occasional candle in a window, I would've guessed all the people had fled. When we lived there, they came and went even in the middle of the night, talking and laughing and singing. Now it was a ghost town.

We reached the port and turned left, towards the piers where the giant Cartager men-of-war had been docked. At first, I thought they'd been put to sea. But as we got closer, I saw the tops of three masts rising from the water like the fingers of a skeleton, and I realized at least one of the warships had been sunk where she berthed.

We turned right at the north end of the port, onto the long finger of land that led out to the fortress. It had taken a lot of damage as well, with a section of the wall nearest the city partially caved in.

There was another exchange in Rovian between the soldiers and the fortress guards before the gates opened to let us in. In the courtyard, they took me down from the horse, cut free the strips of cloth tying my hands and replaced them with heavy iron manacles.

Then they led me through a door and down two flights of stairs to a long corridor, lit only by a torch one of the soldiers held. We passed a series of iron doors before we came to an open one.

They pushed me into a dank, stinking room not much bigger than a closet, with rough stone walls and an earthen floor.

Then they shut the door, and my world turned black again.

CHAPTER 23

THE MAP

I don't know how long they kept me in that cell. The only way I had of marking time was by how often they fed me. They brought six meals in all, so I might have been there six days, or only three, or maybe even just two if they were really being generous.

They gave me beef and milk as well as bread and water, and early on, they brought in a pallet for me to sleep on. Whatever they had planned for me – I was sure it involved writing out the map, but beyond that, I had no idea – they didn't want me too hungry or tired to be useful to them.

I tried not to think about what was going to happen next. Seeing Pella Nonna in Rovian hands – and watching Roger Pembroke trot off towards the palace like he owned the place – had snuffed out the last of my hope that things might turn out okay. So I tried to spend the time living in my memories – of the better times with Millicent, and with Guts when we were first in Pella, and even the odd moment with Dad growing up on Deadweather.

Those two days with Dad at the end put a whole different colour on my memories of him. Looking back, I found moments – like when he wrote "MUST ONE BOOKS" (he wasn't much of a speller) on the ad he placed for a tutor, because he knew how much I loved to read – where it was clear he'd been looking out for me in a way that I was pretty sure proved he loved me.

I wished I'd told him I loved him, the way I had with Millicent. But the truth was, I didn't realize it myself until he was gone for good.

And he'd never been much for that kind of thing, so maybe it was best left unsaid.

There were bad memories, too. I tried to keep them out of my head, but there was one in particular that wouldn't let go of me – or maybe it was the other way around.

It was the old man with the frightened eyes and trembling lips. The one I couldn't kill. I'd done a lot of stupid things to wind up in that cell, but none of them tore me up inside like that one did.

If I'd just had the guts to kill him, it would have all been different. I'd probably be with Millicent and my friends in the wilderness somewhere. Dad might even have joined us. Even if he hadn't, he'd still be alive.

I could've done it. I had the stone in my hand and all the time in the world to bring it down on the old man's head. Why didn't I?

Was it mercy? Was I a good person for not having done it? Was it better to have spared the old man's life, even though it cost Dad his, and was about to cost me mine?

Or was I just a coward?

There's a line about courage in my favourite book, *Basingstroke*. The main character, James, gets impressed into the army, and they're marching off to battle, and the lieutenant tells his men, "Show me courage!"

James elbows the man next to him and says, "How do we do that?"

And the man says, "Nothin' to it. Just see what needs doin'. Then do it."

I'd seen what needed doing, clear as day.

I just couldn't do it.

FINALLY, THEY CAME for me, so soon after my last meal that I knew it couldn't be another feeding. The door opened, and two soldiers beckoned me into the hallway. They led me down the hall and up the stairs, then down another hallway and into a room with a wooden table and three chairs.

In the middle of the table were a pitcher of water and two glasses. Off to the side, an inkpot and a quill pen were carefully arranged atop a short stack of parchment.

They took my manacles off and motioned for me to sit. Then they left the room, closing the door behind them.

I poured myself a glass of water. Under other circumstances, I might have waited to ask for permission. But I'd been parched for as long as I could remember – even after they started feeding me, I couldn't seem to get enough water to slake my thirst – and I figured there was nothing they could do to punish me that was any worse than what was coming anyway.

I kept refilling my glass until the whole pitcher was gone. Then I sat and waited.

Fifteen minutes later, Roger Pembroke entered. He was

clean-shaven, in a blue linen long-tailed coat over a white silk shirt. He shut the door and walked over to the table.

He picked up a glass and the empty pitcher. When he felt its weight, his eyebrows rose a little. He smirked.

"What do you have to say for yourself?" he asked, lifting the pitcher slightly.

"I need to pee," I said. It was true.

Pembroke went to the door and opened it. "Boy needs a privy."

The two soldiers from before must have been guarding the door. They came in and escorted me off to do my business.

When I came back, the pitcher was full again. Pembroke was sitting casually, his fingers entwined over his stomach and his legs stretched out in front of him.

"Sit," he said.

I sat. He poured me a fresh glass of water. Then he stared at me with his ice-blue eyes. They weren't hateful, or angry, or even friendly. They just stared, with no emotion at all.

"I don't suppose there's any mystery as to why we're here," he finally said. "I only hope your memory's equal to the task."

He reached into the inner pocket of his coat and pulled out a worn piece of folded parchment. He slowly unfolded it and placed it on the table in front of me.

"This should help get you started."

I stared down at the smudged figures, scrawled with a charcoal pencil. It was the same sequence of Okalu hieroglyphs that began the map in my head. I'd never seen that particular parchment before – not up close, anyway – but I instantly knew where it came from and who had written it.

It was the parchment that started the whole thing – the one my father had copied from the wall of the tomb before he took us to Sunrise and we met the Pembrokes. The one that made the Moku think Dad was footman to a goddess who'd just floated down out of the eastern sky.

Dad kept it in his pocket. The only way Pembroke could have got it was by robbing his corpse.

I could feel the bile rising in my throat.

"You stole that from him. You robbed his dead body."

The blank stare didn't waver. Pembroke slowly leaned forward in his chair until our faces were just inches apart.

"That's right," he said. "That's exactly what I did."

Then he leaned back again.

"Now finish it."

I didn't move for a while. When I finally did, it was to drink another glass of water.

We stared at each other through the silence. Then Pembroke looked away, pursing his lips as if he'd just remembered something.

"I'd almost forgotten . . . Someone wants to join us."

He stood up and went to the door.

"Could you bring him in, please?" he asked one of the soldiers.

I heard the soldier walk off. As Pembroke returned to his seat, I looked down at Dad's parchment. The lines were thick and shaky, their proportions badly distorted from the original. It looked like a child had drawn it – and for a moment, I felt embarrassed for Dad, and sorry that he'd spent so little time with a pencil that he could barely copy figures.

Then I had to look away, because I thought I might cry. I took a couple of deep breaths to steady myself.

When I looked back, there was a man in the doorway. He was big and rough, with a face so deformed that at first I didn't recognize him. The nose was out of line with the mouth, there were wormy lumps over the left eyebrow, and underneath it the eye was gone completely from its socket, leaving a puckered, red-scarred hole.

His one good eye burned with hate.

"Mr Birch. So glad you could join us. Have a seat." Pembroke waved to the empty chair next to him.

Birch sat down, never taking his eye off me.

Pembroke placed a gentle hand on Birch's shoulder.

"Not to bring up a sore subject, my friend – but remind me again how you lost that eye?"

"Little – kicked it out," Birch growled.

My mind flashed back to Guts in the dingy hold of the slave ship, taking his foot to Birch's head.

Pembroke nodded in my direction. "*This* little – ?"

Birch's lip curled. "Nah. But he'll do."

Pembroke nodded, approving. Then he leaned in towards me again.

"Tell you what," he said. "I'm going to give you two minutes to draw that map. And if you haven't done it by then, I'll leave you and Mr Birch to discuss the situation privately."

Pembroke sat back and waited for me to make my decision.

Birch pulled out a rusty pocketknife and began to inspect the jagged, brown-crusted blade. After a moment, he raised his eye to stare at me again. He was smiling.

"Got plans fer you," he said. "I been thinkin' 'bout this fer a while now."

I looked at the floor.

One way or another, I was going to die. I knew that.

But I wasn't going to let them get that map out of me.

I was going to show them what courage was.

The two minutes passed.

Pembroke got up and left. He shut the door behind him.

Birch went to work on me.

He liked his work, and he was good at it.

I didn't last long.

When Pembroke finally came back, I begged him to let me draw the map.

Once they got Birch out of the room, that's what I did.

I did such a good job on it that when dinner came to my cell after they locked me back up, there was jelly bread for dessert. I cried as I ate it.

THE LAST PIECE of jelly bread was still in my mouth when the cell door burst open. Roger Pembroke stood me up and pinned me to the wall by my throat.

"YOU THINK THIS IS A JOKE? THINK YOU CAN PLAY GAMES WITH ME?"

His face was bright red. A thick, angry vein bulged on his forehead.

I tried to speak, but he was crushing my windpipe, and all I could do was dribble bits of food onto the back of his hand.

He slammed me to the ground and kicked me once, so hard it knocked the wind out of me.

"Don't know . . . what you mean," I managed.

"GIVE ME THE REAL MAP!"

"I did!"

He picked me up and bashed me against the wall again. His burning eyes locked into mine.

"Who wrote that nonsense? Was it the Okalu girl? WHERE IS SHE?"

My whole body was shaking. "Don't . . . know . . . what you're . . . talking about." I gulped air. "I drew the map. From the tomb. Memorized it best I could. If it's wrong . . . I can try again . . ."

His eyes searched mine. The fury was slowly leaving his face.

He let me go and took a couple of steps back.

"You're actually serious?"

I nodded. "I gave you what I had. Right from the tomb. Best I could."

The fire in his eyes fell to a smoulder. He looked at the wall. Sighed deeply. Rubbed his face with both hands.

Then he started to laugh.

"What is it?" I asked.

He kept on laughing for a while. Whatever the joke was, he seemed bent on enjoying it.

When he was done laughing, he sighed again. It was a heavy, worn-out kind of sigh.

"I'm not one for talk of the Saviour," he said in a wistful voice. "But I'll say this . . . If God exists, He's got quite a sense of humour."

He started for the door.

"Why's that?" I asked.

"Because after all that time and trouble . . . the damned thing's worthless."

CHAPTER 24

SENTENCED

After Pembroke left, I lay in the darkness for a long time, trying to puzzle out what he meant by "worthless". At first, I figured he was talking about the map – that it wasn't a map after all, or it was but just didn't lead to the Fist.

But the way he'd said "all that time and effort" – with a sort of heavy weight in his voice – made me wonder if he wasn't talking about something else.

He'd gone to real trouble to track down the map, following it first to Deadweather and then all the way to Mata Kalun. But the kind of regret I heard in those words didn't seem to match up with the loss of what only amounted to a few weeks – during which he'd managed to invade and capture the biggest city in the New Lands, so it wasn't like finding the map had taken up his every waking moment.

And the map wasn't the real prize. It was the Fist of Ka.

Millicent once told me her father had spent years searching for the Fist, digging all over Sunrise, long before he ever suspected there was a map that might lead him to it. I'd seen with my own eyes the long shelf of books he kept in his library about Native tribes and their legends, all part of the research for his quest.

The Fist, and its supposedly godlike powers – that was what had taken years from him. If the map was worthless, there'd still be other places to look, and maybe even other maps. But if whatever I'd copied down from the Fire King's tomb convinced Pembroke that the Fist itself wasn't what he thought it was, and all the time he'd spent looking for it had been wasted . . . well, then his reaction made a lot more sense than if he'd just spent a few weeks tracking down a dud map.

And the more I thought about the legend of the Fist, the more it made sense that the whole thing was just a story, cooked up by people who'd seen things beyond their understanding and were looking for a way to explain them.

What had Kira said were the Fist's powers? To give life and take it. To heal and to kill. To burn and to build.

Everyone I'd ever heard of who entered the Valley of Ka for the first time – me, Guts, my family, all the way back to the first Cartager invaders a hundred years ago – had been struck down by an invisible, deadly force.

And those of us who took the cure had just as miraculously been healed.

But that deadly force was just something in the water. And the cure was a kind of medicine, growing naturally in that mossy plant. It made perfect sense – except maybe to those Cartager soldiers, most of whom never got the cure and wound up dropping dead at the feet of the Okalu they were trying to conquer.

I could see as how both sides in that battle might mistake the mass death of the invaders for the wrath of Ka, even though it clearly wasn't.

Then the power to burn: what was that? If it was the ability to summon fire from nothing, I'd seen Kira do that with the fireballs. It looked mystical at the time, but when she explained the whole thing, it turned out there was nothing more to it than a simple recipe and a lot of practice.

What was left? The power to build. What did that mean? The Okalu had built Mata Kalun, and the massive temple definitely looked miraculous. But from what I'd read in books and seen in pictures, builders on the Continent had created equally miraculous things, from kingly castles to giant cathedrals that glorified the Saviour. I couldn't for the life of me explain how they built them, but I felt sure if I was a builder, it wouldn't seem any more mystical than thatching a hut.

It all made perfect, stupid sense. There was no Fist at all. Or, more likely, there *was* – and it was hidden away somewhere just like the legend said, buried in secret by a dying and desperate king who hoped someday his people would dig it up and rule again.

But it was all nonsense. That Fist wasn't going to save the Okalu now any more than it had saved them a hundred years ago.

It was a piece of jewellery.

And Pembroke was angry because it wasn't going to help him rule the New Lands after all. But he'd figure out soon enough – he probably had already – that it didn't matter. He hadn't needed the Fist to take Pella Nonna. He wouldn't need it to take the rest of the Continent. He was either going to come out on top, or he wasn't. The Fist wasn't going to make a bit of difference either way.

It was cold comfort, figuring all that out now. And it made me feel like a fool. If I'd only realized it, at any point, right up until the end . . . I could have just walked away. We all could have.

That whole time, we were chasing a fantasy.

Why didn't I see it? All I had to do was think it through. Why did I believe the fantasy?

Because everybody else did. And I wasn't strong enough to think for myself.

THE DOOR OPENED. There were two soldiers, and a third man in uniform – older than the others, with grey in his hair and fancy ribbons across his chest that said he was someone important.

The older man wrinkled his nose.

"He stinks. Clean him up."

The old man left, and the two soldiers took me upstairs. They let me have a bath, and gave my clothes to an old Native woman who washed them while I ate breakfast. It was morning, although I wouldn't have known it until I came up from the dungeon and saw the light.

Then they left me alone, wrapped in a cotton blanket. I hadn't had the manacles on for a while now. They were barely bothering to guard me. If I'd been wearing clothes, I would have made a dash for it.

Pretty soon, the soldiers brought the clothes back, which were tolerably dry. I put them on and was just starting to think seriously about how I might run off when the man with the ribbons returned.

"Time to go," he told the soldiers. "Bind his hands. Rope, no chains. And put a gag on him – Governor doesn't want any editorializing."

"Where am I going?" I asked.

"An appointment with justice," he said, in a voice that made me wonder if he was trying to be funny.

They bound my hands behind me and tied a length of cloth round my mouth so I couldn't talk beyond an "unnnngghh". Then they led me to the courtyard.

A double line of six soldiers was waiting. The two in the rear had big drums hanging from shoulder straps. The other four had rifles. They stuck me in the middle of the group, between the two rows of rifles. The two soldiers who'd been escorting me fell in on either side to surround me.

We started to march. When we approached the iron gate, the man with the ribbons signalled to a guard on the wall, and he winched the gate open to let us out.

As we crossed the long spit of land towards the port, the seriousness of the situation started to sink in. They didn't give you an escort like this to take you shopping.

I figured I was headed for some kind of trial. Either that, or they'd skipped the trial, and we were going straight to the execution.

There was no way to run. The soldiers had me penned in so tight I could barely see past them to the ships in the harbour.

We turned down the boardwalk. There were a few merchantmen and importers doing business, but not nearly as many as there usually were. The ones we passed spoke in hushed voices and were careful not to look at us.

We started up the main street, which was just as empty as the boardwalk. Compared to its usual chaos, Pella Nonna seemed quiet as a funeral.

When my brain made that connection, I got woozy.

Halfway to the palace square, the drummers started up. Hearing the drums boom right behind my ears, so loud I could barely think, was almost a relief after that unearthly quiet.

As we neared the square, I saw the first hints of the crowd, and I realized why the streets were so empty. Practically the whole town was there – it was as big an audience as the one that greeted *Li Homaya* when he came back from his southern campaign.

Then we turned the corner, and I saw the gallows. In front of the palace steps was a twenty-foot-tall scaffold with a standing platform about a third of the way up. Hanging down from the top of the scaffold was a rope with a noose on the end.

There wasn't going to be any trial.

As they walked me over to the platform, I saw Roger Pembroke at the top of the steps, flanked by a handful of aides in uniform. He was wearing a starchy, stiff-collared shirt and the long blue coat from the day before.

Two of the soldiers marched me up a narrow set of wooden steps onto the gallows. They positioned me just to one side of the noose, facing Pembroke with my back to the crowd.

The drums stopped. Pembroke slowly walked down the stairs until he stood just far enough above the scaffold to look over it at the crowd.

A short-eared Cartager in a Rovian soldier's uniform walked

behind and to one side of him. When Pembroke stopped, the Cartager kept going until he was a few steps further down.

Then Pembroke began his speech.

"Good people of Pella Nonna! I stand before you today, twice a humble servant – of his majesty King Frederick, sovereign of New Rovia . . . and of this community, which it is my great honour to serve as your governor."

Pembroke paused to let the Cartager translate his words for the crowd. I wondered if the band – Salo and Illy and the others – was in the audience, and whether there was any chance they might intervene. It seemed unlikely, but it was all I had.

"When first I stood before you," Pembroke continued, "I swore upon my honour that I would rule with justice for all – that New Rovia would be a land in which every man, woman and child –" he paused just long enough to glance at me – "would enjoy equal rights, and *equal responsibilities,* under the king's laws."

He paused again for the translation.

"In contrast to the bigoted rule of my predecessor, I guaranteed you no criminal – no matter the colour of his skin or the size of his ears – would go unpunished. And, just as certain – no honest man, however thin of wallet or small of stature, ever need fear the hand of government in his affairs, except as a guarantor of justice and impartiality."

It took an unusually long time for the translator to get through that last bit. I wondered if he was as confused by it as I was.

"When I first took office," Pembroke went on, "certain rumours reached my ears, of the foulest and most despicable nature. It was said that lawless bands of men roamed the lands to the north, taking slaves at will from the Native population. Worse, to my ears, was the allegation that these traitors to human decency were my own countrymen – Rovians who had cast off the laws of not merely their king, but their Saviour."

Now I understood why they'd gagged me. Underneath all the confusing words, the lie he was spinning was so massive it was almost breathtaking.

"I undertook to lead an expedition in order to prove, once and for all, the truth or falsity of this claim. To my great horror, I discovered it to be true, and the perpetrators to be at large in the Valley of Ka. My troops engaged them – and these criminals, with *but one exception,* died in combat rather than face the king's justice."

When he got to the "exception" part, he waved his hand at me.

"The person before you today stands guilty of the charge of trading in human flesh. And though his tenderness of age, and the natural affection I have for him as a consequence of our common nationality, cause me more pain than I can express –"

That was a bit much.

"– my duty as your governor demands that I exact from him the ultimate punishment. For the law is the law, and so help me, I am duty-bound to enforce it without prejudice or mercy – no matter the outcome, nor the price to my heaviness of heart."

He lowered his head, looking me straight in the eye.

"Egbert Masterson, I hereby sentence you to death by hanging."

The drums started up again as one of the soldiers stepped forward to fix the noose round my neck.

I don't know why I wasn't more scared. Even as they tightened the noose and I felt the scratch of the rope against my neck, I hardly felt a trace of my usual stomach-clenching fear.

I didn't feel much of anything. It was like the whole thing was happening to someone else, while the real me floated somewhere above it all, watching the scene like a spectator at a play.

The rope was so tight now I could feel my pulse thump in my neck. As the soldier stepped away, I thought I heard someone yelling, trying to be heard over the pounding of the drums.

The soldier walked over to a long lever that rose up from the platform on the far side of the stage. He put his hand on it, and some part of me registered the fact that once he pulled the lever, the bottom would fall out of the trapdoor beneath my feet, and I'd drop.

The part of me watching from above wondered how it would feel.

Someone was definitely yelling something – the same word, over and over. I hoped they'd have the good manners to stop when the drums did so I could die in a dignified silence.

"GOVERNOR!"

A man leaped onto the platform at a running jump, making the whole gallows shudder so violently it was a wonder it didn't spring the trapdoor under my feet. He was a big fellow, with a thick head of brown curly hair, and my first thought was that he looked awfully familiar.

"GOVERNOR!" he yelled again.

Pembroke raised his hand. The drumming stopped.

"Commodore Healy," said Pembroke, not bothering to hide the surprise in his voice.

It was Burn Healy.

CHAPTER 25

SPRUNG

The part of me that was floating detached above the whole scene suddenly reentered my body. I think it was to get a closer look.

What on earth is Burn Healy doing on my gallows?

Pembroke wanted to know the same thing. "What possesses you to interrupt a vital function of government?" he asked the pirate.

"I apologize for my impertinence," said Healy, directing his answer to Pembroke but making sure he was loud enough for the whole crowd to hear him. "But I think you'll agree that justice holds greater claim to our conscience than manners."

"Indeed, Commodore," replied Pembroke, making me wonder why he kept calling a notorious pirate by a title I thought only applied to leaders of the Rovian Navy. "Which is why your interruption of a justly administered execution –"

"Precisely why I'm here, Governor," Healy interrupted. "As I'm sure you're aware, there is a law, of long standing in the kingdom of Rovia . . . which clearly states that when a minor child commits a crime – no matter how vile – his punishment is to be rightly considered the province not of the state, but of his parent or guardian."

Healy cast his eyes to the top of the palace steps, where Pembroke's minions stood in a line. "Isn't that so, barrister?" he called out.

The other minions turned to stare at a tiny, nervous-looking man with big spectacles, wearing a blue military uniform that was much too big for him.

It was Archibald, the lawyer from Sunrise Island. I was surprised I hadn't noticed him there before. Then again, up until that point my attention had been pretty well hogged by my looming execution.

"I said, isn't that so, barrister?" Healy repeated in that bone-chilling voice of his – the one that said your life would be over in a heartbeat if you didn't give him the answer he was looking for.

Archibald had been watching Pembroke, looking for a cue – but at the sound of Healy's voice, his head snapped back to Healy, and he nodded so hard it must have hurt his neck.

Pembroke's eyes narrowed as he stared over his shoulder at his attorney. But he managed to get his scowl under control before he turned back to Healy.

"Be that as it may . . ." Pembroke replied. "This boy's father, *himself* a slaver, died in the Valley of Ka while resisting the crown's troops. Making the boy a ward of the state."

"Not so, I'm afraid," Healy replied. "If Hoke Masterson is dead . . . *I* am this boy's guardian."

"By what right?" Pembroke didn't even bother trying to hide the anger in his voice.

"By blood," said Healy. "Egbert Masterson is the youngest child of my late sister, Jennifer Healy."

I was so stunned to hear someone speak my mother's name that I missed the next thing Healy said, even though I was staring right at him.

Then I looked at Pembroke – and when I did, he was staring down at me with a look that was so bewildered it almost seemed tender.

Healy was still talking.

". . . to release him to me – just as I thank the brave soldiers of His Majesty –" Healy made a sweeping motion with his arm, taking in every Rovian soldier in the courtyard, from the ones who'd marched me in to the watchmen along the distant city wall – "who were gracious enough to allow me the honour of fighting alongside them in the liberation of New Rovia, perceiving that while I do not wear the colours of our king, I am no less a patriot for that. *Thank you again, my brothers!*"

The soldiers roared back with enthusiasm. Whatever fighting Healy had done during the invasion of Pella Nonna, it had obviously won him some big fans in the Rovian Army.

Healy turned his smile from the troops back to Pembroke – who to my surprise was actually smiling himself.

Then I realized it was a fake smile, plastered on his mouth to hide the rage that burned in his eyes. The tenderness was long gone, if it had even existed in the first place.

"So it seems, Governor," said Healy in a very pleasant voice, "that the only proper course of action is for you to release my nephew to my custody. I can assure you, the men of my ship are heavily armed . . ."

He motioned to the space below and behind him, and for the first time, I noticed he hadn't come alone. A dozen or more pirates stood by the gallows stairs, all of them holding pistols. If the pistols were pointing anywhere, it was at Pembroke.

". . . and they will not fail to ensure that the boy departs Pella Nonna within the hour, with no further disruption to the perfect system of justice you've established in New Rovia."

Pembroke's chest rose as he took a deep, slow breath. When he spoke, his voice was tight and measured.

"Thank you, Commodore. I see that the faith I placed in you militarily has been rewarded beyond my imagining. Take this nephew of yours, and may your punishment of him be swift and just."

Then Pembroke turned his back and walked up the steps towards his aides. I don't think he had much appetite for watching his own soldiers help me slip the noose.

CHAPTER 26

AWAY

"Thank you" were the first words out of my mouth after Healy cut my gag with his knife.

"Don't thank me," he said. "Thank your friends."

He headed for the gallows steps. I followed him. "Which ones?"

"The twitchy one, the Native girl and your brother. If they hadn't found me when they did, you'd be swinging right now."

As I started down the steps, I heard a voice call my name. I looked out over the sea of people and saw Salo from the band about fifty feet back, waving to me as he tried to squeeze through the crowd.

Healy was moving at a fast clip in the opposite direction, towards the port.

"Can I just –?"

"Don't push your luck. We're leaving."

I would've liked to talk to Salo. But it seemed best not to argue with the man who'd just saved my life.

The crowd parted in a hurry for the pirates. Once we reached the avenue, Healy and his men moved so fast I had to trot to keep up.

We were almost at the boardwalk when a voice rang out behind us.

"Commodore!"

It was Pembroke, flanked by a handful of his minions and trying to maintain a dignified air even as he practically ran to catch us. Birch was with them, the only one not in a Rovian military uniform. His good eye stared me cold, and I felt my forehead go clammy.

I prayed Healy wouldn't stop to wait. But he did.

"The man with the bashed-in face wants to kill me," I told him.

Healy shrugged. "Don't they all?"

That didn't exactly put my mind at ease, so I made sure I stayed close by Healy's side – and when Pembroke reached us and began speaking to the pirate in a low, steely voice, I was able to hear everything.

"Why didn't you come to me sooner?"

"Only just found out, old boy. Three little birds flew down from the north and took roost on my ship. Funny – their story's quite different from yours."

Healy started towards the port again. Pembroke walked alongside, at Healy's right elbow. I stayed glued to the left one. I could practically feel Birch's eye drilling into the back of my skull, but I didn't have the courage to look back.

"I'm sure you realize this changes your status all down the line," Pembroke informed Healy.

"I'd expect no less. But I wouldn't advise you to push too hard. I've got friends in Edgartown, too, Reg. And you might be sleeping in that palace tonight – but until you've got *Li Homaya*'s head on a stick . . . and anyone else the Short-Ears send to avenge him . . . you need me more than I need you."

Healy stopped at the foot of a pier, turning to stand across it in a way that said it was a bad idea for Pembroke to try to follow him any further. As the two men stared at each other, most of Healy's crew continued up the pier without him. I could see the *Grift* moored up ahead, and for a moment I considered going with them. But even though it meant more time in the company of Roger Pembroke, with Birch glaring daggers at me, I couldn't bring myself to leave Healy's side.

"Don't be too sure of that," Pembroke warned Healy. "I'm quite certain New Rovia will prosper with or without you."

"We'll see. Best of luck to you, Reggie."

Pembroke's voice turned quieter – and, if possible, even colder. "Don't believe I know anyone by that name."

Healy cracked a smile as he glanced past Pembroke at the aides in their crisp, new-looking Rovian uniforms.

"I do. But don't fret, Reg. Just put another mask on. Soon enough, everyone who knows the truth about you will be dead."

"You're getting pretty close to it yourself."

"We shall see. Life is long – until it isn't."

With that, Healy turned and strode up the deck towards his ship. I hustled after him, a little anxious about the wisdom of turning our backs on Roger Pembroke. But the last pair of Healy's men stayed between him and us, covering our exit.

Halfway down the pier, Healy slowed his pace and turned to look at me.

"You don't look so bad, all things considered. You're a sight cleaner than your friends, anyway. They'll be awfully glad to see you. Except possibly your brother. He's a bit of a meathead, isn't he?"

I nodded.

"More his father's child than his mother's. Still, even Hoke had a certain rough charm . . . I'm sorry, by the way." He put a gentle hand on my back. "There's not many a boy has to lose the same parent twice."

"Are you really my mother's brother?" I asked.

Healy stopped at the foot of the gangway. For a moment, he stared down at the weathered planks of the pier. Then he looked into my eyes.

"I believe the word is *uncle*. Yes. Sorry that had to come as a surprise. Your mother had some bad experience with pirates. One in particular."

He paused to glance back in the direction we'd come.

"She got it in her head that if I ever came round, I'd be a bad influence on the moral life of her children. Not to mention their future careers. Your dad felt the same. Didn't want anything to distract you from the critical business of selling ugly fruit at just above cost . . ."

He gave a dry little laugh, with as much sorrow in it as amusement. Then he frowned. "Sorry. Don't mean to speak ill of the departed. He did his best with what he had, your dad did. And he loved your mother like nothing else in the world."

There was a lump growing in my throat. I think Healy must have sensed it, because he quickly gave me a clap on the arm and nodded towards the gangway.

"Come. Let's go and see your friends."

KIRA HUGGED ME so hard it hurt. So did Guts, which was awkward for him, because he wasn't the hugging type. Adonis sort of grunted and nodded his head at me, which was about the kindest gesture I'd ever got from him.

Healy hadn't been wrong about them. They looked awful – dirty, bedraggled, with fat grey circles sagging under their eyes. And they smelled even worse.

"How'd you get here?" I asked.

"We followed the horses," said Kira.

"What happened to Millicent?"

She shook her head. "They took her east, towards the coast. Probably Turtle Bay, where the slave ships anchor. From there, it's only two days' sail to Sunrise."

"Mind yer heads!"

We all had to duck fast to avoid getting knocked off our feet by a bundled sail that two pirates swung over our heads as they sped by.

The entire crew was in constant motion, rushing with their usual deadly seriousness to prepare the ship for sailing. I felt a pang of guilt when I realized I was the reason for the unplanned departure.

Healy was by the wheel, talking with Spiggs, his first mate. He must have seen us nearly get our heads taken off, because he called out in a sharp voice, "Get below! String some hammocks in a corner of the gun deck and stay in them."

We went below, dodging crew members as we went. The gun deck was as buzzing with controlled chaos as the main, but we found a stash of hammocks in some netting to the aft and managed to string three of them in a corner.

We couldn't put up a fourth without getting in the way of the crew, and at first I thought that would be a problem. But Guts and Kira scrambled into one without a word of complaint, and as I watched them curl up together, it occurred to me that in the time we'd been separated, something had changed in their relationship.

I was glad for them – but it made me sad, too, because it got me thinking about Millicent. I started to wonder where she might be – back on Sunrise, probably – and the name *Cyril* popped into my head, and I had to make conversation quick so I wouldn't start to brood.

"How'd you know to look for Healy?" I asked Guts.

"Didn't," he said. "Just luck. First we heard when we snuck into town last night was they'd be hangin' a boy for slavery in the mornin'. We was down at the port lookin' fer a merchantman Kira knew when I saw the *Grift*. Figgered Healy helped us once, maybe he'd do it again. Didn't know he was yer blood kin."

"What happened? How did the Rovians capture Pella? How did Pembroke get to be governor? And why did Healy help him?" There was so much about the situation I didn't understand that once I started asking questions, it was hard to know where to stop.

"Dunno. Nobody's told us nothin'."

"What did they do to you?" Kira asked.

"Not too much, other than trying to hang me," I said.

"You didn't give him the map?"

"No . . . I did."

The look in her eyes when I said it made me feel ashamed. "It's okay, though," I said quickly. "It turns out it's worthless."

"It doesn't lead to the Fist?"

"No – it's the Fist that's worthless. It's got no power after all."

Kira's look hardened. "That's not true."

"It is. Pembroke said as much."

"He was lying!"

She said it with such force that I knew there was no point in arguing with her. And I guess her reaction made sense. If the Fist didn't have any power, it meant there wasn't much hope for her tribe.

"Maybe you're right," I said, even though I didn't believe it.

Kira didn't respond. She and Guts must have been pretty wiped out, because in spite of the noise from the crew, they were asleep within seconds.

I looked over at Adonis, expecting to see him nodding off, too. But his eyes were open, watching me.

"It's sumpin', innit? Burn Healy bein' our uncle?"

He said it in a quiet sort of voice, without any of his usual dumb swagger. And it took me by surprise – in what little time I'd had to think about Burn Healy being my uncle, it hadn't occurred to me that he was Adonis's uncle, too.

And that when Roger Pembroke ordered Dad's murder, Adonis had lost the same father I had.

"It's something," I agreed, because I didn't know what else to say.

"Figger he wants us to take the mark? Turn pirate, sail with 'im?"

I thought back to what Healy had told me about our mother.

"No," I said. "I don't think he does."

Adonis chewed on that for a while, scrunching up his face in the pained look he got whenever he tried to use his brain for actual thinking.

"Better that way," he said, nodding to himself. "Gotta get back to Deadweather. Get the plantation goin'. Like Dad said."

Something inside me recoiled. I thought back to what my life used to be like on Deadweather, before all the trouble started.

And how much I'd hated it. And how vile Adonis had always been to me.

Maybe he's changed, I thought. After all, in the couple of hours we'd spent together since I found him down in that pit, he hadn't once taken a swing at me.

Maybe it'd be better between us now.

Or maybe it'd be worse.

"It can't be like it was," I told him.

"Wot ye mean?"

"I mean, if you don't treat me proper, I'm not going back."

"Ay!" Adonis sat up in his hammock, his lip curled in a snarl. "None o' yer mouth! Gonna do yer job, or I'll bust yer face. Dad said –"

"Dad's *gone.*" I sat up, too, ready for a fight. "He's not coming back. And I'm not, either, if you don't treat me square."

"Square how?"

"No more beating on me, pushing me around, blaming me for Mum being dead –"

He snorted. "Whose fault do ye think –?"

"*Not mine!* It's a dirty lie. Tell it again, you can jump off a cliff. I'm through with you."

He had six inches and at least fifty pounds on me, and for most of my life talking to him like that would have made me tremble.

It didn't any more.

I think nearly getting executed probably had something to do with that.

Adonis's eyes were blazing. But to my surprise, he didn't jump out of the hammock and take a swing at me.

"Look, you – ye got responsibility! To Dad! To me! As a brother! Gotta help me!"

"You want a brother?" I told him. "Start acting like one. Or I'll never set foot on that plantation again."

He stared at me in disbelief, his lip quivering.

Then the strangest thing happened. He started to cry.

"Ye gotta come back! Help me! Can't do it meself!" Just like that, he was sobbing.

"Adonis, don't . . . please . . ."

It was hard to watch. But he couldn't stop. So I got off my hammock, stepped over to his and put my hand on his arm.

"It's okay . . . It's going to be okay."

"Dad's gone . . ." He let out a snuffling wail. "Gone!"

"I know . . . I know . . ."

I reached over and gave him a clumsy hug. He hugged me back. It seemed to help.

"Ye gotta come back . . . be a brother . . . I'm all alone!"

"Will you treat me right?"

"Course! Yeh!"

He clutched me like he was drowning. I patted him on the back.

"Okay . . . I'll come back . . . Just don't cry."

Of all the strange things that had happened that day, me consoling Adonis might have been the strangest.

He settled down eventually, and after some muttering about the plantation's field pirates – at which I made him promise he'd treat them with respect, too – he fell into a sleep as heavy as Guts and Kira's.

I wasn't tired myself – lying in that cell for days had been rest enough – but I didn't want to disturb the others. And I couldn't get up for fear of getting in the crew's way. So I lay in the hammock with my thoughts until well after the *Grift* cast off her lines and headed out into the bay.

There was plenty to think about. I watched Adonis's face as he slept, and saw my father in it – and for the first time since Dad died, I cried for him.

I thought about how I'd always hated Adonis, and whether – after sixteen years of being almost perfectly horrible – he actually had it in him to become a decent person. And if he did . . . or even if he didn't . . . whether I owed it to Dad to go back to the ugly fruit plantation and try to make it work.

I thought about my sister, raging crazy in that temple in the jungle, and wondered if what Kira had said about the Moku sacrificing her at the next storm was true – and if so, whether there was anything I could do to save her.

I thought about the map. It was still lodged in my head, its meaning no less of a mystery to me. I wondered if there was any point left in trying to translate it – if there was a chance that Kira was right, and the Fist had some kind of power after all. Or, even if it didn't, whether the rest of the treasure – the Princess of the Dawn's dowry, whatever that was – might be worth searching for.

I thought about the fact that the deadliest pirate on the Blue Sea had turned out to be my uncle – and that he was the first family I'd ever had who seemed like he was not only looking out for me, but didn't mind doing it.

I shed some tears over that, too, but they were happy ones.

And as long as I'd gone to sloppy mush, I figured it was a good time to think about Guts and Kira – and how I cared for Guts like he was family, and Kira, too.

And then I thought about Millicent.

And how she told me she loved me.

But she'd also told me – funny how I'd managed to forget this all through those black days in the dungeon, and it was only coming back to me now – that she was going to marry that Cyril fellow.

And when I gave her a chance to take it back, she didn't.

Both of those things couldn't be true. She couldn't love me and marry him.

I had to find her and make her tell me which was right. And if the answer came out wrong, I had to find a way to change it. Because I loved her fierce, and all I wanted in the world was to be with her.

But first, I had to deal with her father.

Way back when I first met Guts, I'd told him I was going to kill Roger Pembroke. But it was an empty boast, tossed off to make myself feel powerful. Back then, I didn't know a lot of things that I knew now – about Pembroke, about myself and about what a terrible, dark thing it was to end a man's life when you had a choice in the matter.

But I had to do something. I had to stop him.

It wasn't just that he'd killed my father, although that was more than enough. Pembroke had real power now. He ruled Sunrise, and now Pella Nonna, and if nobody stopped him, he was going to take over a whole continent and make slaves of everyone on it.

I couldn't let that happen.

It was a tall order. I wasn't sure I had the courage. And on my own, I knew I didn't have the strength.

But I wasn't on my own. I had friends.

And now I had family.

And one of them was a fearsome pirate captain, who seemed to not only know Pembroke well but to hate him. Who had serious firepower at his disposal – *turn round in the hammock, Egg, and just count the cannon behind you* – not to mention what seemed like the goodwill of all those Rovian soldiers who were supposed to be on Pembroke's side.

That roar of approval that went up in the square when Healy thanked the soldiers – it was an amazing thing. If someone asked those soldiers to choose between Burn Healy and a shifty snake who lied through his teeth . . .

Suddenly, taking down Roger Pembroke didn't look quite so hard.

In fact, it seemed like all I had to do was convince my uncle it was a good idea.

I slipped out of the hammock and started for the ladder to the main deck. The chaos had settled down now that we were under way, and the gun deck was mostly quiet except for four men working some kind of giant crank next to the mainmast column. They were shirtless and drenched in sweat, grimacing as their upper bodies lurched in sync with every turn of the crank.

I was so preoccupied with the plan forming in my head that it didn't occur to me to wonder what they were pumping, or why. I trotted past without a word, and by the time I was halfway up the steps of the companionway to the main deck, I'd forgotten all about them.

My uncle – *Burn Healy! My uncle! Imagine that* – was standing at the back of the quarterdeck with Spiggs, the first mate. They were deep in conversation, their backs to me.

"We could put in along the coast . . ."

"That's a gamble on material as well as skills. Say it's nothing but spongewood for fifty miles –"

Healy must have heard me approach, because he turned around in midsentence.

"Hello, Egg."

"Hello, sir . . . Don't mean to interrupt."

"Not at all." He turned to Spiggs. "Think it over."

Spiggs nodded and walked off. I hesitated for a moment, trying to work out the best way to ask Healy to destroy Roger Pembroke for me. But before I could get the words out, Healy asked me something:

"Don't suppose you're trained as a carpenter?"

That was an odd question. "No, sir."

"Your brother? Friends? Any carpentry skills in that bunch?"

"Sorry."

"Not as sorry as I am. Let me ask you another one. You were in Pella for a while before the invasion, yes?"

"Yeah. Quite a while."

"How long ago did you leave?"

I thought about it. The days were a blur. "Couple of weeks, maybe?"

"When you left . . . how many Cartager men-of-war were docked there? The big military ships. North of fifty guns."

"Three."

His eyebrows rose. "Are you quite certain?"

"Yes. Completely."

Healy turned his head. Spiggs was halfway down the deck. "Spiggs! There's two men-of-war still at large. I seriously doubt *Li Homaya*'s in the south."

As Spiggs turned and started towards us, I thought back to the day *Li Homaya* returned.

"He *was* in the south," I said. "But he came back. Just before they took us away."

Then I remembered something else.

"Ripper Jones was there, too."

Spiggs was back with us. At the mention of the Ripper's name, both he and Healy leaned in towards me, deadly serious.

"What do you mean?"

"Some men from his crew went to the palace. They met with *Li Homaya*. When they came out, they said they were looking for you. And he was their new friend."

Healy turned to Spiggs, his voice low and clipped. "Council in my cabin. Five minutes."

Spiggs strode away. Healy took out a spyglass and began to scan the horizon. His mood had changed so fast I was afraid to open my mouth. But I couldn't help myself.

"What's wrong?"

He closed the spyglass. "If Ripper Jones made an alliance with *Li Homaya* . . . and there's two Cartager men-of-war unaccounted for . . . it's a safe bet they went looking for me together."

"What for?"

"Revenge."

"For the invasion?"

He shook his head. "No. Like as not, they don't even know Pella fell to the Rovians. If they did, *Li Homaya* would've tried to retake it by now."

"So what do they want revenge for?"

"For *Li Homaya*, it's the loss of his honour. And his ship, which is the same thing." He gestured towards the *Grift* with a wry smile. "I'm not the original owner, you see.

"As for the Ripper . . . it's mutual. We had a falling-out over a business matter. And we've both concluded we're better off with the other one dead."

He looked out at the horizon and frowned.

"Either man alone is a problem. But the two of them together . . . that's something of a crisis."

"Not for you," I blurted out. "You're Burn Healy!"

He smirked. "Thanks for the vote of confidence. But it's a tricky thing without a carpenter."

"Why do you need a carpenter?"

"Because my ship is sinking."

Bright and shiny and sizzling with fun stuff . . .

puffin.co.uk

WEB FUN

UNIQUE and exclusive digital content!
Podcasts, photos, Q&A, Day in the Life of, interviews and much more, from Eoin Colfer, Cathy Cassidy, Allan Ahlberg and Meg Rosoff to Lynley Dodd!

WEB NEWS

The **Puffin Blog** is packed with posts and photos from Puffin HQ and special guest bloggers. You can also sign up to our monthly newsletter **Puffin Beak Speak**

WEB CHAT

Discover something new EVERY month –
books, competitions and treats galore

WEBBED FEET

(Puffins have funny little feet and brightly coloured beaks)

Point your mouse our way today!

It all started with a Scarecrow.

Puffin is seventy years old.
Sounds ancient, doesn't it? But Puffin has never been
so lively. We're always on the lookout for the next big
idea, which is how it began all those years ago.

Penguin Books was a big idea from the mind of
a man called Allen Lane, who in 1935 invented
the quality paperback and changed the world.
**And from great Penguins, great Puffins grew,
changing the face of children's books forever.**

The first four Puffin Picture Books were hatched in 1940 and the
first Puffin story book featured a man with broomstick arms called
Worzel Gummidge. In 1967 Kaye Webb, Puffin Editor, started the
Puffin Club, promising to **'make children into readers'**.
She kept that promise and over 200,000 children became
devoted Puffineers through their quarterly instalments of
Puffin Post, which is now back for a new generation.

Many years from now, we hope you'll look back and
remember Puffin with a smile. **No matter what your age
or what you're into, there's a Puffin for everyone.**
The possibilities are endless, but one thing is for sure:
whether it's a picture book or a paperback, a sticker book
or a hardback, **if it's got that little Puffin
on it – it's bound to be good.**